LADY LUCK

HAREM STATION

NEW YORK TIMES BESTSELLING AUTHOR, JA HUSS, WRITING AS

KC ROSS

LADY LUCK

NEW YORK TIMES BESTSELLING AUTHOR JA HUSS WRITING AS

KC CROSS

ABOUT
THE BOOK

KC Cross is the not-so-secret naughty pen name of New York Times bestselling author, JA Huss (who normally writes filthy romantic suspense).

Luck knew two things when he left Harem Station months ago.

One. The silver-haired Cygnian princess Nyleena was still safely frozen in her cryopod.

And two. There was a good chance she was his soulmate.

He left anyway.

Nyleena is what you might call feisty. Or sassy. Or maybe just... feral. She is wild. Much too wild for Luck's taste. But now that he's home there's no way to deny it.

Like it or not, she is his.

Lucky for him, all Cygnian princesses have one true weakness. They cannot resist cooking up crazy plans to tackle unsolvable problems. And he's going to use that irresistible urge to tame her savage spirit.

Nyleena has plans of her own and none of them involve Luck. She is out for blood. All the people who made her life hell will be dealt with, and she's going to find every single one of them and take them out.

Right after she solves this one last unsolvable problem… how not to fall in love with your soulmate.

Lady Luck is a sexy hate-fuck of a story about a wild princess, six hot brothers trying to tame her, bad relationship advice from killer sexbots, your favorite evil, but misunderstood, dragonbee bot, and a repentant AI trapped in a sex prison with a succubus.

CHAPTER ONE

LUCK

I don't think people can properly appreciate the immense size of Harem Station the way my brothers and I do for the simple reason that no one outside our immediate family has seen the hidden parts.

It is massive even if you only consider the known spaces. Four hundred levels. And that's not including the hidden lower levels where the docking bays and lockups are, or the hidden upper levels where we all live and keep the harem and the Pleasure Prison.

I know every corner of this place. I know every support beam, every crack in the obsidian floors, every servo bot's name, all the best places to drink, and gamble, and shoot, and shop, and eat on each level.

I know all Harem's secrets too. Of which she has many. I'm standing in one of them right now, so that's the one I'm really talking about.

When you have a massive space station like this you need a massive biosphere. We have a dozen or so levels that would probably qualify as forests if the flora were on a planet. But it's not enough to sustain gas exchange necessary to maintain life.

So we have places like this too.

I look up at the skylight—which doesn't give me a view of the sky, since we're in space. Or even a view of space, since that would defeat the purpose of this small patch of grass and flowerbeds.

It's just fake sunshine. But it's warm and doesn't feel fake. It'll even give you a sunburn if you're not careful because it's actual ultraviolet light.

To get here you have to really know where you're going. These places are well hidden to avoid being disturbed by people, or bots, or little trysts like the one I'm about to have. They're not on any station map or any welcome brochure. They're not even in the Baby ALCOR's data core because he asked me about them not too long ago.

I, of course, denied their existence.

These gardens have always been my job here. Were my first job, actually. When I was about… oh, maybe sixteen or so, ALCOR came to me and said this was my secret mission.

He pulled that shit a lot when he wanted us to do things we didn't want to do. "This is your secret mission, Luck. It's very important."

All bullshit, of course.

Well… except that one thing.

But that's got nothing to do with the flowers.

I fell for it though. Secret greenhouses, some of which were filled with flowers that got you high?

Hell yeah, I took care of that. I had a nice little drug business going that first month people started coming to Harem Station. I made a bundle. But ALCOR shut that down pretty quick. He was pissed. So pissed. And went on a rant like you would not believe. Mostly because I wasn't charging enough. Which, now that I look back on it, is kinda funny and makes me smile.

But also because the essence of the flowers was a potent hallucinogen and two people jumped off ledges.

They didn't die, or course. He caught them with safety bots. But it was kinda fucked up so I stopped. And I was never into the drug myself. I tried it a few times and it gave me some weird-ass dreams that still kinda creep me out when I think about them now.

But anyway, there's a couple hundred of these little mini-greenhouses scattered across the station to help keep the air fresh and sweet in the most densely packed parts of the living quarters. And ninety-nine point nine-nine-nine-nine percent of them do not have psychedelic flowers.

Just regular plants that make good air.

Funny thing about people who live on stations—especially the kind of people who live here on Harem. They get angry and stressed if they don't have enough breathable air. It's not like water, which can be rationed with shower timers. Or food, which has to be earned through servitude or purchased with credits.

Air is free on Harem and we provide more than enough. There are no low oxygen levels on our station. There is no place on Harem where you fear for your health or ability to think because you can't suck in enough air.

Not all stations are like that. Almost all of them make you pay for air.

This would put our organic occupants at a disadvantage because half our inhabitants are bots who don't need to breathe.

We provide free charging stations for our inorganic occupants too.

Free air, free charging. It makes a difference in the mental health of your people.

But I digress.

I'm lying on the grass in one of the hidden patches of green enjoying my fake sunshine. My cocks are hard with expectations because this is where I meet Nyleena.

When we all came back from the latest shit show out at the Loathsome One's Lair Station a couple months ago I knew she was mine immediately.

One shared look between us was all it took to jumpstart my cock and make her eyes glow with white light.

But one more shared look was also all it took to realize—we are not compatible.

She growled at me. This low, threatening rumble in her throat made my cocks deflate immediately.

I growled back. Not even meaning to, either. It was just instinct.

We avoided each other for a week after that. She went her way, I went mine. And for a little bit everything was fine. There were no urges. No irrational thoughts of sex at the most inappropriate times. No lying awake at night longing for her body.

That's because we didn't interact much that first week. Then I bumped in to her at a shooting gallery and I had this irrational urge to stuff her inside a maintenance closet and fuck her brains out.

I didn't do that. That was all her. She stuffed me into a maintenance closet and fucked my brains out. So… after that happened we were a lost cause. Oh, we hated each other. We still growled and she likes to bite. But it didn't take long to realize that we needed each other to continue to operate on a normal level because suddenly she was all I thought about. Every fucking minute all I wanted to do was fuck her. And after a couple of weeks of this lust-filled agony, she confessed she was having the same problem.

So we came to an agreement and arranged these trysts.

I look forward to them now.

Don't get me wrong. They are one hundred percent hate-fucks.

Most of the time I have my hand over her mouth so I don't have to hear her talk. And she always injures me before we're done. Dragging her long fingernails down my back with such force she makes me bleed. Or she'll bite me in the shoulder as she comes. Or grab my balls after I come, when she knows I'll be able to feel it.

She's mean.

Can I just get that out of the way right now?

Princess Nyleena is *mean*.

She is also insane, and unpredictable, and arrogant.

There is almost nothing to like about her.

She does have pretty hair. I'll give her that. Long, silver strands that look like thin wires of pure silver. And really nice tits. And the light inside her makes her skin look a little bit ethereal.

But once she opens her mouth no one cares how beautiful she is.

And she's always up to something. Always finding a way to get in trouble. Last month she organized a bot strike down on level thirteen. Got the maintenance servos all riled up about working conditions. Two weeks ago we found her clinging to the outside of the station with a cyborg, drunk off their asses. I still don't know why they were doing that. A bet, maybe? A dare? Who knows? And just a couple days ago she pushed some guy off level fifty-seven for grabbing her ass.

That last one I kinda approved of, but the point is, she has way too much time on her hands.

Crux has begged me to try to tame her, but you know what? I just don't care that she's wild. She's not my problem. I mean, we fuck and all, but once that's over I'm good for another twenty-four hours before I have to think about her again.

Still, Crux did ask. Sorta begged, actually. He pulled me aside last night and said, "Luck, help me out here, brother. She's just... wild. Can you just give her a job? Or a hobby, maybe? Something? Anything that will occupy her mind and make her stop fucking with people?"

He was getting lots of complaints.

She's restless.

And then he mentioned that Cygnian princesses have this weakness.

If you challenge them to solve an unsolvable problem they becomes obsessed with it. It's all they can think about. That's how most of the runaway princesses up in the harem room escaped the Cygnian System. They came up with these crazy plans that involved stealing ships and blowing things up.

That's how Queen Corla escaped through a spin node back when we were all teenagers. That's how Lyra saved Nyleena out at Bull Station and how Delphi got the Loathsome One—AKA Veila—to send her after Jimmy on a sentient ship to try to free her brother.

Of course, they don't always work. Rarely work, in fact. Otherwise we'd have thousands of runaway princesses here on the station and we almost never have more than a few dozen. It takes a lot of effort to round up that number. Lot of effort.

But Crux said, "The plan doesn't have to work, Luck. Just get her thinking about something other than fighting, and drinking, and causing trouble."

So I planted a little seed in Nyleena's brain yesterday.

I told her she was the only one on this whole station who didn't pull her weight. And then I ticked off all the jobs I have. Like these greenhouses, for instance. And my salvage missions. And taking care of *Lady Luck*, and training with Cha-Cha. Shit like that. I basically challenged her to get a job using shame.

And even though she laughed at me I know she's been thinking about it.

She gave no fucks. Called me a farmer. A junkyard scavenger. Ship sitter.

But I could see the wheels turning in her head and pretty soon the idea that she needs a job will consume her. It will be all she can think about.

"Well, I see you're working hard today," Nyleena snaps, coming into view from the long, dark hallways that lead to our secret spot.

We have a secret hidden calendar with all our prearranged meeting spaces. Something I cooked up using a program left over from my teens when I first took over the secret garden mission, thank you very much.

13

Nyleena is wearing a silver torso bodysuit with a flirty little lavender-lace skirt, the kind the mercenaries all wear these days. Tight, form-fitting, and shiny. When I first arrived she used to wear the kind that go all the way down her legs, the thin fabric disappearing inside her thigh-high stiletto boots.

But she was wearing that when we had our first tryst and it became very clear, very quick, that getting access to her lady parts was gonna be an issue.

She didn't even fuck me that time. Said, "I do not get naked for trysts." Flat-out refused to engage and left. But the next time I saw her she was wearing the torso bodysuit.

Back then we were only trysting every few days but now... that's too long.

So every day now she wears this style of bodysuit. It's like a strapless one-piece bathing suit that has a convenient stick-tab closure between her legs.

And boots.

I kinda love those boots.

They are made of this silver malleable metal. Cold, and hard. But pliable too.

And the bodysuit is a corset. I know, if she were to turn around, there'd be honest-to-God laces zig-zagging up her back.

So fucking hot.

Her silver hair is always wild, like the light in her eyes whenever she looks at me. And her tits always seem to be popping out of that strapless bodice.

She looks like an organic sexbot and even though she's mean, and there's pretty much nothing to like about this wild, feral girl—my cocks stiffen at the sight of her every single time.

It's not fair.

I didn't choose her. They made us this way.

The longing I feel for her when we don't have sex every day is undeniable.

I hate it. It's a weakness I don't want and never asked for.

So that's why we're meeting here on this small patch of grass, surrounded by a bunch of immature space orchids that are just short green stalks with no flowers.

To fuck.

And that's it.

"Stop talking and climb on," I say, fisting both my cocks. I'm ready for her. I want to get this over with as soon as possible. Feel the relief as it floods through my blood. Then go back out into the station and be normal.

Until the satiated feeling wears off and we have to do it again.

Mother of suns, why me? Why was I made this way?

That's the worst part, too. I fucking hate this. I don't enjoy sex with Nyleena. She's like water. I *need* her.

Nyleena reaches between her legs and pulls the tabs that hold her suit together apart with a rip. Smiling that evil smile the whole time she stalks over to me, then steps over me. Straddling my body as she blocks the light with hers.

She lifts up one sharp-heeled boot and places it on my chest, pushing down with force.

I let her do it. I can't feel shit right now. I'm way too hard to experience pain.

And besides. I can see up her little skirt. Her pussy lips taunting me with the relief I'll soon feel.

She has this longing too.

If she didn't have an equal and opposite force of anger and hatred for me inside her the way I do her... if I thought for one second I could talk her into a DNA signature scrambler to make this all go away... I'd do it.

I'd do it and just forget I ever laid eyes on this silver-haired demon.

But we already know we're fated. We already know that this... partnership, I guess you'd call it, is inevitable.

"No foreplay today, Luck? Why do you always have to meet my already so low expectations? Hmmm? Can you, for once, just surprise me?"

God. I need her closer. Not just because I want to stick both my cocks inside her and get the double ejaculation over with, but so I can cover her mouth with my hand and make her shut up.

But I rally. Because I don't want her to know how much she gets to me. "Sit down, princess. I'll show you what foreplay is."

She takes two steps forward, so her pussy is right over my mouth, grins, eyes shining with evil intentions, then lowers herself so she's sitting on my chest. She places both hands on my rough, stubbled cheeks and presses her tits into my chin. Staring down into my soul.

We share a moment then.

I wait for her to scoot forward and place her pussy over my mouth so I can eat her out. But she doesn't move. Just continues to stare at me.

16

"What the fuck?" I ask. "What the fuck are you doing?"

"I'm trying to see if there's anything inside that idiot head of yours worth appealing to."

"Appealing to? Now what?" I growl. "Can't we just fuck and get this over with?"

"That would be giving you what you want, Luck. What about what I want?"

"What the fuck do you want?"

"I have decided that I want to hunt people down and kill them. Veila, specifically, but I'm not that picky. That's my new job."

"You want to be a mercenary?" I ask.

"No. I just want to kill people for personal reasons. I want to get my own ship, leave this place, and go hunting for all the assholes who fucked me over. I want to—what are you doing?"

"What?"

"Why is your finger in my asshole?"

"Because we're having sex," I deadpan. "And that's one of the places fingers go."

"I'm trying to have a serious conversation."

"Yeah. I know." I huff. "That's something we don't do. I've told you that over and over again. Now shut up and fuck me so I can get back to my regularly-scheduled life."

She opens her mouth. Probably to call me an asshole. But I'm done playing around. I wrap my arms around her, flip her over on her back, and mount her. Both of my stiff, hard cocks pressing forward into her hot, wet pussy.

CHAPTER TWO

There are a lot of things to hate about Luck. He's an arrogant prick. He's not all that smart compared to his brothers. And he's mean. Like really fucking mean.

It's not that he flips me over and starts to fuck me without even asking. It's that, once again, he cuts me off mid-sentence.

I hate this habit of his with a fiery, infernal passion.

It makes me want to teach him a lesson. It makes me want to push him off me, slap his face, rip his balls off, and stuff them down his throat.

But… "Oh," I moan, unable to control my building excitement. He feels so *good*. It's like his damn cocks were made just for me. The two of them together are the perfect girth to stretch me wide and push all my magic pussy buttons.

He begins to nibble my ear and that sends a flood of chills up and down my spine. But the chill he inspires inside me doesn't stay there. It radiates out to my limbs until my whole body is buzzing and tingling with erotic excitement.

He thrusts forward, grunting in my ear. And even though just last week that sound was infuriating and kind of disgusting to the point of distraction… this week it's something else.

"Fuck me," I growl.

It's… kinda hot.

He thrusts forward again, harder this time. He grips my face as his mouth lowers onto mine. We don't kiss a lot during sex. But when we do…

"Ohhhhh," I moan past his lips.

When we do it's exhilarating. Maybe even slightly… passionate.

The only thing I hate more about Luck than the fact that we're forced to fuck every day to keep our sanity is his lack of dirty talk.

He refuses to talk to me or let me talk to him.

That makes me ragey. Because dirty talk is my favorite and he won't engage.

But one of these days…

"Come," he commands me.

"Are you kidding?" I ask. "We just started."

He slaps his hand over my mouth and the rage that was only imaginary two seconds ago manifests in all its glorious reality when I wrap my legs around his middle and squeeze him so tight with my thighs, he gasps.

Take that, asshole.

He glares at me, momentarily distracted. And I use that distraction to my advantage by twisting my body and flipping him over so he's on his back.

He's still inside me, the heads of both his cocks swollen in place. Locking us together until we come and relieve the lust hidden deep inside our genetically-matched souls.

My tits bounce on his chest and he grabs my hair, shoots me a warning glare.

I know what that glare says. *Don't make me bleed, Nyleena.*

He shoots this look at me every time, and every time I take it as a challenge.

I raise my hand up.

"Don't," he growls.

"Oh," I say. "He can speak. Tell me more," I purr.

"Do not—"

But I do it anyway.

I swipe my nails right down the side of his cheek and hiss at him like a feral cat.

He wraps his muscled arms around my upper body, squeezing me tight as he pulls me down on to his chest.

I'll admit, Luck is strong. And when he gets me in a lock like this, there's no way I can escape until he lets me.

But I don't make it easy.

I squirm and twist in his grip. All the while his hips are thrusting up with powerful force. So hard that his balls are slapping against my clit.

This momentarily takes my mind off the forced submission and I float a little.

"Come," he commands again, growling out the word in my ear. "Right. Fucking—"

I do.

I come.

The light locked up inside me pulses out in flickering waves at first. And then it stops just as his cocks contract inside me. My luminous flux holds steady for a moment so when his contractions are over, and his sperm is ready to explode into me, my flux knows what to do and it bursts into fractals of geometrically-shaped light that dance and crackle

21

around our bodies. Electrifying them like charged ions flowing out from a sun on a matrix of deep, dark space-time.

He throws me over to the side, his cocks slipping out of me, dripping with our shared release, and breathes hard and heavy.

I lie there with eyes closed. Not caring that he just literally threw me away.

Because this is the best part.

I wait for him to tuck his dicks away, mumble out, "Thank you," as he walks off and leaves me alone.

And then… I let out the last of my climax.

Because I never give him all of me.

I have one little hidden, secret surprise that he will never know about.

I open my eyes and come for real. Silver-laced lavender light shoots up and out, bouncing off the UV reflectors above the grass and flowers, and comes back down to blanket my body, and this entire secret garden, in a soft, purple glow.

And all the plants around me grow ten times taller from my sexy, lust-filled, nutritious light.

When I wake up I have no idea what time it is.

I almost always sleep after sex with Luck. It's not like I have anything better to do.

He's right about that job. About me not having one, at least. Because I am so fucking bored on this station.

Luck always walks out after he's done. Always says, "Thank you," but it's always derogatory.

I don't care.

He always misses the best part of me. He's never experienced my real release. Never seen the plants grow tall. He has no clue who I am.

We never use the same secret garden twice. He's got us on this insane rotation schedule. Says it's part of some protocol Real ALCOR gave him back when he was a kid. No one can get suspicious about the secret gardens or people will start hanging out here. Start having secret trysts like us.

Which I do not care about at all.

In fact, maybe I'll make up a virtual poster today and send out a map to all the secret gardens I know about.

Wouldn't *that* piss him off?

I sigh and smile, allowing myself to be content for just another minute.

But then the smile fades. Because I am so bored. It's late afternoon now. I only just woke up a few hours ago so there's a whole evening and night ahead of me.

I'm sick of getting drunk. I'm sick of fighting. I'm sick of everything here.

I want to be free. I want to go somewhere. And I want to kill people.

Not these people. I don't have enough hate saved up inside me to bother with anyone here. Not even for Luck.

And that whole job thing he mentioned yesterday. He said I was the only person on Harem who didn't pull their weight.

And that kinda pissed me off, if I'm being honest.

Because I do have a job. I'm a fucking bomb. I'm an explosion waiting to happen. It's not my fault they don't want to detonate me. Right?

That's how I see it.

But it would be nice to have another purpose. So I think about this for a while.

What could I do? How could I fill my endless hours of boredom?

I list my skills and come up with... well, I'm not good for much. Mostly just looking good while killing people.

And fighting. I'm pretty good at pissing people off to the point where they want to try to kick my ass.

There's a lot of fighting here on Harem Station. Pretty much everyone is an explosion waiting to happen. Not literally, like me, of course.

But the only jobs I can think of that could use my mad combat skills here on Harem are gladiator fighter and maybe... I could enroll in security academy.

I already volunteered to go hunt down Veila for them. Kill that fucking bitch. That's what I really want to do. But everyone said no. Even fucking Lyra said no.

Who are these people to tell me what I can and can't do, anyway?

I sit up, pull out a disposable wet-wipe from my boot and clean off the remnants of Luck's come, then refasten the sticky tabs of my bodysuit and get to my feet.

And it hits me. *Yeah. I will* get a job, asshole.

I'm gonna get a ship so I can go hunt Veila on my own. Veila and everyone else who ever crossed me is dead. When I told Luck that I wanted a ship I was sorta joking. I was fuming about being stuck here when I walked in and that declaration just spilled out of my mouth.

But you know what? I do want a ship so I'm gonna march up to that fucking harem room. And I'm gonna point my lavender-tipped fingernail in Crux's face. And I'm gonna tell him what's what. I'm gonna make them take me on that Veila hunt.

And if he says no I'll... I'll steal a ship.

No. I'll steal *Luck's* ship.

Ha!

Lady fucking *Luck*.

I will not be fucked with. I will not be trifled with. I will not be forced into some... menial servitude job here on Harem. I will not end up some joke in a gladiator fight or arresting bots and bastards who break rules.

I toss my disposable wipe into the recycle tube as I exit the secret garden, casting one last glance over my shoulder to look at the towering plants I made grow, and then smile.

I've got it all figured out.

CHAPTER THREE

I feel better after the fucking.

Mostly.

At least I'm good on the sex part of my general malaise for another twenty-four hours.

But there's something else that's been bothering me for a long time now.

Valor.

See, Valor and I have been partners forever. Ever since we left Wayward Station as teenagers we've been a team.

Then we got gifted Beauty, our amazing bot. And we only got tighter after that. Valor, Beauty, and me were a tight little crew.

And then we got _Lady Luck_ as our ship and it all seemed so… settled.

So perfect.

Until Beauty sacrificed herself to help blow up that Cygnian warship out at the Battle of Bull Station and everything changed overnight.

Valor lost interest in salvaging. That's our job for ALCOR. Or it was, before everything changed. Because Real ALCOR blew up with Beauty and now we're stuck with the Baby ALCOR copy running the station and the Asshole ALCOR copy, locked up inside the Pleasure Prison with our new AI, Succubus. She was a gift from Mighty Boss himself after the other shit-show we had involving Mighty Minions Resort and the Loathsome One's Lair.

Now all Valor wants to do is work with Tray in the Pleasure Prison control room.

Which, for sure, is an important job. We have millions of people in that sexy virtual adventure game at any one time. Which means we have millions of unconscious bodies in various gaming pods at any one time too.

It's a huge responsibility.

But come on. Valor comes from a military family. His father was some hotshot general back on Wayward Station. He's a commander, for fuck's sake. Not a body babysitter.

And he just handed *Lady Luck* over to me when I hired Xyla's ex-sexbot friend, Cha-Cha, to be our new partner.

I get it. Beauty was like a little sister to us. We did everything together. You might even say we were our own little family unit. And she had our backs one hundred percent.

But she's gone. Just like Real ALCOR is gone. He accepted the Baby ALCOR just fine, but Cha-Cha?

Nooooo. He refuses to even nod hello in her general direction.

I miss Beauty too. But we can't just stop living our lives.

Right?

Draden's dead. And Ceres. And Serpint moved on. He's got Lyra now. And that stupid nannybot, Prince. He only stayed on Harem because *Booty* was trying to find herself inside the Pleasure Prison, but now she's back in her ship body where she belongs so I bet Serpint and Lyra are all gearing up for the next trip.

Does rationalizing this make me a dick? Should I still be mourning for Beauty?

But if I didn't leave with Chach and *Lady Luck*, then Jimmy and Delphi would probably be dead. And we'd have no Succubus reining in the Asshole ALCOR. Not to mention all the Akeelian boys we saved from the Loathsome Lair.

If Cha-Cha and I hadn't shown up to help *Dicker* and Jimmy so many people would still be stuck in that disgusting breeding program. And most of them were kids.

So see? It was fate. I did what I was supposed to.

Still. I miss him. Valor has been my rock for too long not to miss him when he's not by my side.

I was going to go hang out with Chach after my regularly scheduled tryst with Nyleena, but instead I head for the Pleasure Prison control room to try to maybe have a conversation about this with Valor.

The Pleasure Prison takes up twenty whole levels at the very top of the station, just below the princess harem and our living quarters. It's mostly filled with gaming pods and servers powered by ALCOR.

Well, the Baby ALCOR now. That transition was a whole other level of shit show after Real ALCOR died. The Baby was OK to run things for short periods of time but when Real ALCOR didn't come back he dropped the ball. Many times.

29

People died. Lots of people died. Most of them were in the virtual pods when that happened. But we had some atmosphere issues too.

It was bad.

So the new rule is that Baby ALCOR still runs the Pleasure Prison but there has to be an organic humanoid in the control room at all times just in case.

Tray spends most of his time inside the virtual. He's in there several hours a day taking care of shit that needs to be programmed on the inside.

I think it's a mistake to be able to make changes to the virtual environment from inside the program, but Tray has been doing that for so long we'd have to shut down whole sectors of the Pleasure Prison for months to take the code out and put it on an exterior server now. And that would cost us untold billions in credits, since the Pleasure Prison is pretty much the main draw here at Harem.

Aside from the princess harem, of course. But very few people can afford a real princess from our harem. We do have many virtual princess harems inside the Prison though.

Whatever. Tray is the king of that kingdom. He can run it however he wants.

So that's where Valor comes in. He's one of the organic humanoids in the control room now. Every spin, for several hours at a time, he's in charge of monitoring more than a million gaming pods.

Which, like I said. Super-important job.

It's just not *his* job.

His job is with *me*. Hunting down ancient AI parts in the farthest reaches of the galaxy and bringing them back here to keep Baby ALCOR running smoothly.

And, can I just say, that's an even more super-important job than the gaming pods? Right?

Right.

For a game that takes up twenty levels in servers and has an almost infinite boundary once you're inside the virtual, the control room is actually really small.

It's a circle of monitors. Like eleventy-billion split-screen monitors that line the walls and just one control seat. In the center of the small space is Tray's gaming pod.

When I enter he's in there. I can tell because the lid is closed and the glass is all fogged up from his breathing.

Valor is sitting at the one control seat, sipping coffee. He does half a spin in his chair, sees me, nods his chin in my direction, then turns back to the monitors.

There's one big screen directly in front of him that just runs medical stats. All the health statuses of the players are ranked in order of who needs immediate attention. Those in red need to be woken up by medical bots and pulled out.

We don't have any listed at the moment.

There's a few pod ID's lit up in yellow, meaning they might need attention soon, but not yet. We only have about half a dozen of those at the moment.

All the rest are green, indicating everyone's having a good sexy time in there and no one is about to die in the real.

"You need something?" Valor asks, not even bothering to look at me.

And I want to say everything that just ran through my mind as I walked over here.

It was fate, I want to tell him.

I did a good thing.

Cha-Cha is top-notch. She's not Beauty, no one will ever replace Beauty. But she's a good person. And she's got my back. Definitely had my back when all those evil borgs came at us back on the Lair Station.

And then, of course, I want to say... *I miss you, dude. Life isn't the same anymore and I don't know how to change it back.*

But one of the yellow pod ID's goes to red and begins flashing.

Valor doesn't even have to do anything. That's how redundant this job actually is.

Baby ALCOR is on it. And a few seconds later the pod ID lights up white, indicating the player has been pulled and is already receiving medical attention.

Still, Valor doesn't look at me. Just pretends that outcome depends on his care and focus.

But I came here for more than that conversation.

I came here to be close to him. To make this ache go away.

So I grab a wheeled stool from the corner and scoot up next to him. "What's up?" I say. "How ya been?"

He side-eyes me for a moment, then goes back to sipping his coffee and staring at the screen.

"Do you blame me?" I ask.

"For what?"

"Beauty?"

He shoots me a crooked frown. "Why would I blame you for that?"

"I dunno. You just... don't really talk to me anymore."

"I've got a lot on my mind, Luck. It's not personal. I'm just… thinking about shit."

"What kind of shit? Maybe I can help?"

"Well, I guess it is personal." He looks at me straight on. We lock matching violet eyes. "Because I'm not really interested in sharing it with *you*."

And just like that, all that sadness inside me turns to… *rage*.

CHAPTER FOUR

MYLEENA

I like most of the levels here on Harem Station.

Except this one.

The one that actually contains the harem.

Every time I come up here these low-level princesses glare at me like I'm the enemy.

Which… OK. I probably am in their minds. See, they are all golds and oranges. Or greens. Or blues and reds. In Cygnian System, these girls have no pedigree. Only the pinks and silvers have that. So they resent us because we are upper-class.

And that makes me a little screamy. Because look, bitches. You get a real job back home. You get husbands. And homes. And a boy child or two to raise, if your husband is rich enough to buy one. And that means you get to play Mommy. And hang out with your other pretend-mommy girlfriends while those little boys kick balls around or hit them with bats.

It's a fucking cakewalk compared to what my job is.

I'm a goddamned bomb. That's what I want to scream at them. *Which would you rather be? A trophy wife or an explosive device?*

35

But they all know this and they still glare at me every time I come up here.

I'm glaring back at them—daring them to say something to me—when the cyborg master comes up and taps me on the shoulder. "Can I help you with something, Nyleena?"

"Yup," I say, planting my hands on my hips. "I want to speak with Crux."

"Do you have an appointment?"

"Do *you* think I have an appointment?"

His one red eye races across the elongated rectangle on the upper third of his face.

"It was a rhetorical question, OK? Just... where is he?" But then I spy him on the other side of the glass in his office. "Never mind. I see him."

I walk off, half expecting the cyborg master to stop me, or at least attempt to stop me, but he doesn't.

I don't bother knocking, just burst through the door and stand in front of Crux's desk.

Crux taps something out on his air screen, then closes it down and says, with a heavy sigh, "Yes, Nyleena?"

"I want to go on the Veila hunt. And I am not taking no for an answer, buddy. There's no way I'm gonna get stuck fighting like a gladiator for money or busting overzealous bots."

"I'm sorry?" he says, giving me one of those fake perplexed looks.

"You know what I'm talking about. I know you guys are all planning something. Some stealthy trip to go trap Veila and bring her back here so you can free your precious Queen Corla. And I want in."

He leans back in his oversized chair, making it creak a little. Stares at me with those piercing violet eyes. Rubs his hand over his scruffy jaw. Blinks. Then says, "Is there some particular reason you feel qualified to go on this so-called Veila hunt? If there is one, and I'm not saying there is."

"Are you kidding me? I'm a goddamned force of nature." I nod my head.

"So you say. But—"

"So I say?" I huff. "Just ask anyone."

"I mean... what are your specific skills, Nyleena? Can you list them for me?"

"My skills?" I huff again. "I'm tough. I can fight. No, I can kick ass. I'm not afraid to take a punch, either. I'll get my ass kicked a little. That's fine. But I'll still win in the end."

"Hmm," he says. "Can you fly a ship?"

"Asked no one ever." I laugh. "We have sentient ships. No one needs to *fly* them."

"Do you have a sentient ship?"

"Me? Personally?"

"Yes, you."

"I'm sure I could get one."

"How?"

I shrug. "There's always poker games. Or I could talk the Baby ALCOR into giving me one. He likes me."

"Does he now?"

"Mmm-hmm." I nod. I think he does. He calls me into his office all the time. Mostly to yell at me after getting arrested, but still. I think he likes me.

"OK," Crux says. "Well. I can see that you are a formidable princess." I smile. Because I am. "But I'm not sure anyone wants you to go. *If* we go." He leans forward and lowers his voice. "No one likes you, Nyleena. You're kind of a pain in the ass. So if I convince them to let you go on one of their ships— say, *Lady Luck*, for instance—you're gonna have to do me a big favor in return."

"What kind of favor?" I scowl at him. Because I don't want to make deals. I want to make demands.

"You say Baby ALCOR likes you?"

"He does. He's very nice to me. Always checking in to see if I need anything." This is only half true. He does check in on me regularly, but that's mostly because I'm always up to something he disapproves of.

"Well, I need something from Asshole ALCOR."

"Oh," I say. "I don't really have a relationship with him."

"Oh," Crux says, once again leaning back in his chair. "Then I don't think I can do it. I really need this info."

"What info?"

He stares at me. Chews his lips for a moment. Lowers his head a little so he's peering down his nose at me. Then sighs. "Have you ever heard of people being… leveled up?"

"Maybe?" I lie. "It's kinda ringing a bell. But I don't know anything about it."

"Well, Asshole ALCOR does. And I need to know what this leveled-up thing means. Because we've been told that our maybe-dead brother, Draden, was leveled up so he's actually not dead. We'd like to find him. So I'll tell you what. If you can get Asshole ALCOR to explain what this leveling-up bullshit is, I'll make sure you're on the Veila hunt mission. In fact…" He pauses here. Looks me dead in the eyes. "I'll give you your own sentient ship."

"You will?" I say, excited.

"Mmmm-hmmm. Can you do that?"

"Get you information from Asshole ALCOR. Just to be clear, this is the one trapped inside the Pleasure Prison with the Succubus thing, right?"

"The very one."

"How do I get in there?"

"Ask Tray. He can get you in. But getting you a meeting with Asshole ALCOR is gonna be harder."

"Tray, huh? That's it? Just go ask him?"

"Yup. I'm sure he'll be happy to help you."

"OK," I say. "You've got a deal."

"Great," Crux says, pinching the air with his fingertips to open up another screen. "Let me know when you have that info and I'll let you choose a ship from the recent arrivals."

I quickly turn on my heel and walk out before he can see the huge smile on my face.

Holy fucking suns! I totally came out ahead on this deal.

I'm gonna have my own ship by the end of the day. Hell, who needs a Veila hunt now? These assholes can do that. I've got my own list of people I'd like to capture and kill.

I could be gone tomorrow on my own personal revenge mission.

This thought makes me so happy, I don't even bother glaring back at the little princesses in the harem when I pass. I just get in the elevator and take it down to the Pleasure Prison level.

But as soon as I get off and walk down the short hallway to the control room, I can hear fighting.

I run forward and walk in on Valor and Luck slugging each other in the face.

"What the hell?" I say, jumping in between them. "What's going on?"

But just as I say that I notice the gaming pod lid has popped open and Tray is jumping out, face red with anger.

"Oh, hey, Tray!" I say brightly. "I have a question for you about—"

"What the fuck?" he yells. "What the fuck are you assholes doing? Do you have any idea how much the equipment in this room costs? And what would happen if any of it broke?"

"Oh, no, wait," I say, putting up a hand. "I wasn't involved—"

"Get. The fuck. Out!" Tray yells. And there's veins popping out of his thick, meaty neck, that's how pissed off he is.

"But I need—"

"Out!"

"Come on," Luck says, glaring back at Valor as he hooks his fingers around my upper arm and begins to tug me towards the door. "Let's go."

CHAPTER FIVE

LUCK

"What was that all about?" Nyleena asks, once we're back on the main concourse that runs down the middle of the station. There's not much up here at this level. All the fun levels are a hundred or more levels below us. So it's relatively quiet on the large, expansive terrace surrounding the Pleasure Prison control center.

"Not important," I say. Because no way. I'm not talking to Nyleena about Valor. "Why were you up there?"

She stops and smiles.

Like actually smiles. And it's not one of those I'm-going-to-eat-you smiles either. The kind she likes to flash before she punches you in the face, or shoots you with an electrodart, or knocks you out with drugs, puts you in an enviro-suit, and throws you out an airlock.

All things she's been arrested for by Baby ALCOR since Crux decided to wake her up.

It's a real smile.

"OK, don't be upset with me."

I rub two fingers in that little dent in the center of my forehead, right between my eyes. "What did you do now?"

"I didn't do anything. Yet." She raises her eyebrows when she says, *Yet.* "I'm just warning you, because you might not like my plan. That's all."

"What plan?" I sigh. God, she makes me tired.

"I'm leaving Harem Station."

"You are?" I chuckle. "When?"

"Probably tomorrow. I made a deal with Crux."

"What kind of deal?"

"Oh, you know." There's a glint in her eyes. A literal glint. Little crackles of silver flash across her irises, like she's lightning in a bottle, ready to strike. "The kind that involves my own sentient ship." That last part is practically an excited squeal.

She looks different when she's filled with excitement.

Don't get me wrong. Nyleena is bombshell-hot every moment of the day. But it's a dark kind of hot. A dangerous heat that rises up off her skin like steam. And right now it's more like a warm-slice-of-cherry-pie kind of heat. Soft and a little mushy, but still very tasty.

"Do you know how to fly a ship?" I ask, as I start walking towards the private elevators that go to the highest levels. I really am tired. I'm going home.

She stomps her foot and stands her ground. So I turn to face her just as she says, "No one flies ships. For sun's sake. Why do people keep asking me that? I mean, what is the point of a sentient ship if you have to know how to fly it?"

"Well, it comes in handy, you know. In case there's an emergency. Have you set up an interview process?"

"What the hell are you talking about?"

"You can't just partner up with any ship, Nyleena. This is a huge decision. You're not gonna be flying out of here tomorrow on a sentient ship."

"Why not?" she asks, walking towards me again.

I turn and continue heading towards the elevator. "Because you have to choose the right one or things will not go well. Just ask Delphi. Did she ever tell you—"

"Yes, yes, yes," she says, putting up a hand to stop me. "I heard her story. I'm sure I'll be fine."

"And how are you paying for this ship?" I ask, pressing the call button. The elevator doors open and we step inside.

"I'm not paying for it. That's the point. Crux is giving it to me."

"How are you buying fuel, Nyleena? How are you paying for air, and water, and—"

"That's the ship's problem," she says. "I'll just choose one that has a good water generator and life support system."

"And fuel?" I ask, pressing the button for my quarters.

"How much do fuel pellets cost?"

"Where do you want to go? Do you want the ship to have weapons?"

"Oh, fuck yeah," she says. "Cannons. SEAR cannons," she adds dreamily.

"OK, well. That shit takes a lot of fucking fuel pellets. Where are you going? Can you pay for the gates?"

"Pay for gates?"

"Gates aren't free. Surely, you knew this."

She pauses. She did not know this.

43

JA HUSS & KC CROSS

"*Lady Luck* has a pass paid for by Harem Station. We flash it as we enter the gate and they charge us for passage."

"How much do those cost?" Nyleena asks, just as the elevator doors open to my quarters.

I step out, then stop and turn, one hand on the doors to prevent them from closing. "Last time I checked they were like two point five million credits for unlimited access for a four-hundred-spin year."

"Two point five *what?*"

"You're not leaving tomorrow." I laugh.

She deflates. And I admit, I've never, *ever* seen a deflated Nyleena. Her lips pout. I have never seen her pout either. It's very cute. In a dangerous kind of way. The way dragonbee bots are cute the first time you see one. Those pretty filigree wings and that soft buzzing they make. And then you realize they cook up poisons inside their bellies and fart out death.

But I kinda dig that. And even though we just had sex like an hour ago, my cocks are ready for more. It's pretty cool that being with your soulmate means your cocks work as a team and you don't actually have to fuck twice in a row to fully get off. Once the two of you are in sync, it's like all the sexy stars in the universe align just so and work together.

I could go another round though. For sure.

"But I have plans, Luck. Big plans. And once a Cygnian princess gets a plan in her head, she sees it through. I will be leaving tomorrow."

"Well, if that's the case." I grin at her. "You wanna come inside and have one last go at mind-blowing sex before you take off?"

She glances down at the growing thickness under my tactical pants, then back up at my face. "We just—"

"I know," I say, cutting her off. "But…" I shrug. "And if you're leaving tomorrow, then we should probably—"

"Whatever." She shrugs, pushing her way past me. "So this is your place, huh?"

"Yeah, when I'm here," I say, releasing the elevator doors.

She looks around. It's all pretty high-end standard. Dark gray auto-mold couches, a small dining area. Small kitchen with a giant autocook. A large wall screen for entertainment.

"You want a drink?"

"Sure," she says, plopping on the couch. The auto-mold shapes around her hips and she wiggles a little, smiling as it shifts to make her comfortable. "Tushberry juice, if you have it."

"I can order it," I say, walking over to the autocook to tab through the menu. "So what kind of deal did you make with Crux to earn this free ship?" I ask, ordering her some juice. Then decide I'll have a juice too. Not really in the mood to have a real drink. I'm just too fucking tired.

"He just wants some information from Asshole ALCOR."

"So that's why you were up in the Pleasure Prison control room? To go inside and… what?" I laugh, just as the autocook dings, signaling our drinks are ready. "You're gonna ask ALCOR for a favor? He's not that kind of dude. What are you gonna give ALCOR?"

"What do you mean?"

I take the drinks, walk over to her, hand hers off, then sit down on the other side of the couch and lean back, closing my eyes. "He's not called Asshole ALCOR for nothing. He's gonna want something in return."

"Well," she says, pausing to take a sip of her juice.

I open my eyes for this part. Because when a Cygnian princess drinks tushberry juice they recharge. Or something. And they glow a little. And even though I don't really like Nyleena, I do like to look at her. Especially when she's recharging.

She displays more than most princesses when she does this. Both Lyra and Delphi are quite dull compared to Nyleena. But then, she's a silver and they are both pink.

She smacks those perfect lips and smiles. "Whatever he wants, I guess."

"Hmmm." I smile, closing my eyes again. "That's pretty dangerous. He could want anything." I open one eye and peek at her. "He could want you to get him out of there. He's pretty desperate right now."

She shrugs. "So? I can get him out."

"Can you?"

"Sure. I can do anything once I set my mind to it."

"He's an evil, all-powerful AI and he can't get himself out. So how would you do that?"

She taps her head. "I can concoct perfect plans, Luck. You might think, *Oh, aren't Delphi and Lyra so clever?* They pulled off really great schemes. But they are nothing compared to me and my crafty brain. I'm the clever one. I'll figure it out, believe me."

"*If* that's what he wants," I say. "But you know what would be easier?"

46

"What?"

"Just get Tray to ask Asshole ALCOR what Crux wants to know. He's the one in charge inside the Pleasure Prison. Asshole ALCOR would probably do anything to get on Tray's good side right now."

Her eyes open wide. "That's a good idea."

I down my drink, set the glass down, then take hers from her hand and set that down too. Then I grab her and pull her on top of me. Because I would just like to fuck her real fast, then kick her out and go to sleep. Forget all about this scheming and let her bother other people with the crazy inside her brain for a while.

"Oooooooh," she squeals, straddling me. Rubbing herself across my lap. The friction making my cocks jump with anticipation.

The best thing about this little soulmate side show we're having right now? She never says no. And she doesn't need gifts, or sweet talk, or promises either. She's always ready and willing.

I could get used to that.

Maybe I am used to that? We've been doing this for almost two months now. I don't even think about other girls.

Which… maybe that's weird? But fuck it. Why bother romancing strangers when I have a convenient sex princess who needs me, and only me, to release her pent-up luminous flux?

I reach for the upper part of her strapless bodysuit and I'm just about to pull it down to reveal her goods when both her hands grip my wrists.

"What?" I ask.

"Don't do that." And she's serious when she says this. *Don't do that.* It comes out like a threat.

47

"Why not?" I ask. "I wanna play with your tits."

"I'm only gonna say this once, Luck. OK?" She smiles. "I do not get naked for you."

"You're not getting naked. I just wanna see your tits."

She pauses to consider this. And I'm like… what the fuck? Because I don't understand. There's nothing to think about. I pull down her suit, her tits bounce out, and I get to man-handle them.

"How about this instead?" she asks. And then she grabs my t-shirt at the collar and rips it open.

Just like that. Just rips it open.

"Suns, Nyleena." I laugh. "You're crazy."

She smiles and waggles her eyebrows at me, then glances down and ogles my well-muscled chest. Her palms press flat against my skin as she leans forward, her pussy already moving back and forth across my cocks, making them grow even bigger.

Two seconds later and I've got the stick tab between her legs opened up and I'm pushing a finger inside her.

"Oh, shit," she coos, her fingers deftly releasing the tab on my tactical pants. The stick tab comes apart and then she's got her hand inside. Wrapping around both my cocks as she squeezes and jerks on me.

She knows what she's doing too. Nyleena has the erotic skills of a sexbot.

"Do you want me to suck it?" she asks, already maneuvering into position.

"No," I say. Because as nice as her mouth is, I just want her pussy tonight. "Just put me inside you," I say.

"Ohhh," she moans. "Your wish is my command, Commander Luck. I'm your little sex slave, aren't I?"

OK. So we do a little role-playing. She does mostly. Her idea, not mine. But I don't care. I'm not really into it but it seems to be her thing, if you know what I mean. The thing that gets her all hot and ready. And I like sex with Nyleena to be quick and this Commander Luck stuff gets the job done. So I decide to play along and say, "You're my bought-and-paid for sex slave, Princess Nyleena. And you will fuck me whenever I command it."

"Oh, no," she fake-cries as she positions both my cocks at her entrance. "You're going to hurt me, aren't you? You're so big and I'm so tight…"

Fine. It's predictable. Who cares? It works.

"My giant Akeelian cocks are gonna split you in half, princess. You won't be able to walk. Ever again. I will ruin you."

"Ruin me!" she yells, sitting down so both of my cocks slide up inside her.

She is tight though. Oh, God. And her vaginal muscles are like trained performers. They contract around my shafts so hard, I wince.

But she feels so goddamned good I just want more.

I stand up, taking her with me. Nyleena squeals with excitements and contracts around my shafts again, making sure they don't slip out as I walk her over to a wall and press her back up against it.

There is no chance of me slipping out now. Not until we're done. Because the heads of both of my cocks are swelling up inside her, locking us together until our desire to fuck is over.

"You're an animal," she growls. "Keep talking dirty to me."

"Don't scratch me again," I warn. My face still stings from earlier.

"Got it," she pants. "No scratching."

And then she bites me.

"Fuck!" I yell. Because when Nyleena decides to bite, she fucking bites hard. And even though I can't feel it now... I will feel that later.

"Yeah," she says. "Get mad. Get angry. Hate-fuck me, Commander Luck. I want you to pound me—"

I think I lose time when she starts talking like this during sex. Because my mind kinda floats in empty space for a few moments. I see nothing but pin-pricks of light surrounded by deep, dark space as I thrust my hips harder faster. Seeking to be as deep inside her as I can get.

"I want you to fuck me like the universe depends on it! I want you to—"

I put my hand over her mouth. Because now she's just distracting me.

I want to float in the emptiness we create. Just let the feeling of her pussy clenching down on my shafts fill up the entire universe.

She keeps talking under my hand, but I don't care. I'm close. Very close.

Her thighs squeeze my hips. Crushing me like a vice. And I retaliate by reaching up to grab a huge fistful of her sleek, silver hair, and I pull it.

More muffled talking under my palm. My hips rocking into her like they have a mind of their own and then...

And then that moment comes. Not the release. Not yet.

There's another moment we have together. Something I've never experienced with any other woman.

It's a moment of disembodied calm.

Everything ceases to exist except that deep, dark space and the pinpricks of light.

It stretches time out to infinity and we are stuck there.

Happy to be stuck there.

And then, light.

CHAPTER SIX

Rustling beside me draws me up from a perfect dream.

But I'm reluctant to wake, so I linger in that in-between state. It's warm. There's a soft glow.

Not the glow of me. Which is white and harsh unless I fully release the silver-laced lavender inside me. More gold than silver.

And not the energy of me, either. Which is electric and sharp. It's more of a calm buzzing.

Then the rustling that woke me becomes restlessness and something hard and muscular wraps around my middle.

I open my eyes and realize I'm in someone's bed.

I turn my head to see the edges of Luck's dark blond hair curling around my peripheral vision.

What the hell?

How did I get here? Did I just… spend the night with him?

I lift up the light silver sheet covering us and yup. We're naked.

Motherfucker took off my clothes!

I hate that. I fucking hate it. He's gonna have all kinds of questions and... Hold on.

I stop fuming about being naked and instead concentrate on what I'm seeing under the sheets.

Damn. He's got a nice body. One of his legs is draped over my hip possessively. Both his arms are wrapped around my middle, and his mouth is pressed up against my neck.

He's breathing softly and this tickles all the tiny hairs behind my ear, making my nipples perk up into little peaks.

I squirm, trying to break free of his grip. Because I need to get dressed and I need to do that *now*.

He just hugs me tighter and growls, "Don't move."

"I need to go," I say, struggling as I pull a sheet around me.

"Not yet," he hums.

"Why? Why did you let me spend the night here? Sun's sake. I don't even remember getting in bed with you. I don't even remember getting undressed."

He answers me with a soft snore.

"Are you listening to me?"

"No," he mumbles. "Don't move."

"I need to go," I say. "Is it morning? I have shit to do. My ship is waiting."

And I'm naked, I remind myself. I do not get naked with people. Especially *him*.

"Stay here," he grumbles. "That's an order from your commander."

"Why?"

He sighs. Long and loud. "Because I'm fucking still tired, OK? And I'm comfortable. That's all you need to know."

"I'm not your goddamned pillow, Luck. Let me go!"

"Fine," he says, releasing me. Then he takes the sole of his foot and kicks me away. So hard I actually fall off the bed.

"You asshole."

"I told you not to move. But if you insist on moving, then just get the fuck out."

"You're such a jerk," I say, grabbing the sheet and pulling it off him, then quickly cover myself.

He opens one eye. Glares at me. Then closes it again and turns over so he's lying on his stomach.

I have to suck in a breath of air at the sight of his bare backside.

Suns. He is all muscle.

And scars, I realize.

"Either stay and get your ass back in bed or get the fuck out, Nyleena. I'm still. Fucking. Tired."

"Ugggggh," I say in response. "You're such an asshole. I'll have you know I'll be gone by the end of the day. Then you'll have to be nice to girls to make them fuck you. And good luck with that, *Luck*."

"Why are you still here?"

"Fuck you."

I get up, sheet tucked against my breasts, and look around for my clothes.

Not here.

So I walk over to his closet.

"Now what the hell are you doing?"

I don't even answer him. Just pull a t-shirt off a hanger and slip it on real quick. I grab a pair of shorts, put those on too, then walk out of the bedroom and find my sexy boots scattered along the hallway.

Hmm. He must've undressed me as we walked to the bedroom.

But… that could *not* have happened.

I do not get naked with men.

I don't bother putting the boots on. Just carry them in my arms and get in the elevator.

My quarters are one level down. And when I exit the elevator and enter the short hallway, the cyborg master is exiting his quarters.

We share this floor.

His one red eye flashes across his face. "Walk of shame, huh?"

"Fuck you," I mutter, pressing the code to enter my place.

"Always a delight, Nyleena," he calls, just before the elevator doors close and he disappears.

This day is going to be a disaster, I can already tell.

"No," I say out loud. "I'm leaving this stupid station tonight."

I will do whatever it takes to scheme my way off this place.

I'm done with everyone. I'm done with Lyra, and Delphi, and all those stupid brothers. And ALCOR, all of them too. But especially Luck.

Who the hell does he think he is?

He's no one.

I'm the goddamned silver princess in this place. Me. They have no one higher up in rank than *me*.

Not even Asshole ALCOR outranks me.

I'm the motherfucking commander. And if I see Luck today, I'm gonna tell him that. He's the little bitch now.

His plan was dumb too. Just ask Tray to ask ALCOR. And owe him a favor when I leave? No, thank you.

My plan was good.

I'm gonna take a shower, put on my most badass princess outfit, walk up to the Pleasure Prison, go inside, and then find that damn AI and make him tell me everything he knows about leveling up.

Then I'm gonna get my ship and leave.

I'm not even gonna say goodbye to asshole Luck.

"What do you mean you're full?"

The Centurian running the main entrance to the Pleasure Prison is kinda tall and intimidating. And she's got no fewer than four weapons strapped to her body. So even though I'm a haughty silver princess, I try to control my anger.

I'm not sure she'd really shoot me with that pistol on her hip because Baby ALCOR has pretty strict rules about maiming and murdering here on Harem, but you never know.

"We're full," she says again. "Meaning there's no room for more bodies in the gaming pod levels. We have a wait list on the air screen. Put your name on that and you'll be pinged when it's time."

"How long does it usually take to be pinged?"

She rolls her eyes at me, then pinches her fingers together in the air and opens up her air screen. "There's two thousand, one hundred and seventy-two people ahead of you. Probably two weeks."

"Two *weeks?*"

"And did you see what I did here?" she says, closing and opening her air screen again. "Unless you're an idiot, you can do that too. Now move along. I have customers."

"How come they get in?"

"Because they put their name on the wait list and now it's their *turn.*"

"But I'm Princess Nyleena, Luck's... you know. And I'm on a special mission from Crux. Can't you make an exception?"

"And I'm the Queen of Centuria." She pulls that pistol off her hip and presses it right up against my head. "Now get the fuck out of my face."

I turn away and mutter, "Bitch."

"I heard that," she calls after me.

Great. Now what? Two weeks? I can't wait two weeks.

I stop at the edge of the terrace on the Pleasure Prison level and pout. I really want that ship. And I really want it today. Surely, I can make this happen.

And that's when I spot Valor getting off a bot lift and walking towards the little hallway that leads to the control room.

I follow him in a rush and catch up just in time to walk through the control room door before it closes.

He whirls at me, pistol drawn.

I put up my hands. Because I'm pretty sure Valor is allowed to shoot anyone he wants on this station. "It's just me."

"For sun's fucking sake, Nyleena. What the hell?"

"I can't get in the Pleasure Prison. That bitch at the entrance says there's a two-week wait."

The guy at the control center gets up and says, "No problems to report. See ya later, Valor."

Valor says, "Thanks, Mik. Have a good one." Then he turns to me and says, "So?"

"So I need to get in! Can't you get me in?"

"No," he says, taking his seat at the control center.

"But… you have an empty pod right here." I point to the empty pod in the middle of the room.

He laughs. "That's Tray's pod. No one uses it but him. Not even me."

"But he won't know. Can't you just sneak me in real quick?"

Just as I say that, Tray enters. He nods to me— "Nyleena"—then opens up the lid of the gaming pod.

"Tray!" I say brightly. "Perfect. Just the man I need to see. Is there any way to—"

"I don't have time, Nyleena. Whatever you need, get it from Luck. He's your responsible party, not me."

Then he get inside the pod, shuts the lid, and… well, that's that.

"But—" I turn back to Valor, who is not paying any attention to me. "Come on!" I say. "You can get me on the list. I know you can. You're Valor, for fuck's sake."

"Luck can get you on that list too." He shoots me a look over his shoulder. "He's Luck."

"I can't ask him. He's being a dick today."

"I'm busy, Nyleena. Get out."

"No." I huff. "Don't you need something?"

"What?"

"A trade? Yeah. Let's do a trade. I'll get you whatever you want and you push my name up to the top of the list. Today."

"I don't need anything from you."

"Everyone needs something. Just… what about Veila?"

"What?" And this really gets his attention. Because he actually spins around in his chair to look at me. "What about her?"

"I've noticed you're a little bit obsessed with her."

"Am not."

"Please. You watch that stupid message she sent Delphi and Jimmy every chance you get."

"What do you know about her?"

"Lots," I say, nodding my head. "I'm a silver. Just like her. I know lots."

"Like what?"

"What do you want to know?"

He thinks for a moment, then says, "I want to know what happened back on the Lair Station. I want to know what she told Jimmy. Because he's keeping something from me, I can just tell."

"Hmm," I say. "Well, I wasn't there."

He turns back to the controls. "Good talking to you then, Nyleena. Now leave, before I have to call security bots and have you locked up. *Again.*"

"What if I get that info? From Jimmy and Delphi? Then what? Will you push me up the list?"

"They're not gonna tell you shit." But then he turns back to me. "But Luck would. He was there too. I'm pretty sure Jimmy told him more than he told me. So… if you can get Luck to tell you… sure. OK. I'll push you up the list."

"Done."

CHAPTER SEVEN

The door alarm buzzes me out of my dream.

God, it's a nice dream. And one moment it's fully there. I'm immersed in the fantasy world I created. And then... it's gone.

Fuck.

The door alarm buzzes again. "Go away!" I yell.

My cocks are super hard now. And then I remember Nyleena was here. I turn over and find her gone.

Oh, yeah. I sorta kicked her out. But she kept talking. God. Why does she have to talk so much?

Still, if I had been nicer she'd be here right now and I wouldn't have to jerk off to tame my wild cocks.

Note for next time she sleeps over. Be nice to her so I get a real fuck in the morning.

The door alarm buzzes again. "Fuck!" I swing my legs out of bed and walk down the hallway, fisting both my cocks at the same time.

When I get to the door I open up the privacy screen and spy Nyleena on the other side of the camera, leaning in on the buzzer. Scowling with determination.

Well, then. Looks like I win anyway.

I open the door with one hand and jerk my cocks with the other.

She glances down at my naked body, then immediately back up at my face.

She looks... different today. She's wearing yellow, for one. A short, flirty skirt with white thigh-high boots. And her top is a pale pink.

She almost looks... sweet—

"What the fuck, Luck? I've been buzzing this damn door for like ten minutes."

—and then she opens her mouth and all the sweetness goes bitter.

I sigh. "What do you want?"

"I want..." She takes a deep breath. "I want a favor."

"A favor?" I ask, eyebrows rising up my forehead. "From me?"

"Yes. I need to jump the line for the Pleasure Prison so I can go inside and talk to—"

"I told you, that's not gonna work."

"I think it is. I just need you to put my name at the top of the wait list. OK? That's it. Then I'll..." She glances down. I'm still jerking off. But hey, this is a typical morning hard-on. It will not go away until it gets the release it needs. "Gross."

I shrug, then have a bright idea. "Hey, if you let me fuck you real quick I'll see what I can do about that list."

"Right now?"

"Yeah. Right now."

"Fine," she says, pushing me out of her way so she can enter my quarters.

I close the door and smile. Because I can't get her to the top of the list for the Pleasure Prison. People watch that list like a fucking oracle about to spit secrets. There'd be a riot if someone jumped the list. I don't even have permission to do that. No one but Tray has that kind of power.

I don't have to tell her that, though.

At least... not yet.

"OK, take off your clothes," I say.

"What?" she snaps. "No. I'm not taking off my clothes for a sun-fucking quickie. Just..." She lifts up her skirt and pulls her panties aside. "Work around it."

"I'm in the mood for naked sex," I joke. "So yeah—"

"So no. You want this?" she says, panning a hand down her body. "You work. Around it."

"But I'm already naked. It's not fair."

"Life's not fair, Luck. You should've learned that lesson by now."

"OK," I say, walking over to the couch and taking a seat. "But I get lap sex then. I'm not in the mood to fuck you against a wall today."

"Oh, my God. You're so damn romantic I'm swooning."

"Just climb on," I growl.

She huffs, but walks over to me pulling up her skirt. She settles in my lap, then pulls her panties aside and guides my rock-hard cocks to her entrance.

She grits her teeth when I enter her, then lets go of the panties and places both her hands on my shoulders. "Your brother Tray is a dick."

"We're all dicks," I say. "Bob up and down a little."

She does. Without comment. Like she's super distracted.

"I need to get in there," she says, biting her lip when I take charge and thrust upward.

I kinda like that lip-biting stuff. It's super sexy.

"Make your tits bounce," I say. "I like it when they bounce."

She bobs a little higher. Bounces down a little harder. Pretty compliant this morning.

I like her compliant. She's almost tolerable.

"I mean, he's got that gaming pod in the damn control room and he won't even let me just pop in real quick to get the answers I need."

"You can't just pop into the Pleasure Prison, Nyleena. That's not how it works."

"What do you mean?"

"Can we just fuck first and then talk?" I ask. "I'll be quick. I just need the morning hard-ons to go away."

"Fine," she says, her hips moving more artfully now.

God. I really like how she does that. And her tits are right in my face. I want to rip that shirt down the middle and give her a motorboat right now.

"Don't you dare," she warns, reading my mind.

"Then bounce," I say. "Just make me come. It's not that hard."

She lifts up. So high my swollen heads get stuck at the edge of her opening and a powerful wave of pleasure fills me up.

"Shit," I say. "That feels great, baby. Do it again."

She gives me a weird look. Probably because I called her baby. But thank the sun, she keeps her mouth shut and just does as I asked. Lifting up until I'm stuck inside her then bouncing down hard, so her tits smack across my face.

"Yeah," I say. Because this is different. She feels different in the morning.

"Come for me, Luck. Spill your super, double-cocked semen deep inside me and make me scream."

I know she's just winding me up, but I don't care. And it doesn't take much to do that in the morning, anyway.

So I grab her hips and help. Lifting her up until that new feeling swells inside my body, and then slamming her down on my bare thighs with a smack.

"Oooooo," she starts moaning. "Oh, yeah! Fuck me hard! *Harder!*"

I come.

I can't stop myself.

I close my eyes as an intense feeling of total calm and serenity sweeps through me.

She kisses me. Right on the lips. And I'm just about to open my mouth and kiss her back when she pulls away and stands up, adjusting her skirt as she walks off.

"Where are you going?"

"To wipe your come off before it ruins my panties."

"Did you even come?" I ask.

"No," she calls from the hall bathroom. "But don't worry. I'll get off today at the regularly scheduled time." She reappears, still adjusting her skirt, then says, "OK. Get me in."

Well, that was… fun while it lasted. And my cocks are no longer hard. But I somehow feel… unsatisfied.

"Chop, chop," Nyleena says. "I need this now, Luck."

I discard the meaning of my unsatisfactory satisfaction and pop open an air screen. Go through the motions of bringing up the Pleasure Prison list, then press edit, and fake my disappointment when the screen flashes red.

"Fuck," I say.

"What?" she says, walking over to the couch and kneeling beside me so she can see my screen.

"It won't let me edit the list. Sorry, princess. Can't do it."

"You asshole!" she says, slapping my face. "You knew that before we fucked, didn't you?"

I can't even lie. But I didn't need to laugh. Because she slaps me again and then heads for the door.

"Wait!" I say.

"What?" She turns on her heel and seethes the word at me.

"I can get Tray to get you in."

"This was a mistake. I don't need you, Luck. Valor already offered to do that for me. All I have to do is get him info on Veila and it's done. So you can just... fuck *yourself* from now on."

"Wait. What do you mean? Valor wants info on Veila? Why?"

"I don't know. And I don't care, either. He told me to ask you, but you know what?" She points her yellow-tipped fingernail at me. And you know what else I like about Nyleena? She's always color-coordinated. Right down to her nails. "I'm gonna go ask Delphi to get me that information instead!"

"I know more than she does. I was *there*."

"She was there too!"

"Yeah, but before I met up with Jimmy and Delphi in the docking bays I ran into Veila in the hallway."

"And you didn't kill her?"

"I tried. But her cyborgs were there. And I was trying to meet back up with Cha-Cha, who was a few hallways away. But Veila, she told me something. Something I've been holding in. Something everyone would want to know."

"So why didn't you tell them already?"

I shrug. "We got away. Everyone's happy. Why rock the boat?"

She squints her eyes at me. "Explain."

"No," I say. "I want something from you in exchange for this."

"I already fucked you, Luck. You're not getting another orgasm before the regularly scheduled time!"

"Not that," I say.

"Then what?"

"I want to know why Valor is so interested in Veila. If you can get him to tell you that, I'll tell you what Veila told me in the hallway."

"This is getting ridiculous! All I was supposed to do was get one simple answer for Crux and now I'm stuck looking for information on Veila. And in addition to that, now I have to get even more info on why Valor is so obsessed with her?" She stomps her foot. "I just want my stupid ship!"

I shrug. "Hey, sentient ships are valuable. I'm sure Crux knew how hard it would be for you to answer his question. Otherwise he'd just have answered it himself."

She frowns.

"Right?" I ask.

"Maybe."

"But don't feel bad, princess. Some problems are just… unsolvable, ya know?"

She squints her eyes at me.

"I don't think there's an answer for Crux. And if there was, it probably died with Real ALCOR. Crux was setting you up. Don't you see? You were never going to succeed. He was never going to give you a sentient ship."

"That bastard," she whispers. "But if he thinks I can be deterred by a few obstacles, he's dead wrong. This is what I'm good at! All Cygnian princesses will tell you they're expert scammers and schemers, but I'm the *best*."

"The absolute best," I agree with her. "You'll show him, right?"

"I will," she seethes. "And I'll be back with your stupid information about Valor. You wait and see."

She whirls around so fast her little skirt twirls as she disappears out my door.

More determined than ever.

CHAPTER EIGHT

I decide it's time to find my girls and I start with Delphi because she was there when that whole Veila shit-show went down.

This little idea of mine started out so simple. It was a day's worth of scheming and plotting, tops. But now everything is suddenly becoming complicated.

No worries though. If there's one thing a Cygnian princess excels at—besides blow-your-mind sex—it's scheming and plotting. We love solving problems. It doesn't deter us, it makes us stronger. More determined than ever.

And I have two high-performing schemey minds at my disposal right here on Harem.

Delphi was working for Veila before she came here. And she betrayed Veila. And she's still alive. Which means that mission was a total success and so right now she is a shining star of sneaky in my book.

And then I have Lyra. Whom I'm not sure is quite up to Delphi's level when it comes to badass planning, but she's my sister and BFF. And she saved my life. Risked everything to save my life. So Lyra has guts.

Sometimes the nerve to carry on and see things through trumps everything else.

So if Delphi can't get me what I need I'll go to Lyra next.

When I get out to the main concourse of the station I walk over to the edge and look down. It's pretty intimidating from all the way up here at the top. I can't even begin to see the bottom. For one, there are lots of bridge levels. Some parks. A rollercoaster a little ways down the curve in the distance to my left. There's even a river level. You can actually raft down that thing. One time I was down on the low-low levels where all the raunchy outlaws hang out and it started to rain and I overheard someone explain to another newb like myself that the river did that, but it only happened on the low-low levels because gravity is slightly higher down there.

It's a big place, this station.

I open my air screen and tap the little call button for Delphi and her face pops up immediately, all flushed and red like she's been doing something that requires effort.

"What's up, princess?" she says. Then she frowns. "Oh, man. You're not locked up again, are you? If we have to bail you out one more time—"

"No." I cut her off. "I just need to talk to you. Can we meet somewhere?"

She giggles, then squirms, then giggles again.

I scowl at her. "What are you doing?"

"Jimmy and I just—"

"TMI," I say, putting up a hand. I do not need to hear about the sexual exploits of anyone, especially them. Gross. "Meet me somewhere."

70

"OK. Pick a place."

"Scarlet's Shooting Gallery on level nine."

Delphi crinkles her nose. Because level nine is infamous for hosting all the roughest establishments and Scarlet's is like the worst of them. Which in my book just means fun.

"Just meet me there," I say. Because she's still trying to come up with a reason why we shouldn't. "Ten minutes." And then I add, "It's very urgent."

"Why? What's wrong?"

"Just meet me," I say, then end the call and request a lift bot. Because Scarlet's is a long way from where I'm at now. And if I had to take all the various escalators and elevators it would take more than an hour to get there.

I do have to admit—these Harem boys have been good to me. Not only did they give me Harem Station citizenship, but I get a weekly allowance too. Just enough credits to keep me busy shooting things in galleries, or playing games in the arcades, and a free lift bot whenever I want one.

Some weeks I even have enough credits left over to join a semi-serious card game.

Of course... that was after everyone suspected I was Luck's one and they made him my responsible party.

Which is a little bit degrading. But Lyra is Serpint's one and Delphi is Jimmy's one and they both wear something on their person declaring that and I don't have to.

Lyra wears a freaking collar with Serpint's name on it. Sure, it's made of jewels, but still.

No way.

Delphi wears a cuff, not a collar. But it's the same idea.

I think I came out ahead since no one asked me to declare my ownership after they woke me up from the cryopod.

I was a little pissed off that Lyra let them keep me frozen for months after I was rescued, but whatever. I'm moving on.

And if I can just get this info for Crux I know he'll give me a ship. Crux isn't the kind of man who goes back on a promise. So sure, maybe he does expect me to fail so he doesn't have to pay up. But I won't fail. And when I deliver on the deal, he'll *have* to hold up his end.

Delphi is already waiting for me when my lift bot drops me off at the edge of the terrace in front of Scarlet's. She's got an afterglow. A soft pink light radiates up from her skin.

She's very pretty. A little short to be very useful in a proper fight. But she told me about the exoskeletons that Jimmy's partner, Xyla, has stashed inside the *Big Dicker*.

I should get me one of those. After I get the ship I'll scheme up a plan with Xyla.

"OK, what is it now?" Delphi says when I approach her.

"Let's go shoot!" I say enthusiastically.

"You brought me down here to shoot?"

"You need the practice," I say.

She huffs. "I could outshoot you any day of the week."

"Prove it," I say, panning my hand towards the shooting gallery.

One more fun fact about Cygnian princesses. We're super-competitive with each other. We take dares almost as seriously as we take contracts.

Delphi growls a little and goes inside. We pay for a lane, spend more time than I really have choosing weapons—but that's most of the fun about this place. They have all the best projectiles—then get our protective gear and head in to shoot.

"What's really going on?" Delphi asks as she mounts the targets on the automated moving-target system.

I load up my weapon with real shells. No lasers or plasma pistols for us today. Then say, "Tell me what happened with Valor and Veila back on the Lair Station."

She stops loading targets. "Why?"

"Because I need to know, Delphi. This involves me too and I feel like I'm missing information."

She finishes the targets, presses the button to start the automated systems and they go whirring away and start looping around in some indecipherable pattern downrange. Then she picks up her pistol, checks the magazine, and stares at me. "You're lying."

"Which part of that was a lie?" I ask.

"The part you left out. I already know about your little deal with Crux."

"That's got nothing to do with Veila and Valor," I say.

JA HUSS & KC CROSS

"No," she agrees. Then aims at the targets, squeezes the trigger, and the clay target shatters as it whizzes past a hundred feet away. She stops, narrowing her eyes on the other side of her protective glasses, and says, "But I also heard that you're trying to make a deal to get inside the Pleasure Prison. And I'm pretty sure this information you need from me is part of that exchange."

"So what if it is?" I ask.

"Then that means I get something from you." She shoots another whizzing target and looks back at me. "That's how a scheme works, right?"

"What do you want?" I ask, so annoyed.

"Something you can't get." She shrugs and shoots another target. And maybe I underestimated Delphi's skills. Because she's a damn good shot and she's on to me too. "So… this is lotsa fun and all," she continues. "But you're not getting anything from me unless I get something from you."

"Just tell me what it is," I huff. "I can get anything I want."

"Except this," Delphi retorts, still shooting shit.

"What is it?" I demand.

"You really want to know? Because your failure is going to eat you away when you can't deliver."

"Delphi," I growl.

"Fine. I've been meaning to ask you about this anyway. I want to know about a place called Earth."

"What?" I say, squinting my eyes at her. "What the hell is an Earth?"

"A planet. That's the place you and Lyra were going to when you got sidetracked on Bull Station."

"Never heard of it."

"How is that possible? You were *going* there."

"I was asleep in the fucking cryopod for weeks before we left Cygnia. I don't know anything about Earth. Didn't you ask Lyra?"

"Yes. Of course I did. She didn't know anything either. She said she heard someone talking about your destination and that's how she knew where you guys were going."

"Hmmm. Weird. I don't know anything. Why do you need this information?" I don't know why, but I'm suspicious of Delphi.

She sighs. "See, Jimmy's got this thing for this planet called Earth. His mom was there, or something. I'm not really sure. But then we kinda, sorta, went there when we were on Mighty Minions, right?" I open my mouth to ask a million questions about that, but she just holds up a hand and says, "Never mind. It's a long story. But I want to know more about this place. If you can find out more about Earth, I'll tell you what I noticed about Valor when he came to save us on the Lair."

"Earth," I whisper. "Where the hell do I find information about Earth?"

"There is no information. That's why I know you can't deliver." She smiles sweetly, then turns and pops a target out of existence, like she has eyes in the back of her head, then turns back and smiles at me again. "So... nice try. Sorry you're not gonna get that ship."

"This is bullshit," I growl. "Someone has to know something. Doesn't Jimmy know?"

"If Jimmy knew I wouldn't have to ask you, would I?" She frowns. "But..."

75

"But what?" I ask, leaning forward towards her a little, eager for any hint of what to do next.

"But I heard that maybe… ALCOR—the Real ALCOR—knew about it."

"Well," I huff. "He's dead."

"I know, but Baby ALCOR could have something hidden away in his core memory."

"So why didn't you ask him?"

"He's not friendly with me." She shrugs. "I tried. And Jimmy tried too. But we don't know him that well. Jimmy left right after the memorial ceremony for Real ALCOR, so there was no real bonding time."

"Hmmm," I say. "Well, I know Baby ALCOR pretty well."

"As you should." She laughs. "You've been locked up enough times since they woke you up."

"I could ask him," I offer. Ignoring her dig. "I could get that info. Then"—I point my finger at her—"when I do, you will tell me everything that happened with Veila and Valor when he showed up on Mighty Minions to bring you and Jimmy home. And," I say, stressing the word, "I want to know everything Jimmy knows about Veila too."

"Deal," she says, extending her hand.

"Deal," I say, shaking it.

Then I turn to the targets and start popping them off, one by one, as they whiz by.

I'm totally ahead now.

Not only will I learn why Valor is infatuated with Veila, I will get all the info about Veila that Luck is hiding.

Take that, you lucky bastard.

CHAPTER NINE

Even though Nyleena and I already had sex this morning I find myself counting down the minutes until it's time for our regularly scheduled tryst in the garden patch. It's not the same one from yesterday but we have this schedule going, so I expect her to show.

Today our patch of wilderness is located on level one hundred eighteen near the swimming pool sector. It's a little different than the last one, which was mostly grass and short plants. This one is a circular grove of leafy trees with a patch of velvet clover in the middle.

It's very soft. Better than grass, I decide as I lie down in the mottled, shifting light to wait for her. Almost like a bed.

We should give bed fucking a try. Last night, after we both came, she was so exhausted she fell asleep in my lap. Which, can I just say, was weird.

But I was tired. So I think I fell asleep too. Because when I woke up we were both lying haphazardly across the couch and the auto-mold had shaped around us in this weird way, so my neck was killing me.

And it was dark in my quarters. All the lights had gone into evening mode. Which is just this very low-level glow along the baseboards. I tried to wake her. I even unzipped her bodysuit and got it off her, seeing if she'd get pissed and slug me in the face. At least she'd be awake.

But she was out. Like, passed out good. It was weird, but also lucky. So much bare skin. Now I wish I had turned the lights on. Then I could've seen her naked for once.

But the idea didn't occur to me so I took her boots off and just as I was picking her up in my arms, she sorta woke up and snatched them up from the floor, only to drop them again as I walked her down the hallway.

By the time I put her in bed, she was fast asleep again.

I should've had sex with her in the bed. It would've been a nice change.

This secret garden is pretty good though. Not a bed, for sure. But nice.

My fingers splay out on top of the velvet clover, pressing down a little to gauge the depth. Thick. Cushion-y too.

I open an air screen and check the time.

She's fifteen minutes late.

Hmm.

She always shows up after I do, but never this late.

Did she think we didn't have to meet today since we fucked this morning?

Sun, I hope not. I'm pretty sure she mentioned something about our regularly-scheduled tryst this morning, didn't she?

But then again, she was wound tight when she left me. So determined to win this little battle of wills with Crux.

I laugh.

He is not giving that crazy bitch a sentient ship. She has no clue what she's doing. She didn't even know you had to pay your way through the gates. Like... how the fuck would she get anywhere?

I can picture it now. Nyleena gets her ship, leaves the station, and three spins later we get a frantic neutrino call—collect—asking us to come save her.

I laugh again. Ha. That's so Nyleena.

When Crux asked me to take her mind off things by suggesting she get a job I was all for it. But now she's obsessed with the idea of getting her own ship.

What would that look like for me?

I mean... I'm pretty used to this daily sex stuff. And I have to admit, it's so much better when you fuck your soulmate because we only have to do it once. Not that I ever minded having to fuck girls twice to satisfy my second cock, it's just way better not having to explain how we Akeelians are different every single fucking time.

Yeah. Maybe that's what I like about being around Nyleena. The fact that she gets me.

And I sorta get her. I get the way her crazy brain works. I'm even being supportive by giving her these little challenges. She thrives on that kind of stuff.

But here's the thing... I really do want to know what's up with Valor. And Tray. There's something they're not telling me. I can feel it.

Valor does not belong in the Pleasure Prison control room. He belongs with me. And *Lady Luck*. And Cha-Cha.

He just doesn't know it yet.

And we don't belong here, on Harem. We belong out there. In the farthest reaches of the galaxy searching for old AI parts to keep this place running.

I miss it. I fucking love landing on ancient abandoned stations. You never know what you're gonna find on them.

Some alien species trying to murder you at every turn?

Yes. I love it.

Some thousand-year-old booby trap just waiting for you to trigger it so it can cut your head off as you reach for your booty?

Fuck yeah, give it to me.

Long-forgotten secrets written on walls in weird languages?

More, please.

This can't be the end of our adventures together. It just can't. We're so young still. We have many decades of salvaging ahead of us.

I refuse to believe it's over.

But I would miss the princess sex if Valor and I left again. Maybe Nyleena would like to come with us?

Valor would probably hate that too.

Everything has changed since Beauty died.

But there's no way back. There was nothing left of her. There was an old backup of her mind somewhere in Real ALCOR's data core, but the Baby already admitted that she was not in his memory banks.

Not even Asshole ALCOR has it. He was put inside the Pleasure Prison decades ago. So even if he does somehow have a backup of Beauty, it's not the Beauty she was when she died.

It's the Beauty she was *before*.

Which is a whole different person. That Beauty never went to all those places with us. She never fought ancient aliens on abandoned stations. She never dismantled booby traps or deciphered long-forgotten writing on long-forgotten walls.

What's the point then? Can't Valor just accept that she's gone forever? Why can't he see all the good stuff Cha-Cha brings to our little crew?

I open up my air screen and check the time again, then sit up.

"For sun's sake," I mutter. Because Nyleena is more than a half hour late now.

She stood me up!

Fuck that. My cocks were satisfied earlier today but they're far from satisfied now.

I'm gonna find my little maniac princess and get what she owes me.

CHAPTER TEN

"I'll tell you what," I say to Delphi. "I'll take you on my team any day."

"Thanks," she says, doing a little curtsey.

Our lane inside Scarlet's Shooting Gallery is littered with shattered clay targets. Like the whole floor is covered in debris.

"I'm actually glad you invited me out today, Nyleena," Delphi says. "This was fun."

"It really was," I say, meaning it. "We should do this more often."

"For sure," she says. "And for the record, you're not a bad shot."

"Shit." I laugh. "Better than you!"

Which isn't entirely true. We're pretty evenly matched. Which was a nice surprise.

"If I ever find myself in a bind I'll call you first for backup, sister."

Sister. I beam at her. "Same, bitch. And where do you shop for your outfits? Because they are cute as fuck."

"Oh, this?" She does one of those shy shrugs and lifts the hem of her flirty purple mini-skirt up a little. Then she leans in and whispers, "Jimmy's autoshopper has all of Xyla's outfits in it."

"Really?" I say, looking her up and down again. She's got silver boots. Which I own as well, but hers have designs carved in them and I'm pretty sure they're made of some real silver alloy, not aluminum alloy like mine are. Much higher quality. Maybe even designer. They have lots of designer stores on Harem but you need appointments to get them to dress you. I don't have that kind of clout because I don't have access to Luck's autoshopper.

If I had known this when I was in his quarters earlier I'd have asked him to hook me up.

"Yeah," Delphi says. "All I do is pick the ones I like, adjust it for my size, and poof. It appears like magic."

"Damn," I whisper. I might be jealous of Delphi. Jimmy is very good to her.

I wonder if Luck would be that good to me if I ask sweetly?

"What the ever-loving fuck?"

Delphi and I both turn to see Luck storming towards us. His face is all red and contorted into something that might be rage.

"What?" I ask, my hope of getting designer Xyla boots disappearing in an instant.

"You stood me up!" he says. Then lowers his voice and says, "Hey, Delphi. Sorry to barge in on your…" He frowns at the multitude of cleaning servos busy scooping up our target debris on the shooting lane. "What is this?"

"Target practice," Delphi says, closing out her air screen. "And I guess the time got away from me too. Because I'm late to meet Jimmy. We're having a romantic dinner tonight." She smiles as she picks up her unused ammo and says, "Do it again soon, Nyleena?" over her shoulder as she makes for the door.

"Sure!" I call out. "Thanks for the good time!"

When I turn back to Luck, he's still angry. "What's your problem?" I ask. "How the hell did you find me here, anyway?"

"The Baby tracks your every move, Nyleena. You're not only unreliable when it comes to fuck appointments, you're also unpredictable when it comes to being a law-abiding citizen."

"Oh, that reminds me," I say, holding up a finger. "I need to go talk to Baby ALCOR right now." I turn to leave, but he catches me by the arm. "What are you doing?"

"You owe me a fuck!" he says.

"I fucked you this morning," I huff.

"That didn't count."

"Says who?"

"Me," he growls, pointing to his chest. "You told me this morning we were meeting for sex at the regularly scheduled time."

"I did not!"

"Nyleena," he hisses between clenched teeth. "We have an agreement. We both have needs that must be met to keep on an even keel."

I laugh. "I'm fine. You're the one who needs more. And you know what? Once a day is a lot, Luck. You're damn lucky I gave in to that. When we came up with

85

this little schedule it was every three days. Now you want it twice a day?"

"I never said twice."

"Well, then I'll be going."

"Nyleena," he says, grabbing his hard cocks under his tactical pants. "They need it now."

I glance down and holy shit. He's not kidding. "How did you even walk over here without everyone laughing at you?" I chuckle.

"It's not funny," he says. "It's very uncomfortable."

"Hmm. Did it ever occur to you that the more we do it, the more you need it?"

"I'm not the only one who needs it," he says.

"Well, OK. But I'm not the one with blue balls right now and you are."

"Just…" He walks towards me. Leans in to my ear. "Just a quickie. Right now."

I'm about to give in just to get rid of him so I can be on my way, when the door slams open and a group of Centurian women walk in with rifles.

"Oh, we're sorry," one of them says, looking around. "Is this the wrong lane?"

"No," her friend says. "We're in the right place. Are you guys gonna be long?"

"We're done here," I say. I head for the door and look over my shoulder, mouthing the words, "Let's go to your place," to Luck.

Because he needs something from me. Which I am happy to provide. Because that means I get something from him in return.

Autoshopper access.

Luck is silent the whole way back up to his apartment. I do him a solid favor though. I stand in front of him the whole time so no one can see that he's dying to have sex with me and might explode in his pants.

In fact, I take it one step further and accidentally rub my ass against his cocks a few times.

He grunts and moans like he's in pain.

Poor guy.

But a deal's a deal. He doesn't know we're in the middle of a deal yet, but that's OK.

Once we get inside his quarters I head straight to the autoshopper and take a seat on the little stool in front of it, my fingers already tabbing the menu.

But it's locked. Who comes up here that he feels the need to lock his autoshopper?

"Can you open this for me, please?"

"Is that why you wanted to come up here?"

"What?" I ask, turning in my stool. He's already got his pants open. Hand firmly jerking on his cocks. "You only wanted me up here for sex."

"You're trading me access to the autoshopper for sex?"

"Why not?" I ask. "Then we both get something we want."

"So you don't want to have sex with me?" He pushes his pants down just enough that both his cocks spill out.

I stare at them. I can't help it. They are huge. And fat. And fucking spectacular. And the way his hand

JA HUSS & KC CROSS

doesn't fit all the way around them when he's jerking them both at the same time has always been a turn-on for me.

My luminous flux begins to tingle between my legs.

"I do," I say. "But did you see Delphi's outfit? She has access to Xyla's virtual closet. All she has to do is tap a few buttons, adjust the size, and poof. It appears like magic. I want some new Xyla boots."

"Is that what it's come to?" Luck asks. "Sex is just a transaction for you?"

"Everything is a transaction to me, Luck. You already know that. And don't start pulling out your feelings on me. We're not here for the feelings. Well," I amend. "The climax is a feeling, I guess. But that's also biology. We didn't ask to be…" I sigh. "Soulmates, or whatever. Someone programmed that into us."

"Does it matter?" he asks. His eyelids are heavy now. Almost halfway closed. His hand is still pumping up and down his shafts. Slowly, but I can tell he's gripping himself tight.

I glance down again. I can't stop myself. He's very pretty. In a manly way, of course. Because underneath his shirt he has the battle scars to prove it.

I force my eyes back up to his. Violet. Suns, they are beautiful. Not purple. Not blue. Not pink. But somehow they are all those colors at the same time.

"I guess it doesn't," I admit, answering his question. "But it's just sex."

"Just sex, huh?" he says, stalking towards me. He lets go of his cocks and places both hands on my shoulders, twirling around so I'm facing the screen again. "Go ahead then. The code is your name."

I almost snort. "It is not."

"Try it."

I do. And it is. Because the shopper opens up to the home page. "Hmm," I say.

"Surprised?"

"Yes," I say. But I'm distracted. Not by the clothes, though they aren't helping. But by his hands. Because he's massaging my tight shoulders.

"Does that feel good?" he asks.

"What are you doing?"

"What's it look like? I'm being nice to you."

"Why?"

"Because... because... we're tied together whether we like it or not. So the sex doesn't have to be so animalistic every single time."

I do snort this time. "Please don't tell me you're talking about feelings again."

"What's wrong with feelings?"

I brush his hands off me and turn to him, come face to face with his rock-hard cocks, and push them aside for a moment so I can look him in the eyes again. This time, I'm not dreaming about their color. I need to get something straight.

"We fuck, Luck. That's it. Cygnians don't do feelings. We do contracts. We do schemes. We do war. That's it. So if you're after feelings, you're in for a huge disappointment."

CHAPTER ELEVEN

I turn her back around and place my hands right back where they were, kneading the tension in her neck and shoulders. "You can say that all you want. But it's not true."

"Which part?" She laughs. And in that laugh she relaxes. Just a little.

"Go ahead," I say. "Shop. Buy whatever you want. You want Xyla's virtual closet? Do a search for her name, should come right up."

I don't tell her she could do this on her own autoshopper because I like the idea of her having to use my account. It feels a little... possessive. And Akeelian dudes kinda get off on that.

"What are you gonna do while I shop?"

"Pleasure you with this amazing massage."

"Why?"

I can't see her face, but I can see her reflection on the screen and she's narrowing her eyes at me in suspicion.

"Because I'm a nice guy, Nyleena. And like it or not, we're probably stuck with each other for life. I've decided to make the most of it."

"Well, just so we're clear," she says, entering Xyla's name in the search bar. "I'm here for the sex. And so are you."

"Shop," I say. "And I'm gonna talk while you do that."

"Whatever." She sighs. "I'm gonna spend a shit-load of credits."

"Spend whatever you want."

And for some reason this makes her stiffen a little. So I go back to kneading her tight muscles.

"You're wrong, anyway," I say.

"So you said."

"Lyra has feelings. And so does Delphi. Both of them are in love."

Nyleena huffs. "I'm not them. They're pinks. I'm a silver. We're just… made different. Whole other set of factory settings, so to speak."

"Mmm-hmm," I hum, reaching down to grab her breasts with both hands.

She sucks in a deep breath but plays it off by tapping the screen and pulling up a pair of designer silver boots. I pinch her nipples through her pink shirt.

This makes her jerk and her fingertip accidentally adds the boots to her cart.

I want to laugh. Because Nyleena is always so tough and in control. But every time we have sex I feel that other, hidden part of her hiding deep beneath the surface.

The part of her that's sweet, and funny, and exciting, but in a Harem Station outlaw way.

I decide to lure that secret side of her out and I decide to start now.

Because what I said was true. We are soulmates, whether we embrace it or not. We will be together our whole lives. Even if she does manage to talk Crux into her own sentient ship, she's not leaving here without me. She has to know this.

Doesn't she?

I mean… I can't even go half a day now without craving her. And if I'm feeling this way she has to feel this way too.

It's been predetermined.

If I could just get her to drop her guard a little I could find that other Nyleena hiding inside her. This isn't just a transaction. Even though we're literally going through a transaction in this very moment.

It's not a metaphor for our relationship. It's just a coincidence.

"Are those the boots you wanted?" I ask, leaning down so I can whisper that into her ear.

She shrugs up her shoulders, like I'm making her tingle and she's trying to stop that, but mutters, "Yes," anyway.

"Good," I say, pinching her nipples again. "Get something else while you're here."

Then I kiss her neck.

"Oh, God," she hums.

"Go on. Buy whatever you want, Nyleena. I'm paying. Take advantage of me."

I straighten back up and press my hips forward so my hard, eager, ready-to-fuck cocks push into the dent right between her shoulders.

"You're very distracting," she complains, bringing up a whole page of designer Xyla clothes.

"I am," I say, smiling. "But I'm also distracted as well. So better keep shopping."

"You can't buy my affection with clothes," she huffs.

"Good thing I'm not trying to." I chuckle. "You will love me, Nyleena. And there's nothing you can do about it."

I spin her around and lean forward, both my hands coming down hard on the screen. It beeps and blips as things are added to her cart.

But I don't care. The surprised look on her face when my cocks are practically touching her lips has my full attention.

Her eyes get big. Then she squints them, realizing I'm getting the best of her right now.

If there's one thing Nyleena can't back away from, it's a fight.

She grabs them with both hands and begins to jerk me off.

I moan. I can't stop myself.

"Is that so?" she asks, leaning forward as her plump, pouty lips part and she takes the tip of one of my cocks between them.

Her tongue does this amazing swirl move around my head and I fist her hair, urging her to take me deeper.

She doesn't even fight it. And I knew she wouldn't. She needs to prove she's in control all the time. And if I challenge her to a deep-throat blowjob, she's gonna make sure she wins.

Which means I win.

I almost laugh. But hold it in because then she'll know I'm playing her right now.

And I am.

But it's not my fault she's so easy to play with.

She dives down, taking my upper cock deep into her throat. My lower one bumps against her neck, and I let go of her hair and start to jerk on it.

She slaps my hand away and makes a fist around it, sliding her palm up and down my shaft as I slowly fuck her throat.

Damn. I could get used to this girl.

She pulls back and says, "Come, Luck. Come in my throat."

I spin her around, grab both her hands, slap them against the screen so it beeps and bleeps as more things are added to her cart. Then I grab her hips, lift her up into a standing position, and bend her over the autoshopper.

"Ooooooooo," she giggles. "Take what you want, you animal."

"I will," I growl.

I lift up her little skirt, pull her panties aside, and thrust both cocks right into her pussy.

She bends over for me, face pressed up against the screen. It lights up, and beeps, and flashes as more things from Xyla's virtual closet are added to her cart.

"Oh, yeah," she moans. "Fuck me hard while I spend your credits!"

Seems fair to me.

I grab her hair with both hands and wrap it into a ponytail. Fist it as I pull with one hand, while the other presses down on her upper back, forcing her to stay in position.

"Harder," she demands. "Is that all you got?"

"Oh, princess," I chuckle. I pound her until she has to turn her head and allow me to press her cheek up against the screen.

"Come," she demands.

But I'm not about to come. Not like this.

I want a bed.

I pull out, turn her around, pick her up—she squeals with delight—and walk her down the hallway to my room.

When we get inside I throw her down on the bed, rip my shirt off, then crawl up her body. My cocks dangling between my legs. Sliding along the soft skin on the inside of her thighs.

She brushes her skirt away, ready to pull her panties aside, but I rip those fuckers right off her body and slip into her warm, wet pussy.

"Say it," I demand.

"Say what?" she squeals.

"My name," I command. "Say my name and tell me you can't live without this."

She's not in control. Her mastery of this moment has long slipped away. So she does it. She says, "Fuck me, Luck. And never stop!"

Which... OK, isn't exactly what I told her to say. And it's fake because fake dirty talk is our thing now.

But it's close enough.

I fuck her like an animal. And she lets me.

And when we come together, we're both savage, and feral, and wild.

But just as the experience fills me up with her bright, white light I feel her... pull back.

And I know in that instant this sly, cunning little minx is holding out on me.

She's hiding something.

As mind-blowing as the sex is, I can't help but feel like there's more to it.

This isn't real. Not all of it, at least. Something's *missing*.

A different feeling replaces the ebbing satisfaction.

A feeling that... I'm being lied to.

CHAPTER TWELVE

I'll say one thing about Luck. He's not boring in the sex department. Every time we do it, it always feels fresh.

Of course, that's how all new relationships start out. It's always fun and fresh in the beginning. You can't get enough of each other, you make those dreamy eyes at each other, and call each other pet names like *baby*. Gag.

Every 'new thing' is a soulmate connection.

Except it isn't.

Eventually that guy you thought was so hot chews too loud. Or leaves the shower setting on scrubbing bubbles so those annoying pods fly out at you every time you turn the water on. Or his pet bot is an asshole.

And suddenly, if you have to hear him masticate one more meal, or be ambushed by one more scrubbing bubble pod, or laugh at his stupid bot's lame jokes one more time—you're goin' down for murder, *baby*.

Because you can't take another second of it.

And the fact that this thing Luck and I have truly *is* a soulmate connection doesn't make me feel any better.

There are worse things in life than failing at love. That's how I see it. Because spending your whole life with someone you have to be with, but can't stand— that's my definition of hell.

So hey. Sure. I'll enjoy the lucky sex while it lasts.

But as soon as I get that ship I'm outta here.

Even if I go through withdrawals after I leave, I don't care. I'll get through it and I'll come out the other side of that nightmare stronger than ever.

"I could take a nap," Luck says, curling his body up to mine.

I want to push him off me, but it's a little rude and regardless of what everyone thinks about me, I'm not really a selfish, cold-hearted bitch.

So I let him snuggle.

"Did you have fun?" he asks.

"Of course. You're always fun."

He props himself up on one elbow, like he's about to start a conversation with me.

Didn't he just say he wanted to take a nap?

"Are you sure you had fun?"

I look over my shoulder at him and... aw, fuck. He's got that look guys get after sex when they're feeling insecure. "I said I did."

"Yeah, but... sometimes I get the feeling you're holding back on me."

"Luck," I say, turning over to face him. "I'm the most selfish, cold-hearted bitch on this station. Do you really think I'd bother having sex with someone and then just... pull my punch?" I laugh.

He squints his eyes at me. "That's not really an answer."

"I'm not holding back," I lie.

But I don't feel bad about lying. Because if he ever got a hint of the kind of explosive orgasm I'm capable of… well, let's just say he'd follow me around like a sad, homeless servo bot.

"But you're lying," he says.

"Which part am I lying about?" I huff.

"Before. When you said you don't have feelings. Because Cygnians just aren't built that way. It's a lie. Jimmy and Delphi are very happy. And Serpint—I barely recognize that dude these days. Every time I bump into him he's talking about peaches and tushberry juice because he and Lyra are trying to have a baby."

"Uggggh." I groan. "If I have to hear one more stupid lament over the baby they are not having I might strangle her."

"That's not my point," Luck says.

"I'm afraid I don't understand your point, Luck. What's the big deal? Did we, or did we not, just have fabulous sex?"

"We did."

"See?"

"Well, *I* did."

"Oh, my suns. Do you need me to feed your ego? Did I forget to mention how huge your cocks are? Should I have gagged a little more when you were fucking my throat? For fuck's sake! We're basically banging twice a day now. What more do you need?"

"I'm just trying to find out if you're satisfied."

"I'm fucking satisfied, OK?"

"I don't believe you."

I sigh and turn over. "Well, I'm not going to sit here and gush about how much I love your cocks inside me."

"That's not what I'm talking about and you know it. I just feel like you're holding back. And I think you're doing this on purpose."

"For what reason?" I snap, turning back to him.

"So you don't have to admit we might actually be a thing."

"A thing? I thought you hated me?"

"I did. At first. But..." He smiles. And holy hell. His eyes are sparkling.

"But what?" I say, blinking to make myself stop staring at his violet peepers.

"Don't you ever look at Jimmy and Delphi or Serpint and Lyra and ask yourself if maybe this shit is real?"

"If some scientist somewhere had the fate of the gods in his hands when he genetically manipulated my DNA before I was born?" I scoff. I cannot help it.

"But... they knew what they were doing, don't you think?"

"What part of 'we're part of a breeding program' don't you get, Luck? Because you know, there's a lady down on level one who breeds wild space orchids that only bloom in shades of radioactive green. Do you think she gives two shits whether or not the stinking flowers are compatible?"

"Someone's breeding wild space orchids here?"

Ooops. I was not supposed to tell anyone about that.

"Is this real?" Luck asks. "And are you sure they're green?"

"Why?"

"Because it's illegal, Nyleena. Space orchids are drugs."

"Oh, I knew that. But why are you so concerned about it?"

"Because I'm in charge of space orchid breeding here. It's… it's kind of a huge secret. She's not supposed to be doing that. Are they really green? Are you sure they're not pink and purple?"

"No, they're not pink or purple. Maybe a little on the yellow side. But definitely not pink or purple."

"Good," Luck says. "Then they're fake. Don't buy them anymore. And if you ever see her with pink and purple ones, you come tell me immediately. Because then I'd have to do a raid."

"What are you talking about?"

He opens his mouth to say something, then changes his mind and starts looking at my body.

So I decide to change the subject because right now I can practically feel the neurons firing inside that sex-crazed head of his and I don't want to get talked into another round of sex to prove I'm 'satisfied'. I have shit to do. So I say, "Hey, by the way," trying to sound nonchalant. "Delphi mentioned some weird planet called Earth. You ever hear of that place?"

Luck narrows his eyes into slits.

"What?" I say. "What did I say?"

"You're asking me about Earth?"

"So?"

"Really?"

"What's the big deal? For sun's sake, Luck. Are you menstruating or what? Are you hiding a vagina underneath those two cocks of yours? Because you're being super-moody today and I've just about had enough."

He points a finger at me. "You made another deal, didn't you?"

I slap his pointy finger out of my face and say, "I have no idea what you're talking about."

"You and Delphi. That's why you were shooting with her today, wasn't it? You need something from her and she countered with this."

"This what?"

"Info about Earth." He gets up out of bed, tucks his cocks away in his pants, and secures the tabs. "Get out," he says.

"What?"

"You heard me. Get the fuck out. Not only are you lying about how much you're getting off when we have sex, you're using me. You're the worst soulmate in the history of soulmates, you know that?"

"Fuck you!" I say, jumping to my feet and picking up my underwear. Which is ripped, so I throw them in his face and yell, "You're the one who came to me, remember? 'Oh, Nyleena.'" I fake a falsetto. "'I'm so horny. Let me fuck you right here, right now.'"

"Yeah, and you only said yes because you need me to give you information so you can get some other information for Delphi, so then she can give you what you need for... whoever else you're manipulating today!"

"You know what, buddy? Consider our deal over. I'm never talking to you again. And when I get my ship—and I *will* get my ship—I'm not even gonna say goodbye before I leave!"

I turn on my heel and walk out of the bedroom.

"Good!" he calls after me. "And when you get arrested for not paying your gate fees and need someone to bail you out of Prime Prison, don't call me!"

"I won't!" I say, and walk out the door.

CHAPTER THIRTEEN

LUCK

"Good!" I yell. But Nyleena is already gone. "God," I say, grabbing my hair with both hands. This girl makes me fucking nuts.

But actually, I'm glad she left. I don't know what's wrong with me. Trying to have a conversation with a crazy psycho like her is pointless. So what if she's lying about getting off? Plenty of girls have faked an orgasm with me.

Well, no. I'm pretty sure that's wrong. I'm damn good in bed.

But I know she's holding back. I can just feel it.

And I know for a fact that Serpint says Lyra goes into supernova mode when they have sex. Not that I'm comparing Nyleena to Lyra, but hell, they are sisters, right?

There has to be more to this girl than just this super-great ordinary sex we're having.

Doesn't there?

Beeping from the other side of the room redirects my attention to the autoshopper. The whole screen is flashing. I guess we added a lot of shit to the cart during foreplay.

I walk over to it, ready to clear the whole thing out, then sit on the stool and get my shit together.

We did have a deal. So I press the checkout button, then adjust delivery so it gets sent to her quarters, and tap complete.

There. Now you have a whole new cart of designer Xyla clothes for your fantasy trip on your very own sentient ship.

Such a ridiculous plan. What was Crux thinking?

But she is a ridiculous girl.

Now I have a whole evening to myself. I should go drinking. Yeah. I am gonna go drinking. I'll even ask Valor to come along.

Except I can't. We were punching each other in the face earlier.

And I can't go looking for girls. That's just dumb. Not that I want other girls, but now it's not even an option. And not because I'm in love with Nyleena or anything, it's just…

I don't know.

Life is weird.

Maybe I should just make nice with Valor? He's my best friend. My only other best-ish friend is Cha-Cha and I'm not in the mood for sexbot parties tonight.

Maybe Valor is sorry too?

It's not like we haven't always fought. We have. This is what we do.

But we never held grudges so… time for make-up drinking.

108

I look everywhere for him. I checked his location on my air screen first, of course. But his status was blinking the word 'unavailable' at me. So then I went to his quarters because we're on the same level.

No answer when I ping the door.

So I head up to the Harem room to see if he's with Crux.

No. Crux isn't there either.

So at this point I guess I have to face facts.

He's with Tray. He's got to be with Tray. I know he's not hanging out with Jimmy and Delphi or Serpint and Lyra so who else is there?

Just thinking about all the time Valor and Tray spend together gives me a tight feeling in my chest. Because they have never been close. Hell, Tray has never been close to any of us. He's always been a loner.

And maybe all of us have a little loner gene lurking in our DNA, but it's different with Tray. Jimmy always had Xyla. She's been around from the very beginning. Then they got *Dicker* and that's a proper crew right there.

Serpint and Draden have been stuck together like twins since before we left Wayward station. They had Ceres and *Booty* too. And now that Draden is gone, Serpint has Lyra. He didn't miss a beat, actually. Just reorganized because that's all you can do when people die. The only other option is to give up. And that's what I think Valor is doing.

He and I were like Serpint and Draden. We just naturally teamed up. And we had Beauty and *Lady*.

Crux has the cyborg master, and the harem girls, and the Baby, not to mention a whole station of people who work for him.

But Tray… the only thing Tray has is the Pleasure Prison.

I guess, before our world was tipped upside down with the appearance of Lyra and Corla, I'd say Real ALCOR was part of Tray's crew. But isn't that a little weird? To have no one but an AI and a fake reality? Not even a bot or borg in the real to hang out with?

I don't get it.

I don't understand Tray and I don't understand why Valor is suddenly his best friend.

How did this happen? How did a guy with no friends manage to snag *my* friend right out from under me?

Of course, I did take off after Beauty died. But we have a job to do. The station depends on us to salvage AI parts to keep the Baby running. So really, he's the one who left me. Not the other way around. And he bailed on *Lady Luck* too.

So what if he doesn't like Cha-Cha? We have to have an inorganic partner. She can do things we can't. Go out into a vacuum without an envirosuit, for instance. That comes in handy when your job is to infiltrate long-dead stations with no atmosphere.

I think about all this as I make my way down to the Pleasure Prison levels, and by the time I enter the control room, and do in fact find Valor and Tray together—conversing and laughing like they are the oldest of best friends—I'm kinda pissed off and all my thoughts of make-up drinking have disappeared.

"Hey," I say, when they don't even turn around to notice me walking in.

Valor swivels around in his chair and sends me a tight smile.

110

"What's up?" I ask. "What are you guys doing tonight?"

"We're going inside the Prison," Tray says.

"Why?" I ask.

"Because it's fun," Valor says.

"Since when?" I ask.

"What do you mean?" he asks.

I glance at Tray. Shoot him a look of narrowed eyes. Tray is not as tall as me, but only by one or two centimeters. We've got the same build, though. We're both broad in the shoulders, well-muscled, and hard. I can only conclude this is genetics because unlike me, Tray doesn't do manual work for a living.

It kinda pisses me off that we have the same body when I had to earn mine and he was simply gifted his.

He's got dark hair and dark eyes to match. They're violet, don't get me wrong. But they're not violet like the rest of us. There's no bright pinkish ring around his iris like Serpint has. And no mottled purple around the pupil like Valor has.

Sometimes Tray's eyes even look black.

Like right now as he's glaring back at me.

"You never spent any time inside that place before," I say to Valor. "So what's changed?"

"I don't know," Valor says. "I guess I just never understood it until now."

"Hmm," I say. "What's to understand? It's a virtual sex game."

Valor chuckles, then trades a look of amusement with Tray. Like they know something I don't. "That's not all it is," Valor says.

"So what is it, then?" I ask.

"You wouldn't understand," Tray says.

111

"Try me," I growl.

They trade another look and I can feel my blood starting to boil with anger. First the fight with Nyleena, now Valor and Tray are ganging up on me.

"OK," Tray says, turning to fully face me. "If you really want to know, it's a node-flux conduit for quanta packages that can access the core matrix of electromagnetic and gravitational fields using the holographic principle to form a collective of two-dimensional spacetime-informational-directionality and thus access a form of informational phase transition that breaks information and spacetime down into something other than information and spacetime." He pauses. "You know, like how ice turns to water when you heat it up? Same shit here. But with information and spacetime instead of ice."

I blink. But only once so I don't appear confused, even though I have no fucking clue what any of that bullshit nerd-speak means. "OK," I say, playing it off. "Do you think you could use the words 'information' and 'spacetime' a few more times in the same sentence though? It might make more sense."

"See," Valor says. "Told ya. You don't understand."

"I get it," I huff. "I might not understand all those big words Tray just used, but it's still just a fucking virtual reality."

"It is," Tray says. "But only in the most basic sense. Like dreams, for instance. They're a basic virtual reality too. If you want me to use baby words, Luck, I can. It's about data, dude. We're pushing data through transformational phase changes in there."

"Baby words. Right," I say, glaring at him, then turn back to Valor. "So you'd rather go in there and do magic tricks on data instead of staying out here with… you know, *real* people. You'd rather do virtual things instead of real things."

"It's real," Valor says. "That's the part you don't understand."

"It's just a different kind of real," Tray adds.

"OK." I sigh, rubbing a hand down my face as I rethink my approach. Because I'm never going to convince them to see things my way. I try another tactic. "So what's so great in there?" I ask Valor. "What's in there that's not out here?"

They trade another look. Only this time it's not amusement.

It's a secret, I realize. They're keeping a secret.

"What the fuck is going on?" I ask.

They're still trading that same look. I can practically hear the mental conversation they're having.

Should we tell him?

He'll tell—insert your favorite Harem Station Brother, AI, bot, princess, cyborg here.

Maybe. Maybe not. But he's gonna find out eventually.

Sure. Eventually. But not today.

"Nothing's going on," Valor says. "It's just…" He smiles. "It's just a sex game, dude. And I like it. What can I say?"

I point at him. "You're fucking lying. Why are you lying to me?"

"Luck," he says. "We're gonna tell everyone at the same time, OK?"

And Tray adds, "We need more information so we can explain it properly, that's all. It's not personal."

113

"So something is going on in there?" I say. "Is it Asshole ALCOR? The new Succubus AI from Mighty Minions? What's happening?"

"It's not that," Tray says. "I swear to the fucking sun, that's not what this is about."

"Then what is it?"

They trade yet another look and that's it. I'm done.

"Fuck you both," I say. "Just fuck you both." I point at Valor. "You were my best friend. You and I never lied to each other. We never kept secrets. And now that you've teamed up with Tray, all you are is lies and secrets."

And then I walk out before he can try to placate me with yet another bullshit excuse.

CHAPTER FOURTEEN

MYLEENA

Two days.

I've been working on this super-problem for two days and I've gotten nowhere.

I tick off a bullet-point list of things I need to get my ass off this stupid station and back in the game of hunting down all the people I hate.

One. Crux will give me a ship but he wants to know what something called leveling-up is. And to get that information, I need to go inside the Pleasure Prison and ask the Asshole ALCOR if he knows anything about it.

Two. The waitlist to actually go inside the Pleasure Prison is two weeks long.

Three. Tray refuses to even speak to me, so I can't beg for access.

Four. Valor says he'll help me get in by talking to Tray, but only if I find out information about Veila.

Five. Luck knows something about Veila, but he won't tell me unless I bring him new information about what happened to Valor when he went with Crux to pick up Jimmy and Delphi off Mighty Minions.

Six. Delphi knows something about Valor, but she won't tell me unless I get her information about Earth from the Baby ALCOR.

Seven. I'm pretty sure stupid Luck knows something about Earth too, but now he hates my guts.

So I guess my next move is Baby ALCOR.

I'm just about to open my air screen and make an appointment with the Baby when Luck storms out of the Pleasure Prison doors, grumbling and mumbling to himself as he waves a fist around in the air.

I stand still, hoping he won't see me. But we have this almost magnetic attraction and there's actually no way for him to miss me.

His head swivels in my direction and he stops in his tracks to frown.

I feel a little bad about how we left things earlier. I mean, he's sorta right. I am using him. But he's using me too, so what's the problem?

We lock eyes and stare at each other.

Should we talk? that look says.

Are we mad at each other? Or the world? Is this whole thing pointless?

I don't know.

I see the possibilities when I look at Lyra and Serpint. Or Delphi and Jimmy. Both of my Cygnian sisters seem inexplicably happy with their new life. And both of them were like me before. Living a life of outlaw adventure.

Now Serpint is Lyra's partner in crime. Ditto for Delphi and Jimmy.

Is it possible that Luck and I could become close like that?

I just don't know. We're so different. He's kind of a simple guy and I'm so not a simple girl. I mean, what does he really know about pleasuring a silver princess like me?

Nothing.

But there's a little voice inside my head that counters with, *Maybe that's because you hide things from him? Things like what really happens if you don't hold back during sex.*

That's why he's pissed at me, I remind myself. It wasn't the question about Earth, was it? No. He could tell when we had sex that I wasn't as into it as I should be. Would be, if I thought he could handle me.

But what are the chances a guy like Luck would be able to handle me? I mean, Serpint liberates princesses and Jimmy liberates bots and borgs. Luck is basically a junkyard hunter.

Do I really think he's got what it takes to satisfy me for the rest of my life?

Shit. He's coming my way.

"What are you doing?" Luck calls, once he's within earshot.

"I'm about to have a meeting with the Baby ALCOR, actually. To get information about Earth that you refuse to provide."

"Mmm-hmm," he hums, folding his arms across his chest. "Using him too, are ya?"

"I'm not using anyone," I snap. "In case you haven't noticed, everything I get, and I do mean everything—every piece of information and the ship at the end of this long problem—is through trade. I give something, I get something. That's how life works."

"Mmm-hmm. Except with me," Luck says.

"What are you talking about? I have sex with you every day. Twice, lately. You have no room to complain. In fact, I've given you much more than you've given me."

"Is that right?" he growls.

And wow, he's really pissed off. But then I remember he came out of the Pleasure Prison angry. So I decide to change the subject and defuse this little fight we're having. Maybe try a little harder when it comes to Luck. Because like it or not, he is my stupid soulmate. We're going to be interacting, at least at times, the rest of our lives. Maybe I need to make an effort?

So I say, "What happened?"

"When?"

"In there," I say, pointing to the entrance.

"Oh, fuck them," he huffs. Turning to look over his shoulder. "They're a bunch of assholes."

"Why?" I ask.

"Because... because... do you know anything about quanta holographic principles and data spacetime breakdown?"

I squint at him. "What?"

"Or something like that. I think there was a matrix mentioned. And melting ice cubes."

I laugh. "You're not making any sense."

He points to the Pleasure Prison. "They're not making any sense! Do you know what they told me?"

"I hope it's not that stuff you just incoherently burbled."

"It's not. They told me that data is real." He nods. Like this is a revelation.

"Isn't data real?" I ask.

118

"No!" he says. "That's not what I mean. I mean, they said… that… virtual… information… is real." He nods. "Yeah. I'm pretty sure that's what they just said. It's not real, Nyleena. That's why it's *virtual*."

"Hmmm," I say.

"What?"

"I think I know what you're trying to say. Are you talking about node-flux conduits for quanta packages?"

He snaps his fingers and points to me. "Yes!"

"And you want to know more about this?" I ask.

"Yes!"

"OK." I think for a moment. "I can help you." Then I point to him. "And since you're keeping tabs on how much we use each other, I'll give this one to you for free."

"Awesome," he says. And he smiles at me.

God, it really is a nice smile.

"Hit me up," he says. "And I don't need baby words."

"OK," I laugh. "So… this is what I know about the quanta of spacetime—"

"Wait. Maybe a few baby words. What the hell is a quanta?"

"It's… just another word for package, I guess. It's a thing. A quantity."

"Ah," he says. "Quanta. Quantity."

"Right. So… in virtuals you have a matrix of information that lives in its… unique spacetime, I guess. And since information is theoretically… um… indestructible? Maybe that's the best word. It can't be destroyed. It's saved somewhere."

"Where?" Luck asks.

I shrug. "I dunno. Some people think it's saved on the event horizon of a black hole. And they say that it can be saved on the event horizon of a gate too. As a sort of a backup copy."

"A gate?" he asks.

"It's just a theory," I say. "No one really knows because you can't collect information from the event horizon of a black hole or a gate. So who cares?"

"Well, they care!" Luck says. "That's the kind of shit they're doing in there."

"In where?"

"The Pleasure Prison."

"Are you sure?"

"That's what they said."

"Yeah, but you don't really know what they said. You burbled out a sentence of big words that made no sense at all."

"But you still understood it," he counters.

"I'm guessing. Also, the spacetime in the virtual and the spacetime out here aren't the same. So what does that have to do with virtual information being real?"

He sighs. "I don't know. But it's something important. They're gonna call a meeting about this when they figure it out."

"Oh, well, good. Then we'll all know."

"No," Luck says. "That's not good. Asshole ALCOR is in there with the Succubus AI. What if they hear about this real stuff and escape?"

I raise my eyebrows at him. "I don't understand. I thought the Succubus being in there was her idea?"

"*They*," he says, all agitated again, "are doing secret shit inside *our* virtual. And I don't like it. Not one bit."

"Are you sure you're not just jealous?"

"Of what?"

"Who, you mean. I know that you and Valor used to be tight and now he's all about Tray."

"I'm not jealous." He stares at me. But that stare softens as it lingers. "OK. Maybe I'm a little jealous."

I laugh. "OK. How about this? I'm sorry for the fight earlier."

"You should be," he says. "You're keeping things from me too."

"I'm just about to make you a good offer, Luck. Sometimes you need to learn to shut the hell up."

He makes a motion of buttoning his lip.

"I'll find out more about this for you. And it's free. No strings at all."

He unbuttons his lip. "Really?"

I nod. "Yeah. A favor between friends. It's no big deal, really. A quick conversation is all it'll take."

Everything about Luck relaxes in that instant.

And in the next one… he kisses me.

His hands slip down to my waist and his chest presses forward. One moment his mouth is hard and rough, the next it's soft and pliable. Opening up so his tongue can twist together with mine.

It's so unexpected I gasp a little.

This makes him growl. And I expect him to push me into an alley and fuck right now.

Because that's what we do.

But he doesn't.

He ends the open-mouth kiss, then touches his lips to mine very gently and backs away. Like he's rewinding time and what he just did never happened.

My fingertips reach up to touch my lips of their own accord. And I stare at him.

"Thank you," he says. "And there's no strings attached to that kiss either."

Then he turns and walks away.

And maybe, for the first time ever, I don't want him to do that. I want him to stay. I want to be taken into an alley, or a new secret garden, and fucked properly.

I want to show him what I've been holding back.

But he disappears around a corner and I have to shake my head to pull me out of the swoon-state he left me in.

"Sun," I mutter. "Now *that*… I could get used to."

No. The voice in my head is sharp and clear.

Do not lose sight of your goal.

I want this ship. I want to leave this station. I want to kill people and get revenge.

What I don't want to do… what I will not do… is fall in love with my soulmate.

Never. Ever. Ever.

CHAPTER FIFTEEN

I don't know why, but I feel better knowing Nyleena is working my little Valor problem. In fact, I feel so much better about shit, I go hang out with *Lady* in the docking bay and hook into the virtual we have onboard so I can watch her and *Booty* and *Dicker* play poker.

They always cheat. Always cheat. They gang up on the other ships in the docking bay—especially the ones who are just about to pay off their servitude tithe—and take everything they can.

That's all sanctioned by Crux, of course. He wants to wipe out their savings and make a long-lasting partnership with Harem their only real option.

It's a shit move, but hey. By the time these sentient ships pay off their five hundred spins, they've been on missions for us, they've learned secrets, and to be honest, they are an investment at this point.

They technically have to agree to who takes them on as a responsible party, but we strongly urge them to see things our way and take who we assign to them.

It occurs to me, as I watch the virtual game through a pair of goggles, that one of these losers might end up belonging to Nyleena in a few days.

Is Crux serious about this?

I can't tell.

I know he wanted her to start pulling her weight, but letting her take a ship and leave to go get into trouble somewhere far away... that's just not a good idea.

He can't be serious. It's got to be some sort of trick.

I track Nyleena as I hang out with the ships. Watching her go places. She visits the Pleasure Prison first, presumably to hit up Valor and Tray for info on my behalf, but then she leaves almost immediately and I figure they're already inside doing whatever secret stuff they're working on.

Then she goes to grab dinner. Alone. There's a moment as I watch her status on my little virtual station map when I consider joining her.

But no. I stay away.

That kiss was pretty great. And I'd be lying if I said I didn't want to drag her ass into the closest secret garden and have my way with her.

But she'd just fake it again and I'd be pissed off anew.

I don't need that.

So I just stalk her from a distance. She goes to a shooting gallery down on the lower levels after that. There's a fight while she's there. I know this because I can watch the Baby activate security in real time on my screen. But Nyleena isn't arrested, so I deduce she wasn't involved.

Then she goes to an arcade, blows through a few hundred credits, and leaves. Enters and exits a few stores. Stops to sit on a park bench.

Is this what she does every night? Just... wastes time all by herself?

Doesn't she have friends?

I access Lyra's tracker. Find her in Serpint's quarters. Then find Delphi in Jimmy's quarters.

None of them ever hang out with the other princesses up in the harem or the free ones that decided to stay and work in other jobs on the station.

Cygnians have an inherent sense of class division. Because the pinks and silvers seem to be considered outsiders to the regular princesses we keep here.

I don't quite get that. I guess I could ask, but eh. Don't really care, either.

A few hours later I notice Nyleena is on her way back into the Pleasure Prison and I deduce that Tray and Valor told her to come back later.

So I leave *Lady* and the other ships to their game and head back that way, hoping I can catch her coming out and see if she got any information for me.

And even though when I check my air screen for the time and realize it has taken me a full thirty minutes to get back up there, she's still inside when I arrive outside the control room doors.

I wait on the side of the door and press my ear towards it, listening.

Laughing? Do I hear laughing?

Oh, that's definitely laughing. Definitely Nyleena laughing.

I take a step forward and peek through the small slit of a window at eye level.

JA HUSS & KC CROSS

They're all drinking. Nyleena is not dressed in the normal outfit from earlier. She must've bought something in one of those stores and changed. Because she's wearing a tight, shiny-pink plynal bodysuit that shows off every curve of her hips. And she was definitely not wearing that earlier. There's a fat silver zipper that starts at the middle of her back, runs down the crack of her ass, and right between her legs.

I know this outfit.

Well, not this particular outfit. But I know this style. It's her fuck-me-quick outfit. No need to remove clothes, just unzip the parts required.

I palm the door open and say, "What the fuck is going on in here?"

Tray spins around so fast, his drink goes sloshing over the side of his glass. "Oh, hey, Luck. We're just having a drink and shootin' the shit. Your girl is funny."

I narrow my eyes at my most-hated brother.

"And pretty sexy too," Valor says. "That outfit. Sun's sake, princess. You leave nothing to the imagination!"

I take that back. Valor is now my most-hated brother.

"What are you doing here?" Nyleena snaps.

"What am I doing here? What the fuck are you doing here?"

"Someone's in trouble," Tray clowns.

"Well," Nyleena says, flattening out some make-believe wrinkle in her bodysuit. That thing is way too tight to wrinkle. And there's a second zipper in front. One that allows her tits to practically pop out but doesn't connect to the one that stops short just below

126

her hip bones. "I guess I'm outta here. Thanks, you guys!" she calls brightly as she pushes me out of her way. "Maybe I'll stop by tomorrow?"

"Try all you want to get in my pod." Tray laughs. "Not gonna work, Nyleena."

She shoots him a tight-lipped smile as she passes through the door.

I follow her. "What the fuck was that about?" I ask again, once we're outside in the main concourse.

"That was you and your stupid bad timing. That's what that was! I was not only just about to weasel my way into using his gaming pod to get a conversation with Real ALCOR, I had them talking about their big spacetime secret when you barged in like an alpha caveman and ruined all my hard work!"

CHAPTER SIXTEEN

"Hard work?" Luck laughs. "Is that what you call it now?"

I narrow my eyes at him, so angry. I was so close! I practically had Tray wrapped around my little finger. He was going to let me use his gaming pod! He was! And then Luck barged in and ruined everything!

Now I'm right back where I started. And I'm out two hundred credits of next week's allowance for this sexy outfit I bought just for the occasion.

"What I call... *what?*" I growl. And it's a mean growl. I'm so angry at him right now.

"Prancing around in that tight outfit showing your ass and tits off to my single brothers. You're mine, Nyleena. Mine!"

"You're insane! You think I was in there to what? Fuck them? I was leading them on to get information you wanted, remember?"

"I never told you to sleep with them for it! No wonder you offered that info up to me for free! You were gonna get something else in the process! Were you gonna fake an orgasm for them too?"

"Fuck you!" I say. And then I slap him across the face and turn my back.

"Oh," he says behind me. "You did not."

Oh, yes, I did, asshole.

I make it all the way to the elevator before he catches up with me.

"I'm going home. Do not," I warn, "follow me. Do you understand? You've gone too far, buddy. Way too far tonight."

"You're not going anywhere until I find out what they told you."

I get in the elevator and push the button for my floor. Our eyes are locked together. Each of us challenging the other.

The doors close, Luck still on the other side of them. And I allow myself a small smile of triumph.

But then his hand sneaks in at the last second and the doors pop open again.

"What the fuck, Luck?"

He steps inside with me. "You're not going anywhere until you tell me what they said like you promised." The doors close us in.

"Yeah, well, you promise me great sex every day and never deliver. So I don't really feel the need to tell you anything."

"Is that right?" he asks. Just as the elevator doors open to my floor.

I step out without comment and walk quickly to my quarters, punch in the code, and slip inside, fully intending on closing the door right on Luck's face. Then he does that sneaky hand thing again and pushes it back open.

"What?" I seethe.

"I don't *deliver*?" His eyebrows are so high up on his forehead in shocked surprise, I can see every curve of his wide-open violet eyes.

"No," I say. "You don't. In fact, you suck in bed. You'd need four cocks to make me feel good."

"Four cocks, huh?" He points to the ceiling. "You had four up there in the control room at your service. How was it?"

Ohhhhhhhh, no, he didn't.

I slap him again.

He laughs.

Then he pushes me aside, slams my door closed, spins me around, and shoves my back up against the door. "I thought we came to an understanding."

"We did. And then you turned into a giant cocky jerk and ruined all my plans! It's like… you want me to fail, don't you? You want to trap me here, just like you guys do everyone else, and make me stay. I'm this close," I say, holding my pointer finger and thumb together with barely a fraction of space between them. "This fucking close to solving my fucking problem and you barged in and ruined it on purpose!"

"You bought this outfit for them, didn't you?"

"What are you talking about?"

"I was tracking you. I saw you enter those stores. You weren't wearing the pink bodysuit of sexiness earlier! So you bought it just for them!"

"You're stalking me again? What the actual fuck is wrong with you?"

"You're mine," he says. "*Mine.*"

I force myself to be still. And I look him straight in those glowing violet eyes and say, "*Never.*"

131

But in that same instant that my single, determined word bursts from my mouth, he spins me around, drags my bodysuit zipper down to the crack of my ass, then spins me around again, reaches between my legs, and keeps unzipping until he's got an all-access pass to my lady goods.

I cock my head at him. "Really?"

He grabs both my hands, hikes them up above my head, clasps my wrists together in one fist, and then unzips the top of my bodysuit in one, swift motion so that my tits pop out in all their spectacular glory.

I panic for a moment. But take a deep breath and remind myself that he won't get this outfit off me. And he can't see the parts of my body I'm trying to hide. Not with these strategic zippers. That's the whole reason I bought it.

"I suck in the sack, do I?"

"So bad," I seethe.

"Well, let me tell you something, princess. You're no prize."

"Oh," I laugh. "Is that so?" The nerve of him.

"You might be silver. And you might be a bitch. But your glow, Nyleena, lacks *luster*."

"Fuck you," I spit. "You've never even seen my glow! My glow is so powerful I—"

But I stop. Because I don't want him to know that. I don't want anyone to know what my glow does.

"*Prove it,*" he growls.

I am so angry right now my blood is boiling. Rage fills me up and I can feel it. Just on the edge. Just waiting to burst forth and wash this whole station in the bright white inside me.

I wriggle one hand free from his tight grip, pop the tab on his pants, and reach inside to grab those cocks. I squeeze them with all my strength.

"That all you got?" he hisses, yanking my hand away and securing in his grip above my head again.

"Oh, I haven't even started yet," I purr, the anger and rage bubbling underneath my fake, calm demeanor.

I hike one leg up, hook it around his ass, and pull him towards me until his hips bump into mine and his cocks slam against my stomach.

"You know why I fake it with you, Luck?" Oh, he's so mad. So mad. "Because not only can you not handle me, you can't ever even *hope* to satisfy my sexual needs."

He reaches down, fists his cocks, and then shoves them inside me with no care at all about being careful and considerate.

"Shit!" I wince.

"That's right, princess. Now you're gonna get all of me."

He pulls back and thrusts forward so hard, I gasp.

But fuck him. He's not gonna win this. I hike my other leg up, cross my ankles and squeeze him between my thighs as he pushes me against the door.

"Yeah," he says, laughing. His violet eyes bright with light now. Sizzling and crackling like there's some kind of electric current hidden deep inside him. "You want more? You need it harder? I'll fuck you harder! I'll fuck you so hard you'll think there's four cocks inside you!"

CHAPTER SEVENTEEN

LUCK

She moans. And sure. She's moaned a lot during sex. But this one is different. There's white light inside her eyes. Like she's got a sun hidden in there. Like she's about to unleash a solar storm on my ass, the likes of which I've never seen before.

And all I can think is... *Yes. Give it to me. For once, let me see the real you, princess.*

I thrust deeper and deeper inside her. Pounding her back against the closed door. My pants down around my knees from all the fucking. And her legs, all covered in shiny pink plynal, still wrapped tightly around my waist like she wants to squeeze the breath out of me.

Fuck yeah.

I let go of her wrists and immediately her hands drop to my shoulders and her nails dig deep into my flesh.

I don't feel it much. Not in this kind of heated moment.

But I'll feel it later. And I can't wait.

Her body goes stiff for a moment and I know... I know she's close. She has to make a decision to pull

135

back and keep that release inside her like she's been doing… or let it go and fully expose herself to me.

There is only one way for this to end as far as I'm concerned.

Total glow.

That's what I want.

Total glow.

"Do it," I say. "Do it, Nyleena. Or I swear to fucking God I will make sure Crux never gives you a ship. I will make sure you're trapped here with me forever. I will take all your choices away and lock you up in my quarters. Bind you to a magnetic sex wall and then…"

"Then *what?*" she growls.

"Then… I'll never touch you or talk to you again!"

I'm not sure what happens next.

She goes soft and hard in the same moment. Light pours out of her eyes, and her mouth, and between her legs. But then, in that single instance, she goes dark too.

My whole mind goes dark. Everything.

The world is blank with blackness.

There is no glow, there is no light, and there is no white, or silver, or color of any kind.

It's just… space. And time.

So much time passes. A lifetime. A generation. A millennium. An eternity passes by as she comes.

And then my cocks contract and it takes… *forever*. Like the whining charge of a plasma rifle just before it fires. Like the kickback of a SEAR cannon just before it annihilates a war ship.

Only there is no release.

Just space. And time.

I realize I no longer exist. I am nothing but tiny atoms floating in the time and the space. I have been disembodied. I am loose, and sparse, and infinite all at once.

And then the rifle fires. The cannon annihilates.

My cocks come inside her and…

The world is back, the light is there—streaming out from here. The floors are shaking, and the walls might crumble, and her fingernails leave scars on the round muscles of my shoulders.

And I think to myself… *That's more like it.*

That is her and this is me.

And now we are… a *we*.

When we wake we're hugging each other in a heap in front of her door.

I think years have passed. Maybe even decades.

For sure, we've been here in this spot for several eternities already.

But when I finally manage to make my fingers work again and open up a screen I see the impossible.

Because no time has passed at all. In fact, we've gone backwards.

The time right now is the time it was when I came up to meet her outside the Pleasure Prison.

"We went backwards," I mumble.

"Yeah," she says. "Sorry about that. I kinda do that when I let loose too much during sex."

"You do… what, exactly?"

"Rewind time." She flips her hand in the air. "You know."

"I... no. I don't know. What the hell just happened?"

"Sun-fucks, Luck. I just told you twice. I rewind time."

"That's not possible," I say.

"OK. If you say so."

"You really rewind time?"

She huffs out a sigh. "Will saying it four times make it sink in? Just for once can you take my word on something? Believe me?"

Believe her? She's like the liar champion of Harem Station these days. Hell no, I'm not gonna believe her.

"But hey, you know what?" she says.

"What?"

"Guess that fight never happened."

"Huh," I manage to grunt. "But..." I think about this for a moment. "But then... none of this ever happened."

"Nope," she says. Then she sighs. "This is why we silvers can't get pregnant. That's why our race is doomed. And no matter what Veila does, she will never have a baby. Not a silver one, anyway."

I know it's not funny, but I bark out a loud guffaw. "Are you fucking kidding me right now?"

"Do you think I'm kidding?"

"No," I say. "But... how did we get here then? How are we here when we're supposed to be... there? I should be walking into the Pleasure Prison and you should be with Tray and Valor."

"I dunno. I never said I understood it. I just know how to make it happen."

"But Veila," I say, already moving on to the next confusion thing. "Delphi is Crux's daughter. So…"

"Delphi's pink," Nyleena says. "Pink and silver aren't the same."

"But Corla had babies—"

"You can make a pink from a silver, Luck. But you can't even engineer a silver baby without some serious intervention, let alone produce a natural one. Corla is the only one who figured out how to even bring a pregnancy to term. So I guess it can be done. But she's never told anyone how she did it. She was missing that year she gave birth. That's probably why Veila wants her so bad. Veila needs that final secret to make her stupid breeding plan work. Veila needs… well, everyone doing breeding stuff—they all need to make *silvers.*"

"So… why do they blow you up? That makes no sense."

"Because we can do that pretty well. What we don't do well is make babies the natural way. We are all engineered, remember? It's not the same. I don't know what's different, so don't ask. But I do know they are all looking for a natural-born silver princess."

"Is that why Corla is so special? She's a natural silver princess?"

"She cannot be," Nyleena says. "It can't be." But then she whispers, "Can it?"

"So they need us too," I continue. "They think that these violet eyes we have signify some particular genetic component that will make silver babies?"

"No one's having a baby," Nyleena says. "Lyra won't make a silver princess. And neither will Veila—

she's not even a real silver." Then she pauses. "But maybe Delphi—"

"Hold on," I say, still trying to wrap my head around the first part. "How is Veila silver? Because now that you said that I do remember Crux telling me once that Veila was pink. What's up with that?"

Nyleena chuckles. "I'm pretty sure that's what all that leveling-up shit is about."

"Well, fuck," I say. "This is what Crux wants to know? Why didn't you just tell him?"

"He already knows that, Luck. That's not what he was asking about."

"Then what was he asking about?" I'm so confused.

"He was asking about Draden. And that… I have no clue. I don't know what changes you violet-eyed Akeelians are capable of."

My brain feels like it's gonna explode.

"I need to ask Asshole ALCOR for that info."

"But… what was that light? And dark? It was dark, right?"

"Before the light? Yeah." She sighs. "It's dark all right."

"So this happens every time?"

"No. Never, in fact. I've never let loose with anyone before. Just you."

"Then how did you know about the time thing?"

"I just do, OK?" Then she squirms out of my embrace and climbs into my lap. She places one hand flat against each of my cheeks and peers down into my eyes. They're still glowing a little. Lit up with that same electric current, but subdued now. "This is why I hold back, Luck. It's not you, it's me. There's something inherently wrong with fucking up *time*. Don't you see that?"

I manage a smile. And a nod. Because I do, ironically, totally understand that.

But deep down I'm sad. Will she never let me see this again? Is this the one and only time I ever get to feel that true soulmate connection with her?

Are we doomed to a life less lived? In all ways, no matter what we do? Will we have to go backwards each time we want to be close and connected?

"Where are Tray and Valor then? Because if we took back time then everyone around us lost time. Right?"

She shrugs. Then sighs. Heavily. "I dunno. Maybe we should ask them what happened?"

I hug her tight and sigh. "Not tonight. I'm sure if something really bad happened we'd know about it by now."

I manage to stand up, holding her close to me as she wraps her legs around my middle. My cocks have no interest in her right now. Which is a first. And it feels good to have that need taken away. To just… be with her without the instinctual urges.

We walk to the bedroom and I put her down on the bed. I take off her boots, and she lets me. But when I try to take off her bodysuit she shakes her head and pulls away.

"What? Are you telling me no?" I sorta laugh.

She nods. "I'm telling you no. I'm not getting naked with you."

"But why?"

"I'm just not. I'll sleep with you. If you want me to. But I'm not taking off my clothes."

I don't know what to say to that. It's weird, right?

But is it any weirder than everything else going on around me? Any weirder than time flowing backwards when she comes?

And I'm just about to ask like a million more questions about that when she says, "Take it or leave it. I'm not negotiating or explaining."

I sigh. Give in, because I'm tired, and confused, and there are just no answers for me tonight. So I say, "I'll take it." And then I undress, climb into bed next to her, and wrap my arms around her middle.

She lets me spoon her. Exhausted from the light— or maybe the dark, I'm not sure. And begins to relax.

"Thank you," I say. But I get no response. And when I reposition so I can peek over her shoulder and see her face, she's already asleep.

I want to say more though. I want to say… "I like you, Nyleena. I might even love you."

And I do say it. Because I think it needs to be said even if she doesn't hear me.

And then I think about how we all want to tame her. How we all think she's so wild.

But she's not, is she?

How ironic that Princess Nyleena is actually the picture-perfect example of self-control. All this time she's been holding back the power inside her.

How exhausting must that be?

Probably why she's always so restless. Hell, if I couldn't get my sexual release I'd be wild and savage too.

So point to Nyleena.

Still, she's dangerous and unpredictable. And I'm pretty sure if Veila could get her hands on Nyleena and

142

me—or Corla and Crux, for that matter—she would do unspeakable things to us.

Maybe Serpint and Lyra are safe? Maybe Jimmy and Delphi…

Oh, shit. I cut her off earlier. She said something about Delphi. Something like… Veila will never have a baby. Or Lyra. And then she said, "But maybe Delphi—"

Another mystery. Who the fuck is Delphi? I get that she's Crux and Corla's daughter. And she has a twin called Tycho, who we will be hunting for soon, once we get a handle on the situation and figure out where Veila is. But who are these two? What do Delphi and Tycho have to do with anything?

I don't know. And no one else here knows either, so there's no one to ask.

The only thing I do know is that Nyleena can't leave this station.

She can't leave. She just can't. It's too dangerous.

And when she figures that out for real, she's gonna be pissed off. Probably wilder than ever.

But… maybe there's another way to rein her in?

Maybe I'm going about this all wrong?

CHAPTER EIGHTEEN

MYLEENA

There is another world out there. That's the feeling I get as I sleep and dream. It's a world filled with glow. Not coming from me, just a general all-encompassing glow that fills the space around everything.

And in that glow there is... life.

Not organic, not inorganic. Both. Because life isn't about bodies, it's about minds.

And the only thing I know, as I hover there between these two worlds, is that I am part of it.

It's a place where all the elements of the universes swim together like a big pool of potential. And all I have to do is pluck out what I need and bring it back with me.

Or maybe... maybe that's not quite right? Maybe it's not about ripping it all apart but bringing it together?

My waking is sudden and complete.

145

One moment I'm there and the next I'm not.

My eyes are open and I'm staring at the ceiling. Fully aware. Luck next to me in my bed.

"Hmm," I hum. Then draw in a deep breath and let it out. I turn my head to see him, then smile.

He is very beautiful when he's asleep. I turn over so I can just stare at him like this. All quiet and calm. His breathing slow and even. He's flat on his stomach and I don't know why I love that so much, I just do. His cheek is pressed into the pillow, his forearms hidden somewhere underneath. His brown-blond hair just a little too long as it falls over his face.

Luck.

It's a cool name.

Everyone wants luck.

I told him too much last night. He's going to tell Crux and the rest of them. But it doesn't matter. Whatever Veila is doing, wherever she is, it's not going to work. I want to hunt her down and kill her, not because I want to save anyone. I just want to punish her for disrupting the other world that hovers on the other side of this one. The swimming pool of golden-hued potential I know exists but can't seem to find.

I'm gonna find that place. I need to find that place.

Maybe that's the restlessness inside me? It's calling me, isn't it? This in-between world where there is nothing but gold.

That's my mission, I think.

Which means I really need that ship more than ever.

I need to find this place before other people do. Before Veila does.

She doesn't dream about that world the way I do. You either are a silver or you're not. And she is not. I have a theory of what leveling up is now. It's some artificial way to access that pool, I think. And I consider telling Crux this. I consider getting up, getting dressed, and going up to the harem to pound on his door to let him know I know.

I could get that ship right now. Leave tonight.

But I'm not sure. And I have no proof. And... I just get this feeling that there's more to it than that. Like I'm one little piece of the puzzle.

And I don't want to jump the gun. I don't want to let anyone know I dream about this place until I understand it.

I wonder if Corla is dreaming about it right now?

A tingle of jealousy surges through me at that thought. I don't think I would mind being locked up in a cryopod if it meant I could stay in that in-between world longer. Not just a sliver of time while I dream.

I long for it. I want it. Maybe... I have always wanted it?

The ship is still a good idea. I do need to leave here if I want to find more answers. But I'm starting to get the feeling that there's still pieces to find *here*.

Something has changed since I started this little quest. New things have come to light. New things that all seem to be connected.

Earth. The Pleasure Prison. All that mumbo-jumbo about quantum packages of information.

I'm on a path now. That's what this feels like. And there's clues missing. Clues I need to find so I can piece together this puzzle and understand what's at stake.

Because I don't really get it.

Veila is making an army. That's what the Cygnians and Akeelians are doing too. But why? I mean what will they really do with that army? Take over the galaxy?

What's the point? There's hundreds of billions of galaxies. Even if they got control of one, who cares? Space is so big, so open, so empty. It's just not possible to be in charge of all of it.

And the dumbest thing is that there's plenty of room for everyone. There's enough space out there to have a trillion nightmare societies like the Cygnians and Akeelians.

So what is their endgame?

This is the part that puzzles me and this is the question I now need to answer.

I throw the covers off and get out of bed. Then glance over my shoulder to see if I woke Luck.

Nope. He must be very tired because he doesn't even stir.

I change my clothes—not a bodysuit this time, just some tactical pants and a t-shirt—and then grab my deck boots and take them out to the living room to put them on, ticking off the things I know to be true when it comes to this little mystery.

One. Crux is worried about leveling up. Probably because Veila told Jimmy that their brother Draden is still alive due to this process.

Two. Asshole ALCOR is having some kind of existential crisis. That's why he's locked up inside the Pleasure Prison with the Succubus AI from Mighty Minions.

Three. Jimmy and Delphi are fixated on this place called Earth. Also, Lyra and I were headed there to... what? Blow it up? I dunno.

148

Four. Luck thinks Valor and Tray are doing some kind of reality experiment inside the Pleasure Prison.

Five. Valor is fixated on Veila. Which doesn't surprise or worry me as much as it does Luck because come on. We all know Veila is the bad guy here. She's our target. We're all kinda fixated on her.

Six.

I don't have a six yet. I just know there is one. Probably a seven, and an eight, and a nine too.

And ten. There has to be a ten. Ten makes a very nice list. So I'm pretty sure there's a ten.

Once my boots are on I stand up, ready to go looking for number six. I think that starts with Baby ALCOR, so I open up my air screen and press the big red HELP button.

"What can I do for you, Nyleena?" the Baby says.

"Can you tell me about—"

"I'm sorry," he says, cutting me off. "Is this an emergency?"

"Um… no. I guess not."

"Then please make an appointment. I do realize that Real ALCOR was available every moment of every spin, but the HELP button and calendar were put on the air screen for a reason. I need to prioritize."

"Right, but—"

"Please choose a date and time to book your appointment," an automated female voice says.

I stare at the screen. "Did the Baby just hang up on me?"

"Please choose a date and time to book your appointment," she repeats.

"You fucker," I say, closing the screen. "What an asshole."

"Yeah, he's a real piece of work."

I turn to find Luck walking down the hallway. He's naked, hard, and sleepy.

Which is a pretty adorable combination.

"Where the hell are you going?" he asks.

"I was going to talk to Baby ALCOR but he won't talk to me."

Luck stops in my autocook in the kitchenette and starts pressing buttons. A few moments later I smell brewing coffee. "Do you like him?" he asks.

"Who?"

"The Baby."

"I don't know. Should I like him?"

"I kinda like him. I think he's doing a decent job. It wasn't his fault all those people died when Real ALCOR left."

"Left?" I say.

"Died," Luck amends. "Whatever."

"Hmm."

He plucks two mugs of coffee out of the autocook and walks over to offer me one. I take the mug and he smiles at me. "Do you think he's really dead?"

"Real ALCOR?" I say, squinting my eyes at Luck.

"Yeah. Because if what you say is true—that information can't be killed, and he was nothing but information—then do you think that's what Tray and Valor are doing inside the Pleasure Prison?"

Wow. This is some deep thought for first thing in the morning. "I don't know, Luck."

"But aren't you curious?"

"Do you need Real ALCOR anymore? I mean, you have the Baby, you have the Asshole, and you've got all those security beacons out in space. What's the point?"

Luck considers my question thoughtfully. Takes a sip of his coffee. "He's one of us. I guess that's the point. And if I were missing, or Serpint were missing, or Valor, or Tray, or Jimmy or Crux… he'd come looking for us. I know that for sure. He'd never stop until he found us."

"Draden's missing," I say.

"Yeah," Luck says. He sinks down into the cushions of my couch and stares at the mug in his hands. "So's Beauty."

"Beauty," I say. "Your old bot."

"Our old *partner*," he says, glancing up at me with a little heat in his eyes. "And Ceres, too." I don't know who Ceres is. The name is familiar, but I can't place it. So Luck adds, "Serpint's old partner. Died with Draden."

"Well, either people can die or they can't," I say.

"Right," he says. "But I kinda hope that's what Tray and Valor are working on in the Prison. Because it would be nice to get them all back."

I want to… I don't know. Agree with him. Or even build on that dream he's dreaming and get behind it. But I can't. Because it's not logical. Or helpful. For him or anyone else who's lost someone they love.

So I say, "I don't think that's what they're doing."

"Can you find out for me?" he asks.

We lock eyes for a moment. His are sizzling. Little flickers of pink underneath the violet.

"That's… number six."

"Six what?"

"Six things I need to think about today. You want a lot of things, by the way. You want to know why Tray and Valor are hanging out. You want to know what they're up to inside the Pleasure Prison. And now you want to know if people really die?"

"It's really just one thing, Nyleena. It's all related. So what's one through five?" he says.

"Same as yesterday," I reply.

"Right," he says, sighing. "Your quest to get a ship."

"I know you think it's stupid and—"

"I don't think it's stupid, Nyleena."

"You don't?"

He shakes his head. "In fact, I had an idea last night. Would you like me to show you around *Lady Luck*? So you can understand what it takes to be responsible for something so powerful?"

"You'd do that?" I ask, surprised at the offer.

He shrugs. "Whether you stay or you go, either way you're part of me now. And *Lady* is part of us. So you need to know her the way I do."

"Hmm," I say.

"What?"

"That's just very nice of you. Should I fuck you in return?"

He smiles, then frowns. Looking down at his cocks. "That's not necessary."

"Doesn't look that way to me." I laugh.

"I can jerk off," he says. "I've been waking up to this since I was a teenager. I can deal alone." Then he stops to stare at me. It's a long, concentrated stare that starts to make me uncomfortable when it lingers. "That's not why I like you around."

152

"You sure about that? Because you've told me it is dozens of times over the past few months."

"It's convenient," he says. And not as a joke because he's not even smiling. "But lots of things are convenient and you can still live without them. You..." He shakes his head again. "I don't think I could live without you anymore."

CHAPTER NINETEEN

My little declaration feels wrong.

Inevitable, for sure. But a little premature, maybe. Nyleena and I are bound together whether we want it to be that way or not. And I'm not sure this is just something you can walk away from.

My life before Nyleena is over. That's very clear. And if she leaves I will miss her in a way I don't fully understand yet.

"Let me clarify," I say. Because she's just staring at me with this what-the-fuck look on her face. "I'm not saying I love you or anything. I barely know you. But you're here, and I'm here, and we're together now. We are part of something now. So that's what I mean when I don't think I can live without you anymore."

"Mmm-hmm," she hums. "I see."

"I'm not gonna stop you if you do manage to get that ship and leave. That's why I'm gonna help you. But even if you do leave I don't think you'll stay gone long."

"Why's that?"

"Because you need me."

She smiles, looking down at my rock-hard cocks. "I think you need me more than I need you."

"Like I said. Having you around to take care of my needs is convenient. But not necessary."

She scowls. "Well, that's romantic."

I hold up a hand. "I'm just saying… I want you around because we're a team. Not for the sex."

"So you don't want to fuck me right now?"

I stand up, walk towards her, then continue right past her. "I'm gonna take a shower. I'll be ready in ten minutes."

"You're serious?"

"By the way," I say, stopping in front of her autoshopper on my way back to the bedroom. "You didn't even notice your delivery."

"What delivery?"

"Xyla's closet," I say, then take a sip of my coffee while she gawks at the autoshopper stuffed full of clothes and boots.

She looks at me and smiles.

"See, I can be romantic. Order me some clothes, will ya? I don't feel like going home to grab some. You might go off and do something crazy if I don't keep my eye on you."

Then I wink and walk off.

It's nice having Nyleena around to have sex whenever the need calls. But I'm being honest when I say that's not the best part. Maybe it was a few days ago, but ever since she started this whole mission to leave things have changed.

Is it because I'm afraid she actually will leave? Or is it because she has a new spark to her and I'm kinda included in this spark?

I think a little of both.

When I get out of the shower my hard-ons are gone. I told her I knew how to take care of myself and I do. But she did pick me clothes. She even laid them out on the bed for me.

Dark blue tactical pants. Dark blue t-shirt— probably a size too small, but it shows off my muscles, so who's complaining? She even got me socks.

We take the private elevator down to my docking bay where *Lady Luck* lives when we're on the station. She's a sleek yellow bombshell of a ship and I love her. Everyone laughed at us when she got the new paint job, but we just smiled. Yellow says, *Here we come, motherfuckers. Get ready.*

"Well, she sure is bright," Nyleena says as we pull on envirosuits to enter the vacuum in the docking bay.

"Out in space she's so small in the grand scheme of things it hardly matters."

Nyleena stops tugging on her suit for a moment to stare through the window. "Yeah," she finally says. "We're very small out there, aren't we?"

"Practically meaningless," I reply. "*Lady* is not moody like *Booty*," I tell Nyleena. "Or driven like *Dicker*. She's a very calm ship. She likes words and emotions. So everything about *Lady* comes down to feelings. I like that about her. Her voice is interesting and her opinions unique."

"What do you do?" Nyleena asks. "Out there?"

"Why? You trying to picture yourself as a salvager?"

"Maybe," she says.

"Put your helmet on and I'll show you what we do."

I help her with the snap tabs and then she helps me. That's not something Valor and I ever did.

It feels intimate and nice.

We cycle through the bay airlocks, walk over to *Lady*, then climb the stairs and wait inside her airlocks until the door security lights finally flash green, indicating there's enough atmosphere to breathe, then we help each other take the helmets off.

"Wow," Nyleena says. "This is quite fancy."

"Thank you," *Lady* says, her voice very soft and feminine for such a practical ship. "I designed it myself."

"I like it," Nyleena says.

"*Lady*, this is my princess, Nyleena. Nyleena, meet my queen, *Lady*."

Lady chuckles. So does Nyleena.

I want them to like each other, I realize. *Lady* is very important to me so her opinion of Nyleena counts. It counts a lot.

"I'm showing Nyleena around," I explain to *Lady*. "Because pretty soon she'll be the proud owner of her own sentient ship."

"Exciting," *Lady* says. "Have you ever been responsible for a ship before?"

"No," Nyleena says a little stiffly.

"Don't worry," I say. "I promise. This isn't a set-up to talk you out of it. It's just a crash course in everything you need to know."

"OK," Nyleena says.

"So… ask her anything."

"Well…" Nyleena looks around. The interior of *Lady* isn't anything like the interior of any other sentient ship I've ever been in. It feels like a home, not a salvage ship. The walls are all painted a very pale yellow and the trim is white. Even the cockpit has this color scheme. The chairs are soft leather and the console is silver. There is nothing dark about my *Lady* at all. Everything is bright and cheerful.

Not a manly ship, for sure. But she's not a man, is she?

Why should she give up who she is for me?

"OK," Nyleena says, her wits gathered up enough to ask a question. "What's it like to work for Luck?"

"Really?" I ask.

"Yeah. I want to know. Because how your partners see you is important. Is he moody? Or easy-going? Does he yell? Or talk softly? Is he fair? Or unreasonable?"

"He's all of that," *Lady* replies.

"Thanks a lot." I laugh.

"At times," *Lady* continues, "Luck is just… big."

"What do you mean?" Nyleena asks.

"When he's in the room, he's the only mind in the room. Even when Valor was with us, Luck's opinion mattered more because his picture is big."

Nyleena shoots me a confused look.

"Yeah," I say. "She's not a very straightforward ship. Believe me, she runs a million possible word combinations through her brain before she decides on a sentence. So you really have to ask the right question if you need a quick answer."

"I don't need to say much," *Lady* says. "I mostly run in the background and it's very easy to forget I'm here. So when I do speak I like to make you remember me."

"Hmm," Nyleena says. "You're a poet."

If *Lady* had a face she'd be smiling. "Yes. I like that word a lot. I'm a... poet."

"I hope I get a poet," Nyleena muses.

This hurts a little. I can't explain it because I wasn't lying when I told her that this visit isn't about talking her out of owning her own sentient ship.

"There are no other poet ships," *Lady* says. "I'm the only one."

"I like that answer a lot," I say.

We spend the next few hours going over the *Lady*'s parts starting with the cockpit. I can't teach Nyleena how to fly a ship in one morning, but I can give a general idea of what to do if something goes wrong. That mostly involves tapping the emergency life support tab on the screen. I teach her how to send and receive messages, especially neutrino waves. Because that's how the important ones come in.

I show her the salvage units, and the water generator, and the autocook. Then we go through weapons systems and I explain the necessity for a bot or a borg.

Nyleena stops me to ask a lot of questions about this. "What if I just want to go alone?"

"You want to go out *there* alone?"

"I'll have the ship. Won't that be enough?"

"Do *you* think it'll be enough?" I ask.

"I don't know," she admits.

160

"Forget about liking the bots or the borgs. What if you don't like your ship?"

"Hmm. I guess I didn't think this through, did I?"

"You're not leaving tonight, Nyleena. Even if you do solve Crux's problem and he keeps his end of the bargain. You need to think this through very carefully. Forget about how great things will be once you have the freedom of a powerful ship like *Lady* and instead think about how horrible it could be if you and the ship don't respect and like each other. Imagine floating out there in the deep dark, just you and this ship. And you hate each other's guts."

"Will it kill me?"

"It could kill you any moment of any day. And sure, there would be consequences, but it doesn't change the fact that you place your life in the hands of a powerful being when you take responsibility for a ship like *Lady*."

"You're trying to talk me out of this."

"I'm not," I say. "I promise. I'm just giving you a little reality check." I take her hand and hold it. "I want you to be safe. That's all."

"So I need to interview bots." She frowns. "How do I pay them?"

"Well, what will your mission be?"

"To kill people, of course. Bad people, to be clear."

"Unless you find a bot or a borg that has the same mission you do, you have to have a real job. Like salvaging. We go out, find parts for the station, and we get paid when we get back."

"You own this place, it's different."

I shrug. "I still work, don't I?"

"I'm not calling you lazy, Luck. I'm just saying… we're different."

We stare at each other for a moment. Locked in a realization of sorts.

"I don't want you to leave," I say. "But I have two good reasons for that. One, we're partners now. If you leave, you should leave with me. And two, I'll worry about you, Nyleena. I will. I'll never stop worrying about you." Then I pause. Because I have one more thing to say. "Come with me."

"Come with you?" she asks. And she makes a face. "To rummage through junkyards? I'm not saying your job isn't important, I'm just saying… I'm not sure that's how I see *my* life."

"Fair enough," I say. "But I was taught how to survive out there by the best. Real ALCOR spent years training us to leave the station. We started when we were teenagers. It was almost a decade after we came here to live with him before he thought we were ready. You have had no training, Nyleena. And there's no one in charge of you. No one who can say, 'That's a bad idea. Don't do it.' Not anyone you'll listen to. How long will it take you to learn to trust your ship? And then how long after that before you decide it gives advice worth listening to?"

"You make good points," she says, sighing. "But… I just don't see myself as part of your team, Luck. I'm sorry." She looks around at *Lady*'s interior. "This is *your* life, not mine."

"You don't even know what I do," I say.

"I know enough. That's not my plan. I know that's not a great answer, but it's true."

"Then what is your plan? And don't say kill people. That's dumb. You can't live a life based on revenge."

"Why not?"

"I just told you. It's dumb."

"You're dumb," she snaps. "I can do whatever I want. I'm a goddamned silver princess."

"What does that mean? Exactly?"

"It means I have power. That's what."

"Power to do what?"

"Whatever I want."

"To kill people?"

"Lots of people," she says. Then lifts her chin up in royal haughtiness. "I can blow up worlds if I want to."

"And kill yourself in the process."

"Sometimes it's worth it."

"When?"

"I don't know yet. But they made me this way for a reason, didn't they?"

"To blow up places like Harem Station, Nyleena."

"I'm not going to blow up Harem Station," she huffs. "Now you're the one being dumb."

"Whatever," I say, standing up. "You ready to go then? Because I am."

"I'm sorry I can't be what you want. I'm just... my own person now. I spent my whole life waiting for this kind of freedom. I'm not ready to give it up to scour junkyards with you."

"Right," I mutter. And head to the ladder to climb back up to the main level.

Because that's *not* what I do.

But I don't say that out loud. What's the point?

163

Nyleena has a plan and even though I think it's a lot more than just killing people for revenge, she's not interested in building a partnership with me.

Bringing her here was a mistake.

And asking her to join me… an even bigger mistake.

If she doesn't need me then fuck it.

I don't need her either.

CHAPTER TWENTY

NYLEENA

Luck didn't say another word to me the whole time we suited back up, cycled through two airlocks, then took the suits off and hung them back up in his staging room back inside the station.

Not a single word. Not even a grunt or a huff.

And I tried. I asked him what he had planned for today.

He didn't answer me. The only thing he said was, "See you at four," just before he walked off towards some random hallway.

Meaning, our standing appointment for secret garden sex.

Fine.

We're back where we started. That's actually a great place to be. I might not have made much progress yesterday but today is different.

I am on a mission. I am the silver Cygnian princess Nyleena, for fuck's sake. And if there's one thing I'm great at—aside from blowing up worlds with my light—it's scheming and plotting. I'm going to scheme the fuck out of this day starting right now.

And it all starts with Baby ALCOR.

How dare he send me to his automated calendar.

Does he even know who I am?

I take seven escalators and two elevators to get back up to the top levels where I know for a fact Baby ALCOR hangs out.

He has an office next to the harem room and that's where I'm going. I'm gonna sit my ass down in his waiting room until he makes time for me. I'm gonna—

"Nyleena!"

I turn at the shout and find Delphi and Lyra walking my way. I wave and head towards them. Because these two are the only people on this whole station I can really relate to. They are like me. We are alike. We are the same. We all risked everything to leave the Cygnian System behind and start a new life.

If anyone will understand my desire to go out in the deep dark and find my own way, it's them.

"Hey," I say, once they're within earshot. "What are you guys doing?"

"Going to a screen," Lyra says. "You wanna come? It's a brand new Jax Justice action flick. In this one he's fighting the Lorians. Giant cyborg assholes who want to enslave all the Centurian women and force them to have half-breed Centborgion babies."

"Sexy," I say, then frown. Screens are kinda pricey and I already spent next week's allowance on yesterday's outfit. Which was super dumb of me now that I know Luck bought me Xyla's entire closet as payment for extra sex. "I don't have any credits left."

"I'll pay," they both say at the same time. Then, "Jinx!" Then, "Double jinx!"

Then they laugh and laugh. Like they are sisters.

Delphi is not Lyra's sister. I am.

God, I want to gag. Why did I think we were the same again? We're not. I'm not like anyone on this place.

Except Corla. I wish I could talk to Corla.

"Hey. Have you gone to see Corla yet?" I ask Delphi.

"No," she says. "I don't see the point. They're not gonna wake her up until we catch Veila. I'll just see her then."

"Hmm," I say, a scheme forming in my head. "Which beacon is she on again?"

They both shoot each other one of those looks. The kind that say, *Uh-oh. Nyleena's scheming.*

"I just want to *see* her."

"Believe me," Delphi says, "no one is going to let you get within a million klicks of that beacon."

"I'm not gonna wake her up, for fuck's sake. I just… want to visit her."

"Not gonna happen," Lyra says. Then she takes my hand and tugs me along as they start to walk again. "Come see a screen with us. It'll be fun. We never spend any time together anymore. I miss you."

"I'm sorta busy today," I say, resisting her pull.

"Doing what?" Lyra asks.

I shoot Delphi a look, because she's part of my scheme in progress. But she's making a slicing motion across her throat basically telling me to shut up about Earth.

I can respect that. So I say, "Trying to get a meeting with Baby ALCOR. I need info about something."

Delphi smiles. And I scowl back at her. My look clearly says, *You owe me. Get ready to pay up soon.* Because once I get her that info about Earth I will expect her to tell me exactly what happened to Valor back on Mighty Minions.

"We're going to miss the promos," Delphi says. "How about we meet up later, Nyleena? After dinner, maybe?"

"Sounds perfect," I purr. "I'll have what I need by then and we can… *chat.*"

"Great!" she quips. "Come on, Lyra."

Lyra waves as Delphi pulls her off in the opposite direction.

How are they so content to be stuck here? I don't get it.

But you know what? They can stay here and be bored for eternity for all I care.

I have places to go and people to see.

Well, waiting out an AI is probably not the best scheme I've ever come up with. He appears to have infinite patience because I sit in his office for hours. I wait so long my stomach is rumbling with hunger and his cyborg assistant is shooting me dirty looks.

Finally, I've had enough. I stand up and march over to her console and cross my arms in front of my chest, just in case she hasn't caught on to the idea that I'm annoyed as fuck. "How much longer?"

"I don't know," she says, her one red eye racing across her face. "You can always make an—"

"I know," I say, putting up a hand to stop her. "You've told me to make an appointment several times. But the first available is three days out."

"He's very busy, Princess. I'm sorry. I don't control him, I'm just a guiding hand."

"Can't you guide him in my direction? I mean, I really need to talk to him. Baby ALCOR!" I yell, looking up at the ceiling. "Talk to me!"

"That won't help," the cyborg assistant says. "He's not here."

"Where is he?"

"I'm afraid I can't give out his schedule. But," she says, her voice lifting a little, like she's about to be helpful, "I can make you an appointment."

I growl at her and walk out.

Fine. He wins.

For now. Because I'm gonna find a way to get that information about Earth *today*. No matter what.

Anyway, it's time for my regularly scheduled tryst with Luck in the secret garden. I pull up my schedule to see which sector we're meeting in. Then I activate the little button I'm supposed to before I head towards it so no one can track me.

Today we're on level one hundred twenty-two. Right near the Harem Station History Museum.

It's a little hidden gem tucked away in the middle of a huge mechanical room that, according to the station map Luck gave me to find the gardens, runs the interactive content inside the museum.

There's no privacy at all. It's literally a patch of grass in the middle of the room. No walls around it like the others. But it's not the first secret garden that was designed this way. A few others were in huge mechanical rooms and Luck told me it's because the robotic shit inside these rooms is so rudimentary and automated, they do not qualify as minds. They are simply brainless machines that don't require any sort of intervention.

Like an autocook, I guess. That's a complicated set of circuits, for sure. But it doesn't have a brain. You can't say, "Hey, autocook, make me something delicious and sweet." You have to program in a sequence of numbers for your specific recipe. It can't even respond to voice commands.

That's what these machines are.

There are no trees. And that makes me wonder what will grow when I finish myself off after we're done.

Because I have decided that last night was definitely a mistake. I should not have let myself loose like that. It's very dangerous. And telling him my little time secret was my worst mistake yet.

He's gonna tell everyone. Then what? What will they do with me? Lock me up in a cryopod like Corla? I mean, sure. I was just musing this morning about how nice it would be to dream the gold dream inside a cryopod, but how do I know Corla is dreaming? She could be inert. Mindless. She could be floating in darkness.

I don't want to risk it. If they find out I'm holding secrets inside they might shoot me out to one of those beacons and keep me on ice until...

Until what?

I snort laugh. I'm being paranoid and stupid.

Lyra is already here.

The only reason Corla is locked up like that is because Veila was missing and then she turned into the enemy.

Lyra and I are nothing like Corla and Veila. We're a team. We're solid.

I'm fine.

I check the time on my air screen and realize Luck is late.

He's never late for sex. Ever.

I ping him and my call gets routed right to his voicemail.

"This is Luck," his voice grumbles. "Obviously I'm busy or I'd have answered your call. Or maybe I don't want to talk to you? So before you leave me a pointless message, consider that."

Beep.

I don't leave a message.

Obviously he's busy.

Or… he's done with me. I did piss him off this morning. He took me out to *Lady Luck* and showed me around and I insulted his job.

Was I mean?

I wasn't trying to be mean. I just want to make it perfectly clear that I'm not interested in scouring junkyards.

When I leave the secret garden and enter the main concourse again, there's a giant flashing holographic sign in front of the museum telling me that admission is free today.

Was that there before?

I don't know. But I decide to go in and check it out because if this is the history of Harem Station then there should be an interactive teenage Luck running around in there.

And at that thought… I brighten and go inside.

CHAPTER TWENTY-ONE

Stations are so much better than planets because planets are difficult to settle and if you happen upon one that's already settled, it's usually a little bit backwards and doesn't have a lot of humanoid variety.

The backwards part isn't an insult, it's just a fact. Once you're on a planet you're pretty much stuck there. The amount of energy it takes to go in and out of such a large gravity well is the definition of effort.

And unless the planet's system has a nearby gate, it typically has only one species of humanoid on it.

There are over a hundred different species of humanoids on Harem Station. And that's not including the bots and borgs.

Everything about Harem is weird, and mixed up, and… quite frankly, *amazing*.

This is why I don't really understand why Nyleena wants to leave. I mean, I get it. She wants to go places. See things. Explore.

But… that's the definition of my job. That's what I do! And then I come home. To here. This rich, culturally diverse, super-station.

So how can she not see herself in my life? My life has practically been set up to her dream standards.

I don't understand it.

The bar where Cha-Cha hangs out is on level three hundred and nine. High enough up to avoid the riff-raff down below, but far enough removed from the top of the station where we live to feel like you have to make an effort to get there.

It's a dart bar called Erbotica. For some reason sexbots are obsessed with playing darts and whenever I want to find Chach, Xyla, or Ladybug, I check here first.

They are in the back being loud. Xyla is throwing magnetic darts at Prince-bot's spherical body because for whatever reason, he's painted up like a bullseye.

Delphi's evil dragonbee bot, Flicka, is whizzing around Prince, buzzing with excitement as Cha-Cha and Ladybug keep handing Xyla more ammunition.

I'm just about to interrupt and say hello, when Cha-Cha sees me and whistles loudly to make everyone shut up.

"Luck," she says, brightening as she walks towards me, all her mechanical joints loose from the special bot-juice whiskey they drink. "What's up, my master?"

"Nothin'," I say.

"Nothing?" Xyla asks. All the sexbots have articulated features so they can do humanoid expressions pretty well. Xyla's raised eyebrow is a perfect example of this special sexbot feature. She makes this face, which I recognize as her accessing her internal database, and then says, "My calendar says you've got a hot date with Nyleena right about now. So why are you here talking to us instead of sneaking around those secret gardens getting laid?"

"You hacked my calendar?" I ask.

"When don't I hack your calendar?" Xyla says.

Xyla was the only other person here on the station when my brothers and I landed on Harem. It wasn't called Harem back then. Just ALCOR Station. She and ALCOR had been friends for a very long time before we showed up. And even though Xyla and Jimmy immediately became tight once we came on board, she was still very close to Real ALCOR.

She misses him just as much as we do. Maybe more.

That's part of the reason Ladybug and Cha-Cha took her to Blue Sand Beach for a vacay.

They were so drunk when I picked them up and told them we had to go save Jimmy. But when you're a sexbot, being drunk is a choice. They take some kind of antagonist to clear the bot juice from their system and presto. No longer drunk.

They are all a little drunk right now.

Flicka buzzes over and lands on my shoulder. This one makes me nervous. I think she makes everyone nervous. They are banned here but for this one exception. We all know what dragonbee bots are capable of. And according to Jimmy she took out a whole horde of cyborgs back on Lair Station by shooting a few puffs of poison out her ass.

I flick her off and shrug my shoulders to hold down the chill running up my spine.

Prince just hovers there covered in magnetic darts and says nothing.

175

"Seriously," Chach says. "Why aren't you banging Nyleena?"

"We're fighting," I say.

"Here, you poor baby," Ladybug says. "Have a drink."

Organic humans can drink botjuice, but not a lot of it. One mug and you're drunk. Two and you're sick for days. "Thanks," I say, taking the mug she's offering. I sip it, then sigh. "I need advice," I say.

"About what?" Chach asks.

"Nyleena."

All of them trade a weird, suspicious look. Even Flicka gets in on this. She flies over to Xyla and starts buzzing around her ear. Xyla, whether she means to or not, begins nodding her head.

"What's going on with Nyleena?" Ladybug asks. She's staring at me with wide, red eyes. Her whole body is naked of clothes. Just smooth metal. Black and shiny. She's been dressing like this ever since we got back from Mighty Minions and Ladybug goes inside the Pleasure Prison to hang out all the time. One perk about being a bot? No pod necessary to join in on sexy virtual fun. They just access it directly through their minds.

If Tray came to us one of these days and said he wanted us to extract his mind and put it in a bot body, I would not be surprised. Then he could go in there all he wants and never worry about his body back in the gaming pod.

"She wants to leave the station," I say.

They all trade that look again and I'm just about to ask what's up with that when Xyla says, "And that's a problem, why?"

"Because I'm getting used to her. She's not so bad, you guys. But I'm not sure she feels the same way about me. I mean, I don't want her to go. Now she's mad at me for offering to let her join me and take Valor's place on the salvage team. And ever since she revealed a secret to me last night I find her situation to be a lot more sympathetic."

"What'd she tell you?" Xyla asks.

"I don't think I should say. It's kinda personal."

Xyla raises that eyebrow again. "Luck. If you know something about her that we don't, you need to tell us. Do I need to remind you what she really is?"

"I know what she is. And I'm not telling you what she told me. It's very personal. If she wanted anyone else to know, she'd have told you herself."

"She can't have secrets," Xyla explains. "She's too dangerous. And didn't Crux order you to tame her ass down?"

"No," I say. "He told me to tell her to get a job. So that's why I'm so conflicted now. If he really does give her a ship and she leaves the station, then she kinda has a job, right?"

"Do you really think he's going to give her a ship?" Chach asks.

"He better," I say. "He made a deal with her. I expect him to hold up his end."

This time there is no shared look. But the Prince-bot starts beeping and whistling as he picks the magnetic darts off his body using one of his grabby hands.

"I know," Xyla snarls at him.

"What's he saying?" I ask. I open my air screen to pull up a translator, but by the time it starts translating,

Prince has gone quiet. "What was that about?" I ask Xyla.

Xyla looks at me for a long second. Like she's weighing her options. Trying to figure out if she should tell me or not.

But then Ladybug says, "You know what the real problem is here?"

"What?" I ask, turning to meet her fiery-red eyes.

"This is about commitment."

"What do you mean?"

"Nyleena wants to know someone has her back. I mean, think about things from her perspective. She's a silver princess. God only knows what her life was like back in the Cygnian System." Ladybug visibly shudders. "I mean, they made her into a bomb."

"How do you know they made her? Maybe she was just born that way?"

The girls all shrug. Like they're not sure it matters.

But I think it matters. If they made her into a bomb, that's awful. And rejecting that is normal.

But if this is just her—just the way she is—then that's different. She should be allowed to be herself. She should not have to reject something that goes so deep. If silver princesses are just born with this amazing, explosive light inside them, then why should she have to change her inner nature to make the rest of us feel safer?

Fuck. No wonder she wants to leave.

"Not the point," Ladybug continues. "My point is that she needs a champion, Luck. And if you're her soulmate, that's your job."

"To be her champion?" I ask.

"Mmm-hmm," Ladybug says. "Support her."

178

"That's it? Then she'll want to stay with me?"

"I don't know. Who can predict a feral savage like Nyleena?"

"Hmm," I hum. "Could work."

"Trust me," Ladybug says. "Girls love this shit. When they know their man is on their side, they swoon, Luck."

"Swoon, huh?"

"*Swoon*," she purrs back.

CHAPTER TWENTY-TWO

Inside the museum it's actually pretty peaceful and quiet. Not too many people here right now and it only takes a few minutes to get to the first exhibit, which is a holographic image of the station as viewed from space. It asks one question in a deep voice that is just a little bit different than Baby ALCOR's.

"Who would you like to guide you through the exhibits?" Simulated ALCOR asks.

Other holograms pop up and I can't help but smile.

Crux, Jimmy, Tray, Valor, Luck, Serpint, and Draden.

All younger versions of themselves.

"Oh, this is too cute," I mumble under my breath.

I'm very tempted to choose Draden and Serpint, who apparently guide as a team and come with servo-bot minions, because they spend the whole time playing shoot-'em-up with makeshift weapons as I decide.

But I'm here to learn more about Luck. So of course, I say, "Luck, please."

"Good choice," teenage-hologram Luck says, shooting me with his finger. "I'm gonna show you a

181

real good time, Princess. Follow me," he says, then walks off. But I hesitate and he looks over his shoulder and says, "Keep up now. It's very easy to get lost on ALCOR Station. And you never know what's hiding in the dark hallways."

I don't know where everyone else disappeared to, because when I follow Luck into the next room, there's no one here but us.

"This is what the station looked like when we arrived." He throws his arms out wide and the room morphs into a full hologram.

"Wow," I say out loud. It's very dark. Almost no lights at all. The black, shiny obsidian floors that appear very glam and high-end today looked like an endless sea of smooth, danger-filled water back then.

Luck points out landmarks, then and now. And if there wasn't a holographic overlay to illustrate that these levels really are the same, I'd never be able to picture it.

There's nothing here. No stores, no shooting galleries, no arcades, no screen houses. Nothing.

Little Serpint and Draden make several appearances as we go through the levels and Luck describes how they spent their early days. They are so small and young, I can't help but laugh when I think about big, strong, broad-shouldered Serpint my sister fell in love with.

We go into a training room next and I see how each of the boys leaned to build bots and ships, and program autocooks, and fly. They were also taught how to fight and we stop in the gym to watch Crux and Valor spar.

It's pretty brutal stuff. Neither of them pulls punches. It's a fight-your-hardest-and-worry-about-medical-attention-later kind of bout.

"I know how to fight too," I say to Luck. Because I feel like he's trying to convince me not to leave the station.

"Can you take me?" he asks.

"What?"

He snaps his fingers and a holographic figure of me appears in the center of the mat. Crouching in a fight-ready stance as I circle him, ready to pounce.

Luck turns away from me to face… other me. And I walk a few steps to the side so I can see his face.

He smiles at other me, then says, "I'd rather kiss you."

Other me responds by leaping into the air and attacking him. We both fall to the ground and there's some shuffling and grunting… but in the end, Holographic Luck finds his way on top of other me.

And then he does kiss me.

"OK," I say, putting up a hand. "I think we've gone off track here. I want to know more about you."

Other me disappears and Luck turns to face me. "Like what?"

"You know. What you do."

"Ah." He winks. "You want to see my junkyards?" He grabs himself and gives his cocks a shake.

"For fuck's sake." I laugh. "Stop being a perv."

He pretends to blush and averts his eyes. But then he turns again and says, "Come on. Junkyards are this way."

I follow him through several more exhibits. Mostly other holographic images of him and Valor doing

183

things. Meeting Beauty. Who, I have to admit, is a very pretty bot. She's a brilliant gold sphere. Sorta like Lyra's new nanny-bot, Prince. Except you can tell Beauty is no nanny-bot. She's got hidden panels that produce grabby hands holding weapons. And there's a screen playing as we pass through another exhibit that shows a video of her kicking ass against some gruesome alien-looking things on some dark and creepy station.

There's a text crawler on the lower third of the screen declaring it to be "actual footage".

"Hmm," I say. But Luck doesn't stop. Just keeps going until we finally end up in another room. A huge room that isn't a hologram. I know this because my fingers dart out to sweep through the image and scrape bare, ragged rock.

"What is this?" I ask.

Luck peeks over his shoulder and shoots me that charming smile of his. "My first junkyard."

I squint my eyes as I take it all in.

"But… it's a cave." I say. Not that I've ever been in a real cave. But I've seen images and footage of them.

"Not just any cave," Luck says. "This is where ALCOR was born."

"What?" I ask, looking around me.

It is a cave. I'm not wrong. But there's writing on the walls. Picture writing surrounded by weird slashes and chips in the stone. Like it's very ancient.

And there's ice on one side. A whole wall of ice that appears to be melting, because water is dripping down the side. But at the bottom of the ice wall there's a collection grate of some sort. And when I walk over there it's at least twenty degrees cooler than the other side of the room.

"There were lots of caves," Luck explains.

"Where?" I ask. "Where was this? It wasn't a station."

"No, it was a planet," he says. Then he winks. "A very special planet."

"Where's Valor?" I ask. Because I can see another Luck on the far side of the rock-walled cave. He's messing with a technology console, fingers busily typing on an old-fashioned keyboard as he gazes up at green code spilling down a dark screen. Like he's giving commands.

"I went alone this one time."

"Why?" I ask, moving closer to other Luck so I can see what he's so fixated on.

"Because it was a secret," Luck says.

"Hmm," I hum. None of the code makes any sense to me, so I turn back to him and say, "I thought you fought aliens on abandoned space stations?"

"We do that too. Now. But ALCOR sent me on a secret mission once. Back before Valor and I teamed up. And this is what I found."

"But what is it?" I ask, turning back to look at the ice wall.

"Everything," he whispers. "It's everything."

And then suddenly the lights come on and the room—which I was so sure was real—disappears and there's nothing left but blank, slate-gray walls.

"Wait," I say. "Where'd it go?"

Luck points to the ceiling. "He was about to catch me. I had to shut it down. I'm sorry, Princess. But the tour is over now."

And then, before I can even get another question out, holographic-guide Luck disappears.

"What the fuck?" I whisper.

"Nyleena?" a disembodied voice says above me.

"What?" I say, unsure who or what this voice belongs to. Because it's not the Baby and it's not the simulated ALCOR either. It's faked, I realize. A mechanical voice. Like it's wearing a disguise.

"You have a message. Please exit the museum to access it."

"Weird," I say, so annoyed again. All my wonderment at seeing the old station and the young brothers disappears as my reality comes rushing back.

I am the silver princess Nyleena. And I am on Harem Station.

I need to get the fuck out of here. These people have too many secrets for me.

And sure, I have a bunch of those too, but I'm trying to get away from them. Not run headlong into new ones.

It takes me a while to find my way back outside to the main concourse. I have to go through dozens of other rooms, all of which are empty slate-gray walls. Not a hologram in sight. And the moment I step outside my air screen pops up with a message from Lyra.

Her face is bright and happy when she says, "The screen's over. You missed a good one. Come meet Delphi and I at Crusty's and we'll grab dinner."

I'm jealous of her, I realize.

Because somehow, some way, Lyra has found peace with who and what she is.

And I had hope that I too would find that peace.

186

But that hope is fading fast these days.
I need to get the fuck off this station.

When I make it up to Crusty's on the level just below the Pleasure Prison I find Delphi and Lyra already snacking on appetizers in the back of the very crowded restaurant.

I slip in one of the empty chairs, exhausted. "God, I need a drink."

Delphi raises her hand at a passing server who is green from head to toe, hairless, and has the longest fangs I've ever seen on a human. "We need two bottles of wine, please. Something made of tushberry fruit, if you have it. Otherwise we'll settle for passion lime."

"You got it," the server says in a deep, throaty voice that sounds a lot like a growl.

"You missed a great movie," Lyra says, sipping from her half-empty wine glass. "It was fab."

I just stare at her, still very annoyed. "How do you do it?" I ask.

"Do what?" Lyra asks.

"Be so... goddamned happy all the time?"

"I dunno." She shrugs. "I guess I am just happy."

"Here?" I say, then nod my head at the green server. "These aren't our people."

"We're all the same people here," Lyra counters.

"Yeah, I get that," I say. "We're all people here. But... we have *people*, Lyra."

"Like who?" Delphi asks. "Veila?" She snorts. "You know, I've had enough of our people. If I don't

187

see another Cygnian princess as long as I live, I'll die happy." Then she smiles at me. "Present company excluded of course."

"Speaking of her," I say. "When's that mission start? I'm about to get my own sentient ship and I'm totally down for kicking some fake-silver Veila ass."

Delphi and Lyra look at each other. It's one of *those* looks. Again. The kind that say, *OK. We have something to tell her, but not now, right? We don't want to rock the boat and it can wait.*

"What the fuck?" I snap. I'm feeling very much like the savage, feral princess I've become infamous for being right now.

"We're not going on the Veila mission," Delphi says.

"But… your brother," I say.

"Tycho," she says. "Yes. I'm worried about him but Lyra and I have been talking and since she can't go, I'm going to stay here with her. Jimmy and the boys will find Tycho. I'm just… better off here."

"Here?" I say. Then my head swivels to Lyra. "You too? What the fuck, Lyra? You used to be so badass and now you're all meek and soft."

Lyra sighs. But Delphi is the one who speaks. "Don't you get it, Nyleena?"

"Get what?"

"She can't leave. What if they catch her?"

"How are they gonna catch her? There are all these alpha men going with us."

"Us?" Delphi says.

"Not now, Delphi," Lyra says. "We should just drink our wine."

"If not now, when?" Delphi says, looking at Lyra. "She thinks she's getting a ship and leaving here. Leaving *you* here. Like what the fuck, Nyleena?"

"I am getting a ship," I snarl. "It's practically a done deal."

"Is it?" Delphi counters. "You don't seem to be making much progress in that department."

"I got sidetracked today, that's all. Baby ALCOR is playing hard to get but I've got an idea. Speaking of which, where's that bot of yours?"

"Why?" Delphi says, her face scrunching up into wrinkles.

"Because I have a task for her. One I think she'll enjoy."

"You stay away from my bot," Delphi says. "I'm dead serious about that. She's doing really well here. I don't need you fucking up her progress with your psycho schemes."

I let it go and turn back to Lyra. Because I don't need Delphi's permission to talk to Flicka. Isn't that the greatest thing about Harem Station?

Everyone has free will. Even enslaved dragonbee bots.

"But there's more like *us* out there," I say. Then look around nervously and lean in to whisper, "Angel Station, remember? We should be heading there."

"No," Delphi says.

"Would you just shut up already," I snap. "I'm not even talking to you. I'm talking to my *sister*."

"You can't leave Harem Station, Nyleena," Delphi says. "It's impossible."

"It's possible," I counter. "As soon as I get a ship."

"Nyleena," Lyra says calmly. "Crux isn't giving you a ship. I was on board with this—"

"Crazy scheme of yours," Delphi interrupts. And man, I'm really getting sick of her. "But... the truth is, Nyleena, you can't leave because you could be caught. And then someone could detonate you and Lyra and hurt a lot of people."

I sit back in my chair.

They're right, of course. And I knew this. "But Angel Station," I say.

Lyra just shakes her head.

"It's all a lie?" I ask. "This promise Crux made me?"

She and Delphi trade another look. Then Lyra turns back to me and says, "It's not really a lie if you get the ship."

"I just can't leave." I say.

"You can't leave, Nyleena. And neither can I."

I get up and walk out.

Because I'm free.

For the first time in my life, I'm free.

And yet... it appears that I'm not.

I go home.

Is it home? Is this place my 'home' now? Is that how 'home' works?

You end up somewhere by mistake and stay long enough for it become 'home'?

Everything about that seems wrong to me. I should be able to choose where home is.

But what was I really thinking these past few days? That I would... what? Just take off and leave Lyra behind? I knew that wasn't an option and yet... I somehow find myself in the middle of this strange scheme to get a ship.

I didn't even want a ship four days ago. Four days ago I was just gonna go on the Veila hunt with everyone else. It was never supposed to be me alone.

So why do I want a ship so bad right now?

I'm not sure. But the thought of not getting that ship from Crux ignites a fury inside me. I want it. That's all I know. Nothing else makes sense. And all the possible futures I ever imagined for myself up to that moment in time when I asked Crux for a ship are gone now. They just floated away and left this one path forward.

My door alarm chimes.

"Who the fuck..."

I get up from the couch and walk over to the door, then tab on the screen to show me who is outside.

An eyeball.

Specifically, a violet eyeball that's crackling with pink tendrils of light.

"Leeeeeeeeeeeena," Luck drawls. Then he backs up so I can see his whole face. "Open the door. I have something for you."

I roll my eyes and shut off the screen. "Go away."

He chimes the door alarm again.

"What?" I hiss, opening the screen again.

He's leaning against the wall opposite my door. Arms folded across his chest. Huge, charming smirk on his face. Eyes squinting down into little slits. "I have a present for you," he says.

"Let me guess. Is the present hidden inside your pants?"

He laughs too loud and shakes his head.

"Oh, my God, are you drunk?"

He gets serious. Or tries to. Then he holds up one finger and says, "I only had one mug of sexbot juice."

I crinkle my nose. "That's disgusting."

"Open the door," he says. "I need to swoon you with my present."

"Luck, just go home. I'm not in the mood to deal with this shit right now. I'm in the middle of an existential crisis."

"That's my favorite kind," he slurs. "Let me in."

I consider this. We probably should have sex. I can feel my luminous flux building inside me. It's not at critical levels yet, but by morning, it could be.

So I open the door.

CHAPTER TWENTY-THREE

I didn't feel drunk on the way up to Nyleena's place but that sexbot juice really hit me hard when I got out of the elevator.

I'm ninety percent certain she's going to slap my face and send me packing but…

The door opens and she says, "Fine. But this gift of yours had better be good."

"You're using me," I slur, then hurry past her and head right for her autocook and try to remember the code I need. "I love that about you."

Then I laugh. Because I didn't actually mean to say that out loud.

"What are you doing? For fuck's sake, Luck. You're really not helping me tonight."

"Cure," I mumble. Then stab the screen and do a search for the right code for sexbot juice inhibitor. "There," I say, pressing enter. Then turn around to lean back on the autocook before I fall over.

"Why are you drunk?"

The autocook dings and I hold up a finger, indicating she should give me a moment. Then I down the thick, green disgusting drink and hold my stomach as I blink my eyes and grimace.

"God. Never let me do that again. I know better. And my stomach hurts."

She holds a hand over her face to hide a giggle.

"It's not funny," I say. "That drink is gross."

"Why were you drinking sexbot juice anyway? That's so disgusting."

"Because I was in a sexbot bar." I shuffle my way over to her couch and flop down, sinking back into the cushions, then falling to the side so I can lie back. "Oh, my God," I whine. "My stomach feels like shit. And my head is pounding."

I crack an eyelid open and spy Nyleena rolling her eyes at me. "Why are men such babies when they don't feel good? Do you have the man-flu, Luck? Poor thing. Should I make you soup?"

I close my eye and groan. "I don't have the man flu. I have a sexbot hangover."

"Anyway," she huffs. "You said you have a present for me. Hand it over."

I open both eyes and smile at her. "You're gonna swoon."

"Am I?" She chuckles.

"Mmm-hmm. Ladybug said so. And Chach helped me wrap it. She says chicks dig ribbons." I pull a small box out of my pocket and throw it at her. "So there. Swoon."

She catches the small black box in one hand like she's a badass silver princess, then looks down at it.

"Don't worry," I say. "It's not a collar."

"Obviously," she says, holding up the tiny box as proof.

"It's not a ring either. You're never gonna guess what it is." I smile, feeling pretty proud of myself. "And it was my idea. Just because Cha-Cha wrapped it doesn't mean she gets credit for my genius, swoon-worthy present."

She looks down at the box in her hand and studies it. "What is it?"

"Open it," I whisper. "But wait. Come sit next to me first."

She smiles and crosses the room. Plops down on the couch and I put my feet up in her lap.

"Will you please take off my boots?" I ask, holding my stomach as I groan. "I can't reach them."

She pushes my legs off her and says, "You're such an asshole."

"Come on," I beg. "Be my nurse. Just until I feel better. I promise. If you ever drink sexbot juice and need an inhibitor I'll be your nurse in return."

She sighs. But she pulls the tabs on my boots and throw them across the room.

"Socks too," I mumble, suddenly very tired.

"Do I ever get to open my present?"

"OK, you can do that first," I manage to say. But the inhibitor is really kicking in now and I'm ready to sleep.

"I'm opening it," Nyleena says. She throws the silky ribbon on my face and I open my eyes long enough to snatch it, toss it back, and watch her lift the lid off the box.

She holds up the transponder. Puzzled.

"It's perfect, right?"

"What the hell is it?"

"It's a gate pass, Nyleena. One standard four-hundred-spin-year all-access-paid gate pass with Harem Station citizen credentials."

"What?"

"That's right, baby. I got you your very own gate pass."

"Why?"

I open my eyes for real now. Trying to focus on her as I will my stomach to stop churning with disgust at that green gloop I just swallowed. "What do you mean why? So when you get your ship you can fly like a freebird, that's why."

"But..."

"But what?" I ask, forcing myself to sit up a little.

"I can't even leave. The whole thing is a joke. Crux isn't giving me a ship."

I point my finger at her. "Oh, fuck yeah, he is. He promised. If you get him what he wants he has to pay you. If he doesn't..." I shake my head. "I'll have words with that man. And by words I don't mean words."

"Even if he gives me the ship I'm not allowed to leave, Luck. I'm tied to Lyra."

"Fuck," I say. "I never even thought of that."

"Yeah, me neither. I was so caught up in this idea of total freedom I guess I forgot."

"Well, damn. Ladybug's gonna be disappointed."

"Why?"

"Because she wants to be your bot. She's all set to sign up with you."

"Really?"

"Really," I say.

"Well…" She sighs. Then smiles. Then leans over and the next thing I know she's crawling up my chest and kissing me on the lips.

I smile into that kiss.

"Ladybug was right."

"Which part was she right about?" I ask.

"This is a very swoon-worthy gift. I'm sorry I won't get to use it."

Then she drops down onto my chest and even though my stomach is protesting at the pressure of her body, I wrap my arms around her and hold her tight.

"I missed you today," I say.

"You're the one who didn't show up for secret garden sex."

"I was mad."

"I know."

"But I'm not mad anymore."

"Good."

"What did you do today?" I ask.

"I went to the Station History Museum."

"You did not." I laugh.

"Yeah, I did. And who did I bump in to but a teenage Luck who took me around and showed me all kinds of very interesting things."

I smile. Eyes closed. World kinda fading around me.

And the last thing I remember telling her is… "Good night, princess."

CHAPTER TWENTY-FOUR

MYLEENA

"Good night, Luck," I whisper as I sit up and scoot over to the other side of the couch. I look down at the little metal device in my palm.

He spent two and a half million credits to buy me an all-access gate pass. And he even got me a kick-ass sexbot partner.

And I didn't even earn that ship yet.

I let that sink in for a moment as Luck begins to snore softly, then groan as he holds his stomach as he sleeps.

What does it mean?

Lots of things, potentially.

One. Whatever scheme Crux is running with me, Luck isn't part of it.

Two. He's got a lot of disposable money in his Harem Station account.

Three. I'm a citizen. I knew this. But hearing Luck say it makes it all so permanent.

Four. This leads me back to my musing about 'home'. If I'm a card-carrying citizen of Harem Station then this place really is my new home.

How do I feel about that?

It's not any clearer than it was a few minutes ago before Luck showed up at my door.

Five. He believes in me.

I stop again and let that sink in.

He really thinks I'm gonna get that ship. Not only that, he truly expects me to go out into the world and travel through gates.

By myself.

No him. No Lyra.

Me.

I try to think if anyone has ever had such high expectations of me before.

No. Never.

Not even Lyra. I was always the crazy silver sister and she was always the one who needed to protect me. It was her job to shuttle me safely to places. Her job to put me where I needed to be so I could be used as a weapon.

She was the one who saved my life out there at Bull Station. She was always the one people trusted to get shit done.

So fine. I owe her. She deserves to feel safe for once in her life and this is what Harem Station is to her.

Safe.

But I look at the gate pass again and sigh. There is a deep sense of sadness inside me now that I've been forced to rein in my feral side and confront reality.

I am a threat.

I am both a prisoner and free.

I am free to be a prisoner.

It's so fucked up.

Just another paradoxical problem in a long line of impossible obstacles.

There are people out there who will stop at nothing to catch me, and use me, and kill not only me, but Lyra. And probably Serpint too.

Maybe all of us?

Maybe I'm here for a reason? Maybe this was the Cygnian plan all along? What if they knew Lyra would make it out? What if they knew Serpint would be there to steal Corla? What if they knew Delphi would win against Veila?

What if... the three of us—no, *four* of us—are right where we're supposed to be?

What if... we're not on a Veila hunt? What if Veila is on a Corla hunt?

Honestly, I can't picture Veila sacrificing herself to use Corla to blow up Harem Station. But that doesn't mean it can't happen.

Luck groans in his sleep again.

I look at him. Like... really look at him. See him.

He's not a bad catch. I mean, for sure he's beautiful. I will never get tired of his beauty. And he's funny too. And spontaneous. And smart. Very smart. Maybe not smart like Tray, but no one needs to be that smart.

He asked me to help him find out what Tray and Valor are up to. And part of this request is about Valor, who has moved on and left Luck behind. But part of it is about figuring out their secret.

I'm convinced that Luck is right. Those two are up to something. And it's eating away at Luck.

That kinda pisses me off. Valor should not have discarded him after their bot died saving everyone. It wasn't fair.

And if he didn't do it because of that, and instead did it because of the secrets he's keeping for Tray, then that's not any better.

They were best friends. Valor owes Luck an explanation.

I owe it to Luck to figure this puzzle out.

That's my new mission.

If I can't leave here on a ship, then fine. I'll get the information Crux wants but then I will demand a meeting with Tray and he will tell me what's happening.

If not... well, I have a trick or two up my sleeve.

Luck turns over on the couch and stretches his legs out over mine. I pull his socks off and throw them across the room, then move his legs off my lap and stand up.

"Luck?" I ask, leaning over to shake him gently.

No answer. He's out.

I open my air screen, getting a little worried about how quick he fell asleep, and look up 'sexbot juice inhibitor'.

Hmm. Side effects including lethargy, nausea, and drowsiness.

I really want to put him in bed so he's more comfortable, but I try to rouse him several more times with no success. So I grab a spare blanket from the closet and drape it over him.

Then I kiss him on the cheek and whisper, "Thank you."

Because Ladybug was right.

I'm swooning.

I wake up to a warm body climbing in to bed with me.

"Sorry," Luck whispers. "Didn't mean to wake you."

I turn over and look at him in the darkness. For a moment I think his eyes are glowing, but they're not. Mine are. I can see their reflection in his.

"Do you feel better?" I ask.

"Little bit." Then he chuckles and settles face down, hugging a pillow to his cheek. "But don't worry. Not well enough to bother you for sex. Turns out sexbot juice is a great anti-aphrodisiac."

"Well that's too bad," I hum through a smile. "I was all ready to rock your world."

"Liar," he says, his response almost completely muffled by the pillow. "But don't worry. I'll be better in the morning. And then…"

But he trails off. Already drifting away.

He's still dressed and I wish he wasn't.

Will we ever have a normal night together?

Will being with him ever feel natural and true, the way Lyra feels about Serpint and Delphi feels about Jimmy?

I can't picture it, to be honest.

I can picture this. Sex. Friendship.

But there are so many unsolvable problems running through my head right now, I can't imagine that Luck can ever overtake them.

What is leveling up?

Why are Tray and Valor obsessed with that virtual?

Why is Valor so intrigued by Veila?

Why are Jimmy and Delphi looking for a place called Earth? And why were Lyra and I supposed to go there?

What was that place in the museum other Luck showed me?

And what did he mean by everything?

Will Veila come looking for Corla?

What will Corla think about all this once she wakes up?

So many fucking questions. And every single one of them is now an obstacle that stands between me and Luck.

I can't ever be my true self if I'm surrounded by mysteries.

So I make a decision as I listen to Luck's soft breathing next to me. I accept the fact that I'm stuck on Harem Station. I accept the fact that there is no ship in my future.

I accept my fate.

And I decide that I will unravel all these mysteries anyway.

For me.

Not them.

Because maybe that's the true meaning of freedom?

Maybe knowing the truth is all the freedom you need.

CHAPTER TWENTY-FIVE

LUCK

I wake to a hand firmly gripping my morning hard-ons through my pants.

"Good morning," Nyleena purrs.

"Well," I chuckle, still half asleep. "It certainly is."

She throws the covers off me, straddles my hips, and begins rolling my shirt up my stomach.

"What are you doing?" I ask.

"Helping you out this morning. I have tons of things to do today, so probably not gonna make the afternoon tryst. Figured we'd do it this morning and then, if you're horny again later, we can meet up after dinner."

"After dinner?" I try to picture what big scheme Nyleena has planned that she will be missing for an entire day. "What do you have—"

But that's as far as I get with my question. Because she leans over and kisses my lips.

Her silky, silver hair brushes against my bare chest and sends a chill through my whole body.

Her smile is both seductive and devious as her hands wander down to the button of my pants. She kisses me again, just as the button pops open.

"You're feisty today," I say, kissing her back.

"Always and forever. Besides, I need to show my appreciation for last night."

"Oh, yeah." I chuckle. Remembering what I did. "The pass."

"No," Nyleena says, her voice a little bit growly. "Not the pass. Just you, Luck. Believing in me so fiercely. That's what I'm appreciating right now."

"Well, to be completely honest, you're an easy woman to believe in."

"Liar," she whispers. Just as she grips the waist of my pants and pulls them down. Not all the way to my knees or anything. Just enough to release both my rock-hard cocks. She says it again as she slides down my body, her perfect lips puckering as she goes. "Liar."

I'm about to start a fight over this, because she doesn't get to tell me what I think about her. But I lose track of that thought pretty much immediately when her mouth closes over the tip of one of my heads.

"Fuck," I moan. Because even though it's only been one spin since we had sex, it feels like we've been apart for an eternity right now.

She slides her hand up and down my other shaft as she opens her mouth wide to take my cock deeper and I reach down and get a good two-fisted grip on her soft, silky, silver hair.

She looks up at me, her lips sealed around my dick as she smiles. Clearly enjoying her part in this morning tryst.

I push her down on my cock, making her take me deep, and she gives in. Willingly. She lets the tip slide right up against her throat and then pulls back until my fat, swollen head pops out of her mouth and she wipes her lips.

"Take off your clothes," I say. Because we never do it naked. It's always hurried and quick and for once I'd like to just enjoy her. Feel her bare skin next to mine. I hate that I spent the night here again and still we haven't been naked together yet.

"No," she coos. "I like to keep my clothes on."

I grab her hips and throw her off me, then climb on top of her and start unbuttoning her too-large button-down shirt.

She swats my hands away. "Don't."

And she's serious. Her eyes are narrowed down into slits and her smile is gone.

"Why not?" I ask. "You're so fucking beautiful. I just want to look at you."

There is a pause. I can't explain the pause in words but something inside me understands what it is.

Fear.

"Nyleena." I half laugh out her name.

"What?" she replies too sharply.

"What's wrong?"

"Nothing's wrong," she says. Then she grabs my hair with both hands and tugs until I lean down and kiss her lips. "I want you inside me," she whispers into my mouth. "Right now."

I reach down and push one of her thighs open, hiking her knee up to her chest as I position myself between her legs. She's wearing the tiniest pair of fluffy pink shorts that leave almost nothing to the imagination.

So her long, beautiful legs are bare, and smooth, and my hand caresses the muscle of her calf for a second. But the moment I slide it up under her large nightshirt, she grabs a hold of it and pushes it away.

"Nyleena," I say again. "What the fuck?"

"What?"

"Why won't you let me touch you?"

She forces a laugh. "You're touching me in a lot of places right now, Luck. Why are you complaining?"

"Because…" I stare down into her eyes because they're lighting up. Not just a small, erotic glow as a preamble for the show to come. But something different. Agitation, or anger, or… "You're afraid of something," I say.

"Ridiculous," she coos, grabbing my cocks with one hand as she slips her shorts to the side. She pushes them both towards her entrance. Eyes still narrowed and bright, mouth tight now.

I let her. Because it's morning, and I'm hard, and it's not a great time to start a conversation.

But I have questions.

Lots of questions about lots of things I should've noticed before now, and didn't.

The minute both of my cocks are inside her she relaxes a little. Closes her eyes. Settles into the mattress and both her hands come up to my shoulders. Her fingernails—pink today, I notice—gripping the thick round curve of muscle as we begin to move together.

I prop my hands on the bed on either side of her face and lean down to kiss her mouth as I thrust forward.

"Harder," she begs, playfully nipping at my lips. "I want you to fuck me harder."

"No," I mumble. "I want it slow today."

She smiles, letting out a small breath of air. "I want your cocks deep inside me, Luck. I want you to pound me until I explode with light."

"No," I say again, still kissing her.

But if there's one thing I've learned about Nyleena over the past few months, it's that she's tenacious when she wants something. So she ignores my refusal and just fucks me harder instead. Her hips moving, and grinding. The muscles of her pussy clamping down as hard as they can on my dicks as her legs wrap around my waist and squeeze.

It's a power play, I realize.

Which isn't unusual. She's always the biggest personality in a room. Always the loudest voice.

But she was fine until I tried to take off her shirt.

What the fuck is going on?

"Fuck me," she says, continuing with the dirty talk.

And why not? This little trick of hers has worked every time so far, hasn't it? Every time I've tried to take off her shirt she's stopped me with dirty talk.

So I play it cool. I give in. I thrust forward. Giving her exactly what she asked for. I fuck her so hard she inches up the bed with each hard push. Until her head bumps into the headboard and there's nowhere else to go.

I lift her knees up. Allowing myself to penetrate her fully. Deeply.

She's moaning. Eyes closed. Light safely hidden behind those lids.

I lean down into her neck and kiss her. Nipping at the soft skin behind her ear.

And she responds in kind, but with more force, when she turns her face into my shoulder and her mouth finds the hard muscle.

I hiss air through my teeth when she bites. Not because it hurts, exactly. I can't really feel it. But because I know it *should* hurt and I'll have a bruise later.

"More," she says, scraping her fingernails down my back. "More."

But there is something so fundamentally wrong here and I'm distracted.

I want her to take off that fucking shirt.

I don't know why I feel this so acutely. I just do.

"Fuck me!" she says. Like she can tell I'm still thinking too hard. "Fuck me, Luck. Fuck me!"

"I am fucking you," I growl.

She opens her eyes and stops.

Like… everything stops. I stop, she stops. Time stops.

And that's when I know. It comes to me immediately. The reason she won't let me see her bare from the waist up.

We're staring in each other's eyes when this happens.

She knows I know. And I know she's about to get up and leave.

And I do not care that we're not done fucking. That neither of us has had our release yet. Nor do I care that she might never let me fuck her again if I do what I'm planning.

She reaches for my hands before they even grip her shirt. But by the time she clamps her fingers around my wrists like a vice, it's too late.

I rip her shirt open.

Buttons go flying.

She gasps in horror.

I gasp too. But not in horror.

I gasp in shock.

Because there is a thick, pale, white scar down the middle of her torso. A scar that explains more about Princess Nyleena than any words that ever came out of her mouth.

"What the fuck is *that?*" I ask, first staring at the horrible gash, then her brightly glowing silver eyes.

She throws me off her.

I'm talking… two hands to my chest and the power of a pissed-off princess kind of push. I go reeling backwards, my cocks slipping out of her because I was so not into the sex we were having, they hadn't started swelling up yet. And the next thing I know she's standing on the mattress above me. Legs open, straddling my body.

Rage in her face. Full-on fucking feral, savage, Nyleena's-wild-side-is-showing kind of rage in her face.

"You motherfucker!" she says between gritted teeth as she points her finger at me.

"What the hell is that?" I say, scooting backwards towards the edge of the bed. Because I'm pretty sure this girl is going to punch me in the face.

She lifts one foot up and I see it coming. But there's nothing I can do. I've run out of retreat room. And she kicks me flat-footed right in the middle of my chest so hard, I get the breath knocked out of me as I fly backwards and crash to the floor.

"Get the fuck out!" she screams. "You get the fuck out of my quarters right now!"

And for a moment—a long, silent moment where the only noise is her hard breathing, and my hard breathing—I almost do this.

I almost leave.

But then... you know what? I remember just who the fuck I am.

She might be the silver princess. She might be an explosive device made to take out planets. She might be wild, and mean, and beautiful all in the same breath.

But I am motherfucking, sun-damned *Luck* of Harem Station.

I have fought slithering ancient alien species that no one calls a people. Slimy, snake-like creatures that want to eat you whole and spend the next decade digesting you slowly.

I have forced myself through more narrow cave tunnels filled with creepy poisonous insects than I can count to get what I want.

I have clung to the outside of an abandoned space station for days trying to steal parts from an old AI that still had a working defense system inside.

I have flown through thousands of gates, and seen hundreds of examples of evil, and still, I come home every time with the things on my list.

I have been though a spin node and I command time. I am the motherfucking *time commander*.

I am one of the seven violet-eyed, true-blooded Akeelian teenagers who tamed the evil AI, ALCOR, and made that dude love me.

I took on two dozen warrior cyborgs at Lair Station and won.

I looked Princess Veila in the eye on that station while she filled my head up with so much tragic bullshit and didn't blink an eye when I pointed my plasma rifle at her center of mass and shot her.

She didn't die because she was wearing armor. But that's not the point.

The point is… I did not *blink*. Not once.

I shot that bitch and never thought twice.

So I get to my feet and I point my finger up at this one wild girl, and I say, "No."

"Get out," she rages, clutching her shirt closed to hide her secret.

Her legs are shaking and unsteady on the mattress. And for a moment I think she's about to lose her balance and fall, so I reach for her. But she jumps off the bed and lands on her feet to my left.

She narrows her eyes at me. And there's so much wild light spilling through those lids, it comes out as a beam that lands on, and spotlights, me. Her new enemy.

"What the fuck is that scar?" I ask, moving to the left and positioning myself in front of her bedroom door to cut off her escape.

"None of your damn business," she snaps.

"Did they…" Fuck. I grab my hair and try to make sense of it.

Because this is no ordinary scar. It's what you see on dead people after an autopsy.

Something that says so clearly that this body has been split open. That someone has put their hands inside her chest. Touched her heart, or taken it out and put it back in.

"Nyleena," I say.

"No," she says, pointing at the door behind me. "Get out."

"Just tell me—"

"Get OUT!"

And then... I don't know what happened. Because when I come to, the only thing I remember is light, and pain, and I'm on the floor in front of her bedroom door.

And Nyleena is gone.

CHAPTER TWENTY-SIX

NYLEENA

I am not a weapon.

I am a person.

This is my mantra. I've been saying it since I was a little girl back in the sister harem back in Cygnian System.

Because every day I lived there, for as long back as I can remember, they'd tell me the opposite.

"You are not a person, Nyleena. You are a weapon."

The first time they told me that I imagine I was too young to have an opinion on the matter. I didn't talk back until I was about nine.

I just… decided to disagree one day. Lyra and I were never close in the harem back home. She was just another sister. I had a lot of them. But I was the only silver one. I was special that way just like Lyra was special because she was our genetic father's seventh daughter.

So we were alike in that respect. Meaning we did things differently than our other sisters, who were all pink, like her, but weren't born with a programmed destiny, like us.

So one day I'm sitting in the medical facility waiting on my daily exam, and they, the nurses who were assigned to me, come in and that's the first thing they had to tell me before we started.

"You are not a person, Nyleena. You are a weapon. Do you understand?"

I guess this was their way of getting my tacit permission to do what they did next.

And every day I said, "Yup. Got it. I am not a person, I am a weapon."

Every day.

Except that day.

Luck slams into the door with such force, I panic and start reciting my mantra.

I am not a weapon, I am a person.

But I am a weapon. There is no way around that. And I just proved it because Luck is unconscious on the floor of my bedroom.

"Shit," I say. "Shit, shit, shit," I say again, and again, and again.

I walk over to him, hands shaking as my fingertips reach down and press against the side of his neck, checking for a pulse.

Thank the suns, he's alive.

I stand back up, dress quickly in a pair of plain black tactical pants and a white t-shirt, then pull on my boots and leave.

He'll wake up.

He'll wake up and he'll remember we had a fight. And then maybe he'll remember that I shot him with light... but that's it. That's all he knows.

But he saw my scar. I wish I could make him go back in time. What good is controlling time if you can't use it for your own personal nefarious purposes?

So fucking stupid.

But Luck knows something else now too. He knows I am a weapon, not a person. Because that really is the truth. And it's better that way. We might be genetically-engineered soulmates but that doesn't mean we have to fall in love.

We will not fall in love.

I admit, I got a little distracted by him recently. But that ends now.

I'm on a mission today. A mission to find answers and solve problems. I have a whole list of them still.

I tick them off in my head as a way to keep focused.

One. Crux wants to know what it means to level up. Tray has this answer and so does Real ALCOR. But...

Two. Tray is an asshole and refuses to see me. And...

Three. Asshole ALCOR—also, obviously, an asshole—is inside the Pleasure Prison and can't be contacted. And...

Four. Valor could get me into the Pleasure Prison to ask Asshole ALCOR and get what I need, but he wants more info on Veila. So...

Five. Delphi and Jimmy know more about Veila and Valor than they've told me, but they want info on some place called Earth. Which leads me to...

Six. Luck knows something about Earth and Veila, but refuses to tell me unless I find out what craptastic evil Tray and Valor are doing inside the Pleasure Prison. Which leads me back to…

Seven. Flicka. Well, specifically, Baby ALCOR. Because he might have some hidden data on this Earth place hidden deep in his core programs. However…

Eight. Baby ALCOR is avoiding me. So…

Nine. Back to Flicka. Dragonbee bots are the *best*. They're the equivalent of a silver Cygnian princess in bot form. Evil and dangerous. They mix up the little poisons in their bellies and fart out little puffs of death.

I really need to get me a dragonbee bot. Delphi is so damn lucky.

I'm kinda of embarrassed that I've now spent four whole days on this little quest and have gotten absolutely nowhere.

That ends now. I will solve these mysteries and it all starts with Baby ALCOR.

Well, with Flicka, actually.

I have decided that Delphi doesn't deserve such a kick-ass sidekick. If I could steal her away for real, I would. But… that's never gonna happen. So I'm just gonna borrow her today and we're going to combine our super-silver, poison-farting powers and *get shit done*.

When I get out into the main concourse I open up my air screen, find Flicka's contact, and send her a message.

The message says:

Hey, did you know there's another dragonbee bot here on the station? I met him last night and told him all about you. Wanna meet up?

It's a lie. But who cares? Lying is just another weapon in my silver princess arsenal.

Flicka messages back a text that barely makes sense. She's not the best speller. But I get the gist.

She's having breakfast now but she can meet in ten, and where would I like that to be?

So I text back my current location near a Centurian clothing store and then log out of my air screen, delete my account, and essentially disappear.

Take that, Luck. Put a tracker on me? Fuck you.

Plus, I don't want Baby ALCOR to know we're coming.

Flicka shows up a little bit late, and I immediately regret deleting my air screen account before she gets here because I have no translator program and I don't speak dragonbee bot.

But she understands me, so I just go off on my spiel and make her a deal. I will hook her up with the new beebot if she helps me hack into Baby ALCOR's data core.

There's a lot of buzzing, and she farts out a puff of something that makes me start coughing, but a security bot shows up right quick and threatens her with lockup if she does it again, so thirty minutes later she's still fuming at me, but each time she buzzes, I just put up a hand and say, "I just need to get some info and he's avoiding me, OK? Please, just hack me in. I promise to put in a good word with my new beebot friend."

A few more minutes of fussing and I'm assuming she's in on the plan, because she flits around doing loop-the-loops in front of my face, then takes off towards a fast-track escalator that leads down to the bottom levels.

219

Baby's office is up here near the top, but apparently the databanks are down below.

So I just follow, because I have no clue.

Now listen. No one thinks that breaking into Baby's core databanks is going to be easy and not many people are as ballsy as I am, so most don't even bother trying. He is locked up tight. I'm talking full-on cyborg security detail standing guard outside the unmarked main entrance to this secret hiding place where he keeps his servers.

And there's little Baby ALCOR eyeballs everywhere, just in case someone, like me and my new BFF here, get any crazy ideas about infiltrating his artificial memory.

But dragonbee bots are a very special species of evil. Their puffs can do anything from kill any species alive to disable whole stations, depending on what their little internal kitchen pantry has inside it when the need arises.

Kinda makes you wonder why more people don't own them or at least conscript them as part of their teams or armies.

Two reasons, really. One. They don't take direction well. And two. They're not very loyal. How Delphi got this one to behave and stick with her is beyond me.

There's a third reason too. They have limited powers unless you have a whole swarm of them.

Flicka can't take down Harem Station by herself no matter what deadly recipe she cooks up. She'd need thousands of partner beebots to do that.

But the point is, even one dragonbee bot is super-helpful on pretty much any stealth mission imaginable.

And two of them is double the power she has now. So this promise of mine to hook her up is kind of a big deal.

She pretty much handles shit once we get to the bottom level. She's already flying ahead once I get off the escalator. And I can see the cyborg security force off in the distance, diligently standing guard in front of the massive steel door.

As I follow her I notice that all the little Baby ALCOR eyeballs are blinking red, meaning they are offline. And by the time I reach the steel door, the cyborgs have all fallen to the floor like they're dead.

I don't think they're dead. I really hope they're not dead. Because killing the Baby's cyborgs will probably get both of us locked up in a cryopod out on some security beacon in space like Corla.

There's not much time to think about it though, because Flicka is clinging to the security panel on the door and a moment later, it opens.

Probably should not be this easy to break into the Baby's memory servers and something tells me from this day forward Flicka will be on the Baby's shit list.

But that's a problem for another time.

Because we go inside, then Flicka clings to the security panel on this side of the door, and they close up after us. Essentially sealing us in.

Wow. I have to hand it to this little mechanical insect. When she goes in on a job, she goes all in. No bet-hedging or second thoughts for her.

Flicka flies off down a long, dark hallway. No lights come on until I walk forward, then they are tripped by motion sensors and light up as I reach them, then go dark again when I pass. Which is not super-stealthy at all. But fuck it. We're inside.

We end up at a dark screen connected to a console, but it doesn't stay dark for long. Flicka buzzes busily at the access port and in just a few seconds the screen lights up with code.

"Shit," I say. "I don't speak code, Flicka. And I can't even fake it because I deleted my air screen account."

She buzzes, then settles down on the screen built into the tabletop of the console and begins hopping around, the tiny pads of her feet triggering commands.

"Holy shit!" I laugh. "Where do I get one of you? Delphi is so lucky!"

She ignores me and continues to type in commands.

"OK, look for something about…" And I'm just about to say Earth. Because that was the whole reason we came down here. But at the last moment, I change my mind. "Look for something about the Pleasure Prison, Flicka. Plans. Blueprints. Anything that will tell me if there's some secret hidden in there."

She hesitates for a moment.

"What?" I ask. "Luck wants to know what Tray and Valor are up to and believe me, after what just happened between us up in my quarters, I owe him. I have to find this out."

Still, she hesitates. Then she gets back to work, but I notice almost immediately that she is not looking for Pleasure Prison plans. She's looking for Earth.

And there's a hit.

Which is totally interesting and the reason I came in the first place, but not what I asked her to do.

222

"Flicka," I whisper. "Look for the Pleasure Prison stuff first. That's more important."

But again, she isn't listening. Or she's deliberately ignoring my request. Which… see? Totally the reason people don't keep dragonbee bots. They're just not team players.

"Flicka," I say again, a little bit bitchy this time. "I'm not going to ask again. I want to know about—"

"Can I help you with something, Nyleena?" a female voice purrs.

I whirl around, stunned that someone was able to sneak up on me so quietly.

But that mystery dies almost immediately because this isn't just any old someone.

It's the Mighty Minions AI, Succubus.

All dressed up in demon red and black.

Looking pret-*ty* fucking pissed off that I'm down here fucking with her borrowed systems.

CHAPTER TWENTY-SEVEN

LUCK

So... feelings.

Right now I'm conflicted on how I feel.

Am I angry that Nyleena knocked me out with a burst of light so powerful I slammed against the door and I might have cracked a fucking rib or two?

Yes. Yes, I am. You might even call me furious. Or irate. Or possibly even enraged.

But then, when I think back on how I happened to be here, crumpled up on the floor like a pile of old clothes in the doorway of Nyleena's bedroom, I get sad.

That scar. What the fuck did they do to her?

And then I feel guilty for not ever wondering before now. Like... what is my problem? Just because Delphi and Lyra seemed to escape the Cygnians with no permanent damage doesn't excuse my ignorance when it comes to Nyleena.

She is as different from them as night is from day.

You only have to look at her to see that. Forget about what's inside her. Even if you didn't know she was a weapon, one glance and you get it.

225

She's silver.

They're pink.

They have totally different jobs so it stands to reason that they had totally different... training? Is that the right word? I'm not sure.

But that scar, though.

Son of a god, I've never seen that on a living person.

Once, when I was on a station near the binary stars Iota Apodus I was kind of involved in a murder. Not the actual murder-*er*. But I was there. And the Iota Apodians have this weird custom where they make all the murder suspects go view the dead body they may or may not be responsible for killing, and this particular dead body was in the middle of the autoautopsy. All sealed up inside a pod as robot arms split it open and scanned it, then closed it back up.

It's a really quick process. Like couple minutes tops. So I witnessed the whole thing from start to finish and when it was done that guy's chest had a scar like the one I just saw on Nyleena.

Except, of course, he was dead and she isn't.

So do I feel angry? Or sad? Or guilty?

I don't know.

My air screen pops open with an alarm and a red screen to match, letting me know there's an emergency.

Succubus appears.

"Uh... hello there," I say. "What's up?"

"Do you know where your princess is?"

"No..." I'm about to elaborate further, explain that she knocked me out with a beam of hot light, but then decide it's probably better not to.

"Well, right now she's in lockup."

"Fuck. What'd she do?"

"She broke into the Baby ALCOR data core."

"What? What was she looking for?"

"Well, the dragonbee bot she lured into this little scheme tells me she was supposed to be looking for a planet called Earth." Succubus pauses here.

For what? I have no clue. But I feel like I'm supposed to say something. So I say, "OK."

"Did you know about that?"

"I mean… everyone seems to be talking about it, but no. I didn't know she was going to break into the data core."

"Is that all you have to say about the subject?"

"The subject?" I ask. "Are you asking me about Earth? Or about Nyleena's little impromptu crime spree? Because I get the feeling you're asking about Earth."

She moves on without directly answering my question. "Did you instruct her to look for information about the Pleasure Prison?"

"What?"

"Luck," Succubus says with practiced patience. She isn't angry. At least she's not displaying anger. But that could just be how she was trained on Mighty Minions. It's a family resort, after all. Surely she has been programmed with family-friendly responses. "I do not like to repeat myself," she continues. "Did you, or did you not, instruct Nyleena to go poking around looking for secrets inside the Pleasure Prison?"

"Are there secrets in there?"

"Are you going to answer my question?"

And now… yeah. I have settled on an emotion and it's anger. So I say, "I'm sorry, who the fuck are you

227

again? Because I'm *Luck*. And I don't answer to you any more than I answer to Baby ALCOR. And actually, you aren't even a station partner. So I don't have to answer shit when you ask. You, on the other hand, do have to answer me. So let me ask my question again, because I don't mind repeating myself if that's what it takes to get what I'm after. What the *fuck*. Is *happening*. Inside the Pleasure Prison?"

Another pause.

And something you need to understand about an AI who pauses like this. They can run simulations in their artificial minds by the trillions in a pause of five whole seconds.

Her pause isn't that long, but it's long enough to know she's running a lot of them before she answers me.

"You'll have to ask Tray. He's in charge."

"Right," I huff.

"In the meantime, security would greatly appreciate that you pick up your princess from lockup ASAP. They're tired of her."

And then the screen blinks out.

Mother of suns. I massage my temple because my head suddenly hurts like hell. I might've hit it on the door when Nyleena blasted me.

I get to my feet, realize my pants are down at my knees because we were in the middle of having sex when everything suddenly went sideways, and pull them up, tucking my cocks away—still hard, which is just fucking wonderful—and zip up.

What am I going to do with this girl?

I'm stuck with her for the duration. Like… until one of us dies we are connected.

Then I try to picture life without her. Not just separated, but her dead. And that triggers the sadness again.

God, I'm like a teenage girl with all the emotions flowing through me right now.

I jerk off in her bathroom real quick—because I refuse to bail Nyleena out of jail with two hard-ons—and then head down to lockup to pick up my naughty princess.

She's sitting on a bench looking like she's about to murder everyone in the cell with a hot beam of light when I show up.

Usually they don't make you go back to the lockup area to pick up your criminal friend, but apparently all the old rules have been rewritten when it comes to Nyleena.

Flicka is there too. Buzzing away busily on Nyleena's shoulder when I walk up to the laser beams that denote the perimeter of the cell.

All the other occupants—mostly drunk men of various races, and nannybots—are pushed up against the other side of the cell where there's an actual wall, and not a fire-hot fence of plasma, keeping their distance from my princess and her new friend.

"Well, well, well," I say. "Look who fell in the well."

Nyleena shoots me an angry frown. "What the hell does that even mean?"

"It means you got something you deserved."

"Did I?"

I sigh, then look over my shoulder to the security guy shadowing me. "You want me to take the dragonbee bot off your hands too?"

"I'd really appreciate that, Luck," the dude says in a very deep voice. He's a huge Dracoian warrior with dull, gunmetal-gray organic armor covering his whole body. His eyes are white with no color at all and he's got dozens of white tentacles around his mouth that dance when he speaks.

I've always found that creepy as fuck and every time a Dracoian speaks to me the only thing I see is the mouth, but being creeped out by the way other races look is frowned upon here on Harem, so I try to act natural around the Dracoians I interact with. So I look this guy in the eyes.

Which are blank, and white, and also creepy as fuck.

I never said I was a very evolved guy.

"Can we go now?" Nyleena says, getting to her feet.

Flicka flies off her shoulder and slips right through lines of hot plasma before the guard turns them off to let Nyleena out.

"Show-off," Nyleena grumbles, slipping past me, just in time before the plasma fence is turned back on.

Flicka doesn't seem to care. In fact, she just buzzes right ahead of us like she's got places to go and people to see.

But another guard at the door is shaking her head as Flicka arrives. She points to me and says, "You're with him. So I don't care what you got stuffed up that ass of yours, you're gonna wait."

It's a short wait, since Nyleena and I arrive a few seconds later. But the guard seems pleased that Flicka is buzzing her complaints for that small interval of time.

I stop at the guard. "I'm not responsible for this thing, right? I mean… I already got this one to deal with."

"What the hell?" Nyleena growls.

But I shoot her a look that says, *Shut your mouth, Princess.* And she takes me seriously.

"Sorry," the guard says. "But you know the rules, Luck. The dragonbee bot is only here on special directive from the Baby. Someone has to take her to Jimmy."

"Fine," I mumble, then point to Flicka and say, "You better stay close. I'm not in the mood for any more bullshit." And I shoot Nyleena a similar warning in the form of a glare.

She has the good sense to not say anything.

"One more thing," the door guard says. "The princess here deleted her air screen account. So she can't leave until it's reactivated. It's a condition of bail. Also, she needs to appear in court in ten spins."

"Fucking hell, Nyleena!" I say.

"What?"

"I'm not paying for your lawyer. Just so you know. So I hope you have a lot of credits saved because I'm getting the impression the Succubus doesn't like you very much right now. And if you think the Baby will go easy on you because you're mine, don't count on it."

"I'm not yours," she hisses.

But the guard slips a bail bracelet on her that says *Luck*, and totally contradicts her little declaration.

I smile at that. And I'm totally ready to get the hell out of here, but it takes another twenty minutes to reactivate her air screen account and fit a teeny-tiny leg bracelet on Flicka which, thankfully, says *Jimmy* instead of *Luck*. Because I have no desire to be responsible for her too.

Once we're out I ping Jimmy and tell him to pick up his bot at the Station History Museum.

Because that's where I'm taking Nyleena now.

We're going to sort this shit out.

We have to. We're soulmates.

And I'm going to take the initiative and spill a secret or two.

Then maybe… just maybe she will learn to trust me.

We meet Jimmy in front of the museum. He is pissed and Delphi isn't with him.

"I didn't tell her," Jimmy explains. "She knows that no one is happy about Flicka living here and even though I'm pretty sure I can smooth this whole thing over with the Baby and the Succubus, I don't need Delphi worrying about it right now."

I catch Nyleena smirking. Because if Jimmy gets Flicka off, he'll get her off too.

Whatever.

I grab Nyleena's hand and lead her into the museum.

"What are we doing here?" she asks with attitude she has no good reason to have.

"I'm going to show you something."

"What?"

"Just wait and see, for fuck's sake."

"Aren't you going to yell at me for knocking you out earlier?"

"No."

"Why not?"

I sigh. "Because... I should've respected your privacy. I just didn't know what you were hiding underneath your shirt."

"I don't want to talk about it."

"Good. Because we're not going to talk about you at all. We're going to talk about me."

"I can't wait."

I just smile. Because you know what? I'm a goddamned interesting dude. And what I'm about to show her might just change her mind about her plans for the future.

We don't stop at the first exhibit that asks who you want to be your guide. Whenever I come in here Little Luck automatically appears and starts telling me about his life.

Which would be dumb, because his life is my life, except for the fact that Little Luck is actually an AI with his own life. So he's always got a lot to say because he's me. And I'm cool like that.

All the Littles are AI copies of us. There's a Little Jimmy living in here and a Little Crux, though they weren't really that little when we arrived. And a Little Tray, who I sometimes visit in place of Real Tray because Real Tray creeps me out almost as much as that warrior guard back in the lockup. And a Little Valor, who I actually don't care for because he's turned into kind of a dick over the past decade.

But there's also a Little Draden and Serpint in here.

Almost everyone who comes into the museum chooses to be shown around by Little Draden and Little Serpint. They were just too fun as kids.

So after Draden died, in that in-between time after ALCOR died and before I left on *Lady Luck* to go back to work without Valor, I came in here a lot to talk to Little Draden.

Little Serpint was always there too, because they were programmed to be a team forever in the museum. I think that's why Real Serpint never came in here to visit Little Draden, even though he probably wanted to.

Too painful to see himself with his best friend as they were as kids.

So Little Luck says, "Hey, asshole," as soon as he pops up in front of us. "Where the hell have you been for the last five hundred and seventy spins?"

"Out," I say. "Doing man stuff you can only dream about."

We bump fists and laugh. I like Little Luck. He's pretty cool. But as soon as that's done I say, "Hey, fuck off for a while, will ya? I've got things to show my princess here."

He waggles his eyebrows at me, then smiles at Nyleena and says, "Have fun, princess. And hey, when you get a chance? Can you ask Tray to make me a Little Nyleena? I could use the company."

I roll my eyes but before I can tell him to beat it, he disappears.

"So what is this about?" Nyleena asks, turning to look at me.

"I'm gonna show you something. And I'm even going to explain it a little. Not everything, because I've been sworn to secrecy and I'm starting to think the Succubus AI has an ulterior motive for coming to Harem Station. But enough for you to get an idea of what I do for Harem and why it's not really about scavenging for AI parts in junkyard stations."

She blinks at me. "Why, though?"

"So you will trust me." She starts to say something but I put up a hand to silence her. "I'm not asking you to spill your secrets today, Nyleena. But one day. If I share with you, then one day... you might share with me."

She shrugs. Like... *Whatever. You do you.*

"OK," I say. "Come with me."

I lead her into the first hallway. If you come in here with any of the Littles this room appears as the station the way we found it that first day we arrived. And depending on who your guide is, it shows a different part of that day. If you're with Crux, it shows the upper level where we met ALCOR. If you're with Jimmy, it highlights Xyla. Stuff like that.

But since we're not with a Little, the room stays blank when we pass through it. So does the next room, and the next one, and all the others we walk through.

"I don't get it," Nyleena says. "Where's all the exhibits? When I was in here before Little Luck took me into a whole bunch of rooms."

"Just... be patient. It's a secret room that only ALCOR—Real ALCOR—and I knew about."

"Hmm," she says.

"Though from what you've told me, I suspect Little Luck knows something about it too. But not the real story. He doesn't know about this."

Finally we get to a locked steel door with an old-fashioned combination lock on it. Real ALCOR once told me that this is an old-time vault. Totally mechanical. Analog, not digital. Meaning it can't be hacked. You either know the combination of the safe or you don't.

And if you do, you just dial up those numbers in the right order and go inside and if you don't... well, I guess if you have a lot of explosives you can get in. But even then, the initiation sequence inside can't be activated digitally, either. So it does you no good to get inside unless you know that.

And let me tell you... it's a really long combination.

We get inside the vault quickly because that's just eight numbers in the correct order. But once we're inside and I've closed the door behind us, it takes me a while to start up the initiation sequence.

This whole time Nyleena is patient, and calm, and still, and silent. Just watching me. Fascinated, I think. Because this is really fascinating stuff.

Dangerous as fuck, but no less interesting just because it could kill us and everyone else on this station if someone besides me was spinning this thing up.

Finally a point of light appears in the center of the room.

It's literally a point of light.

One photon.

You can't see it with eyeballs, so Nyleena is oblivious to its presence until I tell her, "Look at the center of the room," as I increase it to two photons.

I can see it because I have this special vision implant in my optical nerve that gives me this one special superpower. It's not vision, actually. It's called luminography.

"Hmm," Nyleena says.

"What?" I ask, still fucking with the controls on the console. Adding another photon to the collective I'm building.

"There's this weird light in the center of the room. Are you doing that?"

I turn around and stare at her.

"What?" she asks. Shielding her eyes from the near blackness, but not quite total blackness, in the center of the room.

"You can see that?"

She narrows her eyes at me. "What do you mean? It's so bright it blinds me when I look at it."

I glance at the center of the room, see the three photons of light that are very clearly *not* blinding, then turn back to her. "What?"

"My God, can you just turn it off for a second? I can't fucking think straight with that spotlight blaring in my face."

"It's three photons, Nyleena."

"It's a sun-fucked sun is what it is! Turn it *off*!"

I whirl around, dial the photons down to one, then turn back to her.

"That's a little better," she says. "At least I can look at it now."

"What are you talking about?" I say, thoroughly confused.

"The baby sun in the center of the fucking room," she spits. "For fuck's sake. I don't know what you're up to, but that hurts my eyes."

I turn back to the console. There's a long shelf with cubby holes and inside the cubby holes are different sets of goggles. One set is used to look at the photons once you build up the node to a hundred total points of light. Then another set for the second hundred. Then another, and another and finally, the last set of goggles so you can look directly at the spin node.

I take out a pair of those and hand them to her. "Put these on. That should help."

She takes them. Looks at them dubiously, then slides the elastic band over her head and adjusts the eye pieces.

I turn back to the console and say, "OK, this is two photons. What do you see?"

"A white hole," she says.

"What?" I turn back around to look at the room. "It's two photons, Nyleena."

"I don't care how many photons it is. You asked me what I see and I see a white hole. Which is stupid because white holes are just theoretical opposites of black holes."

"Huh?" I say.

She turns back to me, slips her goggles down, eyes squinting because it's pretty clear that the light still bothers her, even though she's not looking at it. "You know what a black hole is? Swallows light?"

"Sure," I say.

"Well, a white hole is the theoretical other side. Where all the light goes. But it's not real."

I point to the center of the room. "Then what's that?"

She slips her goggles back on, turns to look at the center of the room, which to my eyes is still pretty fucking dark. Then turns back to me, slides her goggles down again, squints, and says, "It appears to be a white hole."

"OK," I say, reaching for another pair of node goggles and slipping them over my head. "Then what's this?"

I turn that fucker all the way up. One thousand photons.

"Holy mother of suns!" Nyleena says.

When I turn back I see a spin node. Gates, upon gates, upon gates, upon gates that go on for infinity.

So I say, "Do you see a spin node?"

And she whispers, "No, Luck. I see…"

"What?" I ask, searching the center of the room for whatever it is I'm missing and she's not. "What do you see?"

"I see… wow. It's so pretty."

"What do you see?"

"I see a galaxy. A spinning spiral galaxy."

And then she reaches for me. And she takes my hand.

And the moment we make contact I see it too.

CHAPTER TWENTY-EIGHT

MYLEENA

"I've been there," Luck says.

I'm reluctant to turn away from the amazing silver spiral in front of me, but I do. Because I want to look at him.

"Luck," I say.

"What?" And there's a pause. Like he wants to look at me, but not look away either.

"Luck," I say again.

He turns to face me. "What?"

"You're..."

"I'm what?"

"You're glowing."

A laugh bursts out. Almost too loud for this reverent moment. "What?"

"You're glowing, Luck." I turn my back to the center of the room, slip my goggles down real fast, then slip them back on. "But just in this galactic spin-node light."

He looks down at himself. "I don't see it. What's it look like?"

"Purple." I laugh. "You're purple."

"Like an ugly, gaudy purple? Or a pretty purple?"

I smile at him. Everything that happened this morning just melts away.

"Like… Am I Xyla lavender? Or Akeelian eyeball violet?"

"Does it matter?" I chuckle.

"Yeah. I wanna be a cool purple."

"Eyeball violet," I say. "And it's a very cool purple."

We both turn back to the galaxy and he says, "I've been through this thing and it wasn't this. It was just a spin node. What is this?"

"I have no idea. I've never seen anything like this. When did you go through it? And where did you go? Where is this place?"

"I was young. Maybe sixteen? Long before we ever left."

"So this was here when you arrived?"

"Yeah. Must've been. ALCOR came to me one day and said this was one of my jobs. But no one could know about it, not even Valor. And then he showed me how to spin the node up and he told me to walk through."

"Walk? Through a spin node?"

"Yeah. And I did it. I kinda knew it was crazy. I mean I was there when Crux shot Corla through the spin node when we all escaped from Wayward Station. But he and Jimmy took care of all the details. I didn't really understand it. So I wasn't afraid. It was ALCOR, you know." He turns away from the spin-node galaxy to look at me through his goggles. "I trusted him."

"And what happened? Where did you go?"

"I went to a planet."

"Which planet?"

"We called it Sol 7. But..." He pauses, still looking at me. "But I think Sol 7 is Earth."

We both look back at the center of the room, quiet for a few moments.

"Do you want to walk through?" he asks.

"It's not a planet," I say. "It's a galaxy. I don't think we should."

"Yeah," he says, once again facing the anomaly in the room. "Maybe it's different now. Or maybe it always looked like this, I just couldn't see it."

"Did you ever go through again?" I ask.

"Once. The day we had the memorial for Draden."

"But that was just last year."

"I know."

"And was it fine?"

He shrugs. "I guess."

"What did you do there?"

"I didn't do anything. I just... walked through and came back."

"What? Why?"

"I think it has something to do with time. I think... there's no time in there. Or... it, like, goes backwards or something."

"It's like a reset?" I ask.

He stops laughing. "Yeah."

And then at the same time we both say, "Draden."

"Shit," he says. "So when Draden was thirteen he had this accident and everyone thought he was fine. But Serpint came to me when I got back from saving Jimmy at the Lair, and he told me that Crux told him that Draden died that day. That ALCOR let him fall and then... *fixed* him."

"Leveled him up," I say.

"Yes," Luck says.

"And the last time was when? When did that memorial ceremony happen?"

"A few days after he died, I guess it was. Serpint came straight home, and then we all came straight home. And then as soon as I got to the station ALCOR took me aside and told me to meet him in here. And he made me walk through and come back."

"Holy fuck," I say. "It's a time machine."

"No," Luck says. "No. I don't think that's what this is. I think it's some kind of stop gate. Yeah. A stop gate. Because when I came back that last time I walked out into the concourse and I felt like I was from the future, but in the past. I can't explain it. I think it stops things and then rewinds them."

I'm silent as he's saying this. Because…

"Hey, isn't that kinda what you told me yesterday? That time rolls backwards when you… you know. Come."

I nod. "Yup," I say. "That's what I do. Part of it, anyway."

"How many times have the Cygnians… you know, actually *used* you?"

"Me personally?"

"Yeah."

"Never." Then I reconsider. "At least, I don't think so." And then I'm sorry I said that because there's a secret lurking just below the surface and we continue down this path of questioning it will try to come out. "But they have used other princesses. I know they ran some practice runs before they sent me out with Lyra."

"Practice runs," Luck says. "With people who explode."

244

"It's all pretty fucked up." I sigh.

"But… OK. Hold on. Let me regroup my thoughts. Because this wasn't even why I brought you here."

"Why did you bring me here?"

"Because I wanted to convince you my job isn't boring. I do cool shit, Nyleena. Looking through ancient civilizations. I was just gonna impress you with the spin node first and then show you all the cool shit I've found over the years. Show you some vid of me kicking alien ass on dark stations. But I've been thinking about that too. And you know what?"

I smile up at him. Because he's right. He's not boring. He's pretty fucking amazing, actually. "What?"

"If you want a ship, I'll go with you. We can take your ship. I'll be your partner. And we'll take Ladybug and Cha-Cha."

"What about *Lady Luck*?" I say. "Won't she feel left out?"

"Valor can take care of her for a while. She's just as much his as she is mine. I'm with you now. So if you need your own ship…" He shrugs. "Fuck it. I'll go where you go."

He doesn't say a single thing about Lyra. Not one word about me being a prisoner here on Harem Station.

We stand there in silence for a few moments. I don't know what Luck is thinking but I know what I'm thinking.

This little puzzle hunt I'm on to get Crux that information to get me that ship… fuck that.

I'm gonna hunt down all these answers people have been asking for, but not so I can get a ship.

I'm gonna figure out what the hell ALCOR was up to. And what Tray and Valor are doing in that Pleasure Prison.

Because I think all this stuff is related.

Me.

Corla.

The virtual.

Time.

This spin-node galaxy.

And now… the Succubus.

She was nasty when she caught me. Simply nasty. Growling, and pacing, and circling me with her swishing dangerous tail. She gave me the creeps. And then she had us arrested by a whole crew of borgs who were not gentle. One of them even smacked Flicka and she bounced off a wall.

I was pissed.

But helpless, because they already had me cuffed.

And that Succubus bitch just smirked at me. She's evil, I decide.

And Luck felt it too.

She's here for something and it's got nothing to do with coaxing Asshole ALCOR into taking on more responsibility and helping out the Baby.

I am a lot of things.

I am mean. I am wild. I am savage.

I am silver, I am dangerous, I am Luck's.

But above all else… I am a problem-solver.

I admit defeat in my other problem.

I'm in love with this crazy violet man. There's no hope of breaking this soulmate bond and I'm probably stuck here on this station forever.

But all the other questions... all the other assignments these people have asked me to figure out like this is some kind of crazy scavenger-hunt game...

Well, they're gonna regret that.

Because now I just want answers and I will tear this whole station apart to get them.

And I know just where to start.

With Lyra.

CHAPTER TWENTY-NINE

LUCK

Nyleena stands still and quiet just a little too long and it begins to make me nervous. A quiet Nyleena is a scheming Nyleena.

"What are you thinking about?" I ask.

She waits just long enough before she answers to let me know whatever she's going to say isn't really what she's thinking about.

"Do you think it's programmed to go somewhere specific?" she asks. "Or did ALCOR program it each time and now it just goes there? To some random spot in that beautiful galaxy?"

"I'm not sure. And I know it's not safe to try, but I have this sudden overwhelming urge to walk into that thing."

"Don't do it," she says, squeezing my hand. "Please. Not until we know what it is."

"How will we ever know?"

"We could ask Asshole ALCOR," she says.

"Like he'd tell us, even if he knew. And that's risky too. Because he's been inside the Pleasure Prison for decades. It's possible he doesn't even know about this. Fuck. I wish Real ALCOR was still alive."

"He is. In so many places."

"It's not the same. I need *that* instance of ALCOR. Not the security instances. Not the Asshole. Not the Baby. *Him.* And he's fucking gone."

"Maybe Tray knows something?" she offers.

"Maybe," I say. "But he can't be trusted either. Whatever he and Valor are doing inside the Pleasure Prison, they're guarding that secret closely. I don't know what to make of that."

"But you're guarding this secret closely too."

I look at Nyleena. Because she's suddenly turned into the voice of reason. "Yeah."

"So maybe their secret is like this secret? And hey," she says, perking up a little. "What if... *what if* ALCOR gave each of you secrets to keep separately until such a time that all the secrets are revealed to make one gorgeous scheming plan?"

"Hmm," I hum. "If that's true, then why did Tray tell Valor?"

"I dunno." She shrugs. Then she's quiet again. Clearly planning something. Finally she says, "If Crux had a secret he was supposed to keep, what would it be?"

I think about this for a few moments. "Probably everything to do with Corla."

"OK. And if Serpint had a secret? What would that look like?"

This one isn't so easy. "I dunno, Nyleena. He's just a princess hunter. He's not a very complicated guy, ya know?"

"Maybe not. But he's soulmated to a pretty kick-ass pink princess. There has to be a reason they made them mates. Don't you think?"

"If there is, I can't imagine what it was."

"They have to complement each other."

"Why do they have to?"

"Because that's just how it works."

"Is it?" I chuckle. "Then how do we complement each other?"

She holds up my hand, looks me in the eyes. And then drops it.

The galaxy disappears and the spin node returns.

"What do you think?" she asks.

"Point made," I say. Then grab her hand again because I feel like the spin node is calling me forward and I don't want to accidentally walk in there.

At least... not without her.

"So there has to be something Serpint and Lyra do as a team. What about Jimmy? How are he and Delphi connected?"

"They're not, remember? He's not her one. That kid who came back with us is."

"Oh, yeah," she says. "I totally forgot about that." She's silent for a few moments, brain wheels spinning. "Well, that's not good."

"Why not? They love each other. Should be OK."

"No. It's not OK. Because if Delphi is connected to that kid, whatever his name is—"

"Leonis," I say.

"Yeah, him. If she's really connected to him then they have a purpose. And that means Jimmy's connected to... gross."

251

"I know," I say. "He's connected to Veila. What could their purpose be?"

"Take over the universe?"

I laugh, then say, "That's not even funny."

"No, it's really not. But there has to be a connection."

"You don't really know that, Nyleena. Just because we have this," I say, raising our hands, "doesn't mean anything."

"But it could."

"It could also just be your over-active scheme gene."

She huffs. But it's a good-natured one. I can tell the difference now.

"Who could Tray be connected to?" she asks.

"I can't even begin to imagine," I say. Then I turn to her. "Do you know where any other princesses are? Or know their names and shit?"

"Sure. Lots of them. Back home. But none out here."

"What do you think about Delphi?" I ask.

She shrugs. Makes a face. "I don't love her the way I love Lyra, but she'll do."

"Hmm," I say. "I'm worried about that. The bond she doesn't have with Jimmy, I mean. When you get your ship we need to hunt that Veila down and bring her back here. Alive."

"When I get my ship." She laughs. "Sure. We'll do that."

"I'm detecting sarcasm, princess. What's up?"

"I'm not getting a ship."

"You are getting a ship," I say. "Crux made a deal. If you give him that info he will give you that ship. And now that you have a gate pass, and me, and Ladybug, we're all set as far as I see it."

She looks up at me, eyes glowing through her goggles in this weird, muted way that makes them look slightly blue. "Why don't you just tell me what I need to know?"

"About Earth?"

"About the leveling up stuff."

"I don't know anything about that. That's all Tray."

"Well, you could tell him to meet with me."

"We're really not that close, Nyleena. He and Valor are friends now."

"And Valor will get me a meeting, but only if I get him more information about Veila. Which you know. And refuse to share with me."

I sigh. Because I could help her get that info, which would satisfy Valor and get her a meeting with Tray, which would get her a meeting with Asshole ALCOR.

But I'm not sure I want to tell anyone the things Veila said to me in that Lair Station hallway just before I shot her with a plasma rifle. It will definitely upset the equilibrium we've settled into since Real ALCOR died.

"I get it," Nyleena says, dropping my hand. The beautiful, spiral galaxy disappears and the spin node returns.

I don't try to take her hand back. Just turn away from that siren song calling me into the node and walk over to the console to dial the photons down to zero.

The room goes dark again and I slip off my goggles. Nyleena is already handing hers back to me, so I put them away, still silent about her request.

"That's fine," she says when I turn back to her. "I can get what I need without you."

"It's just… I'm not sure anyone needs to hear what Veila told me. It's probably lies. And that's not helpful."

"So you're never going to tell me? Even if I find out why Tray and Valor are so tight, like you promised?"

I don't have an answer for her. So I just… shrug.

"OK," she says, completely reasonable and calm. "That's fine. But I have my work cut out for me so I'll see ya later. Thanks for the show."

She walks over to the massive steel door and waits.

I don't want her to leave. I don't want to leave either. I have a sudden urge to stay here in this room forever.

But only with her next to me.

Me alone next to the potential spin node seems like a very bad idea right now.

So I open the door, lock it up behind me, and lead her out of the museum.

We don't say another word.

Not even, *See you in the secret garden for a tryst.*

Not even, *Goodbye.*

We just go our separate ways.

I end up in Crux's office, sitting in a chair in front of his desk as he has a conversation with one of the engineers down in the docking bay about fuel pellets and exit protocols.

I don't mind waiting. And if he's bothered by me sitting here listening in on his call he doesn't show it.

His walls have lots of pictures, and plaques, and certificates on them. I don't think I've ever really noticed that before. There's a plaque from the Draco Assassins' Association, who used to have their headquarters here. Maybe they still do. I actually don't know.

And apparently Harem Station sponsors kids on some planet called Visa who raise karkadanns, because there's a picture of a kid holding a lead rope for the winning karkadann in some race and there's a big THANK YOU FOR YOUR SUPPORT banner written across the bottom of the frame.

Then there's a certificate with an official seal and everything, declaring Crux to be a member of the Prime Governors' Association. Weird. But OK.

And finally, there's Crux shaking hands with the current dude who plays Jax Justice in all those screens. They filmed a vid here a few years back. I was out somewhere with Valor, *Lady*, and Beauty so we missed all the excitement. But Crux is smiling pretty big.

Crux ends his call but leaves his screen open in the air like any second now he'll just have to open it back up again. He says, "Sorry about that. This fucking place. It's always something."

"So are you gonna give Nyleena a ship? Or are you just yanking her chain?"

"What?"

"That deal you made with her?"

"Oh, that." He chuckles.

"So it's bullshit?"

"I didn't say that."

"So it's real?"

"I didn't say that either."

"Well, which is it? Because I bought her a fucking Harem Station gate pass and everything."

"You want her to leave?" Crux asks, confused.

"I'm going with her, asshole."

"Oh," he says, raising his chin up in that superior I'm-the-fucking-governor-here way he does. "Well, sure. I'll give her a ship. But she has to get me the info I want first."

"Leveling up," I say.

He nods.

"I suspect there's a 'but' coming," I say. "'I'll give her a ship... but...'"

"But only if you go with her. And"—he narrows his eyes at me like we're about to argue—"she has to wait this Veila shit out, Luck. You know that. We can't have her loose out in space somewhere. She could get caught and then poof. Harem Station goes down in flames because someone blew Nyleena up and that blows Lyra up."

"I get it," I say. Because I do. "But I don't like it. It feels wrong. If Nyleena wants to leave, she should be able to leave."

"Well, I don't like it either. I'm not out to hold people captive. But I'm running a fucking station bigger than most Prime cities. I've got millions of other people to think about besides Nyleena."

"Like Corla," I say. I don't know why I say it. It's kind of a low blow. But fuck it. If he's allowed to have an opinion about my soulmate I'm allowed to have an opinion about his.

He leans back in his chair, making the leather creak. "And as you can see, I'm holding her captive too. She's been frozen in my possession for almost a fucking year now. Now Lyra… Lyra is different."

"How so?" I ask.

"She's smart. And reasonable. She knows what's up. She's not constantly plotting insane schemes to fuck up all my plans."

"What plans?"

"All the fucking plans," Crux says, annoyed now.

"What about Delphi?"

He narrows his eyes again. "What about her?"

Delphi is Crux's and Corla's daughter. And so far neither Delphi nor Crux have really acknowledged that fact. So this whole thing bugs me. But I decide to tread carefully because I imagine this could be a sore spot for Crux. So I pick another direction to approach the subject and say, "She's not Jimmy's soulmate. She's Leonis'," instead of what Veila told me back on the Lair about her.

"So? They don't seem to mind."

"Yeah but… don't you think there's a reason we're all paired up? Like… we have some kind of destiny. So shouldn't Leonis and Delphi make a go of it, or whatever?"

Crux laughs. "Are you gonna be the one to tell Jimmy he has to hand his princess over to some *kid*? Because I'm not. I might be her genetic father but she's made it very clear I have no say in her life."

"Well, now that you bring him up, what are we gonna do about Jimmy and Veila?"

"You mean because she's Jimmy's true one?"

"I guess," I reply. Because that's all I can say about that at the moment.

257

"It seems to be working so I'm not gonna rock the boat, if you know what I mean."

"I do," I say. "I get it. But there's more to this story than just letting everyone pick and choose what princess they're genetically tied to, don't you think?"

"What are you trying to say? Because I have a fuck-ton of shit to do today."

"OK," I say, gripping the arms of my chair. "OK, I'm just gonna say it. We don't even know what Delphi *is*."

"Excuse me?"

"I remembered something on my way over here."

"Yeah? What's that?"

"Back when we shot Corla through that spin node and landed here and you had to explain things to ALCOR, you told him what she told you." I lean forward. And now it's my turn to narrow my eyes. "You told him she said that these babies we're supposed to make are monsters."

I lean back, feeling a little relieved to actually get those words out.

"You know what you said when you talked to ALCOR for the first time?"

"What?"

"Don't you remember? You had a message to deliver. All of you, except me, had a message. You spurted and sputtered out a bunch of burbled words, Luck."

"Oh," I say. "I did. Didn't I?"

"So what was that about?"

"How should I know? It was more than twenty years ago."

"Well, you're the one up here demanding answers about questions from the day we arrived. If you're suddenly all concerned about what I said, I'm suddenly all concerned about what you said."

"Dude. You're an asshole. The two things have nothing to do with each other."

"Does Delphi look like a monster to you?"

"No. But Corla and Nyleena don't look like bombs that can explode planets, either. And I don't understand. Why is everyone just OK with letting Serpint and Lyra try for a baby?"

"Well, in case you haven't noticed, they haven't been successful. So who cares?"

"Who cares?" I say. "What the fuck are you gonna tell them when they are? 'Sorry. That baby you just spent a year trying to conceive needs to be put on *ice*?' I mean… what the fuck? Just because they haven't been successful yet doesn't mean they won't be. We should have rules about this."

Crux sighs. Rubs his forehead with the tips of two fingers. Leans back in his chair again. Sighs one more time. Then says, "Fine. I'll call a meeting and we'll discuss it."

"With or without the girls?" I ask.

"Without," he says. "At first, at least."

I nod. Feeling a little better. But then… "You know there's more to this, right?"

"Which part?"

"All of it, Crux. None of it makes any sense. Not even when you factor in the fact that they want to breed us for more weapons. There's got to be more to it than that."

259

"Like what? You got any ideas? Because I have a feeling the only one who knows is ALCOR. And he's dead."

"The Asshole might know."

"He doesn't. He's... not *our* ALCOR."

"And what about Succubus? I'm getting a bad feeling—"

"For fuck's sake, Luck. Is there anything you're satisfied with right now? I don't have all the fucking answers, OK? I'm just doing the best I can. If you only came in here to complain about shit, well, I don't have time for that. And if you came in here to figure shit out, I suggest you go talk to the cyborg master when he's wearing his elbow-patch jacket. Because I'm not a damn therapist. I'm just the guy in charge."

I stand up and point my finger at him. "You're hiding shit. That's what I think. You're hiding shit."

"About what?"

"*Delphi*," I hiss.

And then I walk out.

Because I am righteous. I am right.

And you know how I know I'm right?

Because I'm hiding shit too.

About Delphi. About Jimmy. About Veila. About Valor.

Nyleena was spot on.

We all know something we're not saying.

And every bit of it goes back to Real ALCOR.

CHAPTER THIRTY

MYLEENA

I'm fine.

It's all good.

I'm not angry or feeling the least bit vindictive. If Luck wants to hold his secrets close, that's OK. I have secrets of my own I'm holding close.

Everyone has secrets.

Or at least… everyone has parts of other people's secrets.

I smile. And while it's not a vindictive smile, it is a narcissistic one. Because I am the fucking queen of secret unraveling.

It's a new title for me. Normally I'm the cunning plotter. The clever schemer. The shrewd opportunist.

But I quite like Queen of Secret Unraveling. It could maybe flow better. Perhaps. But it's the thought that counts. I'm pretty sure everyone says that.

Except me.

I'm all action. And today is my day.

I'm gonna rip the rest of this day to pieces. Shred this fucker into the answers I want.

JA HUSS & KC CROSS

And then watch out, Harem Station. Because I'm on a mission to out everyone.

OK. Maybe I'm a little bit vindictive. But no one likes to be left out and right now I feel left out. Like I'm floating in space on the other side of this station's outer hull. And everyone inside is watching me. Just standing there enjoying my struggle.

Well, fuck that.

I enter the docking bay where Serpint and Lyra are hanging out with *Booty* now that she's back where she's supposed to be, then walk over to her, climb the stairs, and enter the airlock. A few minutes later I'm pulling my helmet off inside and undoing all the sticky tabs on my suit.

"Hello!" I call.

"Hello, Nyleena," *Booty* says.

"Where's Lyra and Serpint?"

"I'm afraid I hacked your messaging system. They're not here."

"What?"

"But that's because I'm on your side."

"You are?" I ask. "Which side is that?" Because you just never know what this ship is up to. She's always been nice to me. Which I appreciate since she risked her life to help Lyra save me out at Bull Station. So I'm not as inclined to be suspicious of her as everyone else is these days.

Still. She is the *Booty Hunter*. You really don't fuck with this woman.

"The one where you need information to get what you want."

"How'd you know about that?"

262

"Please," she says. "This Baby ALCOR is a child when it comes to security. I should be running this station, not him. And certainly not that Succubus thing."

"Yeah," I say, taking a seat on a nearby bench. "I don't trust her either. So... how can you help me?"

"I know you're looking for information about Earth. And I know that Lyra and Serpint have nothing to say about that. They don't know anything. But they do know something about why Valor is hanging out with Tray these days and not Luck."

"Hmm... interesting. Which means you know too. So you're gonna tell me right?"

Wishful thinking. Because she says, "I need something from you first."

"Of course you do. What's the fun of a psycho scavenger hunt if I don't have to go on yet another mission to get one more thing in a long line of things just to get a fucking meeting with the Asshole so I can figure out what leveling up is? I should've known." I stand up and walk back over to my suit and start putting it back on.

"Just hold up a minute. I'm asking for benevolent reasons."

"Sure you are."

"I'm asking for Lyra. She needs something, Nyleena. Something I think you'd be happy to help her with, even if you got nothing in return."

I do one of those snort-laughs.

"She wants a baby. And she and Serpint are having trouble conceiving."

"I wonder why," I mutter.

"But there's this flower, you see. And it grows in one of the secret gardens."

Oh, shit. I go still and pretend like my whole body isn't buzzing about this. Before this little hunt started I don't think I've said the word 'flower' more than ten times in the past ten years. Now, all of a sudden they're popping up everywhere. "What kind of flower?" I ask, so nonchalant.

"Something that could help a girl out in the reproductive department."

"Hmmm," I say. "It's probably bullshit. It's just not that easy for us."

"For you," *Booty* agrees. "But Lyra is a pink princess. She operates on a different set of standards in this area."

"What do you know about it?"

"Enough. I know Lyra should be able to conceive. She just needs a little help."

"And you want me to get this flower?"

"Sure."

"And what do I get? Because I'm all for helping Lyra out, but I'm on a tight schedule here, *Boots*. I don't have time for side missions."

"Well… I'm not blaming or faulting you for being ignorant, or anything—"

"Gee, thanks."

"—but you asked the wrong person to help you hack this Baby simpleton."

"Oh." I laugh. "OK. Go on."

"So if you get me that flower so I can gift it to Lyra, then I'll hack baby ALCOR for you. I'll tell you anything you want to know that he has. If it's in his data core, I'll find it."

"Really?" I ask, suspiciously.

"Really."

"That's it?"

"Well, I might have an ulterior motive."

"Spill," I demand.

"Not until you agree to help me."

"Fuck." I sigh. "Fine. Where is this flower? Which garden?"

"I don't know. They're secret, remember? And not in the Baby data core. But Luck knows where all of them are because he was the one in charge of planting them when he first arrived. You know some of them. I know you two meet there. So I'm sure this would be a very quick and easy side mission for you."

"If you know we meet there, then why don't you know where they are?"

"Because there's some kind of disruption field around them. Since I've been following you two I now know their general locations. And by general I mean one moment I see you guys, then next moment I don't. You enter into these fields and disappear, then reappear when you exit out of them. And I have asked a few bots—OK, like dozens of bots—to follow you guys for me, but the minute you enter the disruption field your tracking device shows you to be some place on the other side of the station. Do you and Luck have some kind of secret tunnel system?"

OK. That was a test. I knew all this because Luck already told me. There is a weird disruption field around the gardens. And she's right about the tracking because one time I was on my way to our tryst and I wanted to see if Luck was already there. He wasn't. But he was almost there and then… poof. He was suddenly in his quarters. And when I tried to retrace his tracking it had all been erased. He was simply… in his quarters. Even though he wasn't. He was in the garden.

It's kinda weird how secretive it is. I mean, it's just plants, for fuck's sake.

But when *Booty Hunter* comes to you promising the world, but in the same breath admits she doesn't know something, suspicion is warranted.

Still, I'm not a hundred percent convinced. "You could just send Lyra. Or Serpint."

"I could. But Serpint would get suspicious if I told him about this."

"Why?"

"Because this is not his part to play. It belongs to you and Luck."

"Whoa," I say, holding up a hand. "Back up there, *Booty Hunter*. What are you talking about?"

"You know what I'm talking about, Nyleena. We're all here for a reason. We're all part of a bigger plan."

"What is it?" I ask, so anxious to get her secrets.

"No, I don't think so, princess. You play your part, I play mine. And mine is to get you to do me this favor because once you do, there's gonna be a solution."

"That's a whole bunch of stupid double-talk, *Booty*. I'm not falling for it."

"Just… do me this favor and I'll tell you everything I know about Earth. That's where you're stuck, right? You need info about Earth?"

She's right. I am stuck. There's no good way to get this unless I get help.

So I say, "Fine."

"Great!"

266

But then I add… "Except for the part where you hack Baby ALCOR. I'm only half interested in delivering on the deal Crux and I made. I'm not sure I need a ship anymore. But you know what I do need?"

"Tell me," she purrs.

"I not only want answers about Earth, I want to know why Valor is hanging out with Tray *and*… I want to know what they're up to inside the Pleasure Prison. Because I know you know. You were in there for a long time."

"So you can tell Luck?"

"Yes. So I can tell Luck. Why? You got a problem with that?"

She pauses here. Three whole seconds. Which tells me she does have a problem with that. "You're going off mission, Nyleena."

"So no deal?" I say. "Because I think I could get your space orchids. That's what you need, right?"

"Sorta."

"Well, make a decision. Because if you're not gonna tell me what I want I'm moving on to Plan B."

"Which is what?"

"Wouldn't you like to know?"

In the end she does agree. But I move on to Plan B anyway. Because it turns out that *Booty*'s plan and my Plan B were pretty much the same.

Who knew?

I don't understand it yet, but as soon as I get what I need, she's gonna tell me everything.

So I head back to the Baby's office and I look that assistant of his in her one racing red eye slit and I say, "Look. I demand a meeting with the Baby ALCOR or I'm gonna tell everyone on this station just who and what Corla and I are. And then I'm gonna tell them about *Delphi*."

Her eye races a little faster at my threat.

"You have three seconds to decide. One—"

"Very well," Baby ALCOR says. "Send her in."

And now… yup.

My smile is vindictive *and* narcissistic.

Because I am the SILVER PRINCESS NYLEENA.

All caps, motherfuckers.

Because once I commit to solving a problem I will not be stopped.

CHAPTER THIRTY-ONE

LUCK

I wander for a while, thinking about how life has changed over the past few days.

And the spin node.

I really want to go back there and walk through that portal. I haven't been there in a year and didn't think about it once. But now... it's like an old addiction rearing its ugly head.

I think about what Crux said back in his office too.

What did I tell ALCOR when we landed? I'd forgotten all about that. We did give him a message. I clearly remember Corla whispering something in my ear before we left Wayward Station. And I do remember repeating her message out loud once we arrived here.

But I don't know what it was.

What was it?

Dunno.

I stand on a lift bot, just kind of aimlessly floating through the station. That's kind of a cool thing about living inside a ring. You could theoretically go around in circles forever. It's a long trip around the whole

JA HUSS & KC CROSS

perimeter. Draden and Serpint used to do it all the time back when they were small and they'd be missing for most of the day.

So I don't even know how long I've been riding the lift bot around the perimeter when I suddenly realize it's past time for my tryst with Nyleena.

I open my air screen and check our little private calendar. We're supposed to meet on level three hundred forty-two today in the third quadrant.

It's a long way from where I'm at right now, but still. The idea of standing her up doesn't sit right with me. Even if I'm late I should make an effort.

I'm not surprised when I find the secret garden and she's not there, but I am surprised to pull up my air screen, enter her location, and find her in the Baby ALCOR's offices.

Hmmm.

Should I go see what she's up to? Check on her? Make sure she's OK?

These are all excuses, of course. If there's one girl on this station who really does not need to be checked up on, it's Nyleena.

Not because we don't need to check up on her. We absolutely do. But she doesn't need to be checked on.

She's a fighter. And even though pretty much everyone who knows her thinks she could tame that fight down a little, it's grown on me.

And that scar.

God, that still bothers me.

Maybe that's why she's so aloof and self-sufficient?

She had to be. Whatever they did to her back in Cygnian System before she got out with Lyra, it was bad. But somehow she survived.

I pull up the lift-bot app on my air screen and check Lyra's location.

She's at home.

I program the lift bot to take me there and when I finally get off and press the door chime, I realize the urge to go through the spin node is gone.

Maybe not completely gone, but definitely way in the back of my mind.

Princesses, I muse. Universally good for one thing, no matter who you are.

They command attention.

Lyra opens the door. "Hey, Luck. What's up?"

"Is Serpint here?" I ask, peeking over her shoulder to get a look.

"No, he's down visiting *Booty*."

"Oh. Well, I didn't actually come to see him. I came to see you."

"OK," she says, smiling. So different than her silver sister. "Come on in."

I haven't been to Serpint's quarters in ages. It doesn't look anything like how I remember it. Almost everything is still gray, like my place. It's the standard decor color here. But now there's pink everywhere.

"So how've you guys been?" I ask.

"Pretty good," Lyra says.

"Still"—I glance down at her stomach—"you know, trying?"

"Still trying," she says. "But we're ready. We just finished decorating the nursery. Wanna see it?"

"Sure," I say, then follow her down the hallway. "Hey, did Serpint always have two bedrooms?"

"No," Lyra says. "We put a wall and split the master in half."

271

"Damn," I say. "You guys are really serious about this baby stuff."

Lyra just smiles at me over her shoulder and walks into the new second bedroom. "Ta da!" she says, panning her arms out wide.

And I don't really know what nurseries are supposed to look like. I swear to the Sun, I have not even looked at a picture of a nursery ever, in my life. But this one seems... over the top.

There's a crib. But it's not just any crib. It's round for one. And huge. And has a canopy over the top so it sorta looks like a tent a nomad might use on some flat planet covered in frost. But it's all in shades of pink and violet.

There's two of those auto-mold gliding loungers that have that simulated perpetual motion thing going. Two changing tables for the little shitters. Two closets, open and filled with tiny clothes hanging on tiny hangers.

There's even two toy boxes.

"We're not going to separate our twins," Lyra explains as I take in the room.

"Good," I say. "That's great." And even though I know this whole thing is a very bad idea, I can't help hoping that Lyra and Serpint get their babies.

"Sorry," she says. "I didn't mean to make you talk baby with me."

"No," I say. "I'll be an uncle." I smile. And the smile is real.

"So what's up?"

"You know that scar Nyleena has on her stomach?"

Lyra shakes her head. "No. Does she have a scar?"

"It's…" I want to say huge. But instead I say, "Tragic."

"Tragic how?" Lyra says, narrowing her eyes.

I picture it in my head again, then hold my hands out in front of me, palms facing each other. "Like this long, Lyra. It's… I don't know what it is. But it's bad. It's a very bad thing. And I want to know how she got it."

"I don't know," Lyra says. "We didn't spend much time together as kids. Not until about a year before we left on our mission. She wasn't part of my routine. Though we are super-close genetically," she adds. Like this is important. "She is my closest kin."

"Did you ask her about her life back then? Like… what they did to her? Because she won't talk about it with me."

Lyra takes a deep breath and then says, "Sometimes… things are better left unsaid, Luck. Maybe you should just leave it alone?"

"Do you know why she wants this ship?" I ask.

Lyra shrugs. "Because she's got the wanderlust? Maybe?" Then she smiles. "She's always been that way. Always a little too loud. Always a little too strong. Always a little too ambitious."

"No, Lyra. I mean, yeah. She's those things for sure. But she wants this ship to go kill people. Who does she want to kill?"

I expect Lyra to hand me an immediate, *I don't know*. Because how could she know? It's not like Nyleena's broadcasting her plans. She keeps her secrets close, that one.

But that's not what Lyra hands me at all.

She says, "Everyone, probably."

I spend a few more minutes pushing Lyra for some real answers, but she's noncommittal and finally I just say goodbye and leave. I pull up my air screen to check Nyleena's location and find that she's still in Baby ALCOR's office.

So I head that way.

Because I don't know what's going on in there, but whatever it is… it's not good.

CHAPTER THIRTY-TWO

NYLEENA

Being inside Baby ALCOR's office isn't any different than being outside Baby ALCOR's office. Because he's not physically here. Just a disembodied voice coming from everywhere and nowhere all at once.

"What do you want?" he asks.

"Damn," I say. Because his voice is deep now. And commanding. I don't remember him being this… self-assured the last time I talked to him. "You seem to have grown into your station body, Baby."

"You can call me ALCOR," he says.

I glance at the empty desk. Not even a chair on the other side. No papers. No tablets. No chairs in front of it for guests, either.

It's kinda creepy.

Cygnians do not have AI's like this. I'm not sure anyone has AI's like this.

Maybe Mighty Minions. But I've never been there, so can't really say.

"You're here because you threatened me. What do you want, Nyleena?"

JA HUSS & KC CROSS

"I want answers."

He laughs. An honest-to-God laugh. I've heard others talk about Real ALCOR laughing but I've never heard it myself.

A chill runs up my spine.

"I would like some answers as well," he says, still laughing.

"About what?" I ask, spinning in place trying to find a focal point to address him. You'd think he'd have a hologram or something. A screen with a face. Anything to help you feel like you were talking to a real person and not some *ghost*.

"Everything," he says.

And even though it comes out kinda innocuous, I have a flash of Little Luck telling me about that wall of ice back in the museum.

Everything, he said. *It's everything.*

"Well, I can't really help you with everything," I say, playing it off. "But I can help you with one thing."

"What's that?"

"Draden," I say.

And I swear to the Sun and all things holy in this universe. I can feel him narrow his nonexistent eyes. "What about Draden?"

"You don't have any real memories of him, do you? I mean, sure. You can go into the museum and hang out with him. But that wasn't you he loved, was it? In fact, you don't really have a relationship with any of the boys, do you?"

"Nyleena, if I have to ask you to state your purpose one more time I'm going to lose my patience. What do you *want*?"

"I want to help you," I say, spinning around to focus on a screen that shows a view outside the station. A fake, virtual window, I realize. "I want to help you build a relationship with your Akeelian partners. And I think I can do that by giving you memories about Draden so you can share them with the guys."

"I have memories of Draden."

"You have *recordings* of Draden. But Crux, and Jimmy, and Luck, and Valor, and Tray, and Serpint, they don't need recordings. Because it's all up here in their heads." I tap my head.

"So what is your offer? And what do you *want*?"

"I want to know where the secret gardens are. I need a flower, you see. A very special flower. And if you tell me that I'll get Luck to spill his memories of Draden. Then I'll tell you about them so you can all bond and become family again, and you'll give me the location of the space orchids."

I wait now.

Because there's a real high probability that he knows I'm lying. There's a really good chance that he's been tracking Luck and me on our afternoon trysts.

But I'm waiting to see if he's lying too.

Because he doesn't know where these gardens are.

And he doesn't know I know that. Because he can't hear or see anything inside of *Booty Hunter* and she's the one who told me he doesn't know.

"Very well," he says. "It's a deal. But what about your *threat*?"

"Oh, that," I say, waving a hand over my shoulder as I walk towards the door. "I was just trying to get your attention."

But as soon as I open the door and leave, I bump right into the rock-hard chest of Luck.

"Shit!" I laugh. "You scared me."

"Oh." He frowns. "I didn't mean to."

"You didn't really scare me, Luck. It's just something you say when you're suddenly surprised."

He nods his head but doesn't say anything.

"So… what are you doing here?" I ask.

"What are you doing here?"

"I asked you first," I say.

"Looking for you."

"Well, I'm not here for you… but…" I grab his t-shirt in my fist and pull him towards me. "I kinda miss you."

"You just saw me like an hour ago."

"You wanna go to your place?" I ask. "We haven't…" I glance at Baby's cyborg assistant. "You know. I bet you're dying."

"Not really dying. I'm fine. But yes, I would like to take you to my place."

"Great!"

That's what I say. But he's got a weird look on his face. And I really wanted to make a dramatic exit out of the Baby's office. And then seconds ago there was a chance that Baby wasn't gonna track me, but that chance is gone. Because now he's gonna listen on our conversation for sure. And then he's gonna figure he's got all the information about Draden he needs.

So that sucks.

But…

"Well," Luck says. "You wanna go? Or do you just want to stand there and look blankly past my face as the wheels inside your brain turn?"

"Sorry." I smile up at him. "Yeah, let's go."

But it doesn't matter if Luck tells me about Draden in private or the Baby hears it while spying. The fact remains I will deliver. And I will do it very quickly.

Things are about to get a lot more interesting around here.

CHAPTER THIRTY-THREE

"What were you doing in there?" I ask her once we're in the elevator that goes to my quarters.

"Just... getting to know the Baby."

"Nyleena." I chuckle. "I know you're up to something. Everyone knows you're up to something."

"Luck," she says. "Everyone is up to something."

"Truth," I say. "But really. What were you talking about with the Baby?"

"Just commiserating on being newbies around here, that's all."

The elevator doors open and we enter my quarters. I've been on the station for a while now. In fact, these past several months might be my longest continuous stay on Harem since Valor and I first went out into the galaxy to look for ALCOR parts.

"Got anything to drink?" Nyleena asks. "I could use some tushberry wine."

"Sure," I say, walking over to the autocook to order her some sparkling wine. "So what did he say about that? Did he complain?"

"No, not at all."

"Did you complain?"

"Absolutely not," she says.

The autocook dings and I hand her a flute of sparkling tushberry wine.

"Thanks," she says, then greedily gulps it down and sets the glass aside. "So," she says, and her eyes brighten a little. Sparkle with crackles of light from the infusion of nutrients that recharge her luminous flux. "I've been thinking about things."

"Our little secret?" I ask.

"No." She glances up at the ceiling. And I know what that means. I've done it myself enough times over the past twenty years. She's wondering if the Baby ALCOR is listening in on our conversation.

He is. I'm sure of it. She just came from his office. Something happened in there. And whatever it was, it's got his attention now.

She's got his attention now.

She's got mine too.

But not in a good way.

Still, I like Nyleena. She's my soulmate. And even though that bond was formed without my consent or desire, it is what it is and I'm ready to make the most of it.

In fact, I more than *like* her. I like her a lot.

But she's always up to something. And she still doesn't trust me. I showed her my biggest secret.

Well, maybe second biggest.

But she has given me nothing in return. Yet.

I take her hand and lead her over to the couch and we sit. "I want to talk to you about something," I say.

"You do?" she asks, swinging her leg over mine so she can settle in my lap. Her hands slide against the top of my shoulders and then her fingertips lightly caress the back of my neck.

And normally I would not mind this gesture of dominance and hint of impending sex. But I want to *talk*. "Yeah," I say, reaching for the hem of her shirt.

Immediately her hands clamp down on my wrists and we lock eyes.

"Take off your shirt, Nyleena."

"No," she says.

"Take off your shirt," I say again, lifting up on the hem.

"No," she insists, pushing my hands away. "It's none of your business."

"I'm not trying to pry. I just want to... look at it."

"Why would you want to look at it? It's ugly. It's the ugliest thing ever. You don't want to look at it, you want me to talk about it. And I don't want to talk about it."

I sigh. "I'm not trying to upset you."

"I'm not upset. I'm just... firm on this. If you want to talk, let's talk about you."

"What about me?"

"I dunno," she says, relaxing a little. Her hands go back to my shoulders. Slide around my neck. Fingertip caressing resumes. "How about... Draden?"

"Draden?" I ask. "Random. Why Draden?"

"I don't know. I guess because he's the one I'll never be able to meet. And Little Draden isn't quite the same."

"Well," I huff. "Maybe not. Maybe he's not dead. Maybe what Veila told—"

"We don't need to talk about that," Nyleena says, cutting me off. "Tell me something about him from your childhood."

"Childhood," I repeat. "What do you want to know?"

"Hmmm," she says. But it's all an act. I'm suddenly sure this whole thing is an act. This is Nyleena being... Nyleena. She's using me for something.

No, not just any something.

"What was he like as a boy? What kind of relationship did he have with Real ALCOR?"

"What are you doing?" I ask.

"What do you mean?"

"You know what I mean. Asking me questions about Draden. Coming out of Baby ALCOR's office. This is all part of your scheme, isn't it?"

She looks at me. Bites her lip. Breathes deep. "Not exactly," she says in a flat, even tone.

"Not exactly?" I say, raising my eyebrows at her. "Then exactly what is this? Because to me, this looks very much like you're trying to finish this deal with Crux. And to be clear, I don't care if you get a ship. I don't even care if you leave. I told you, we're partners so I'll go with you. But what the fuck are you doing *right now?*"

"I... I don't understand," she says.

"Yeah, you do," I say. "You know exactly what I'm talking about. What do you need to know, Nyleena? Huh? Tell me what information you need about Draden. What do you want me to tell you so you can go running back to Baby ALCOR, or Crux, or who the fuck ever it is that needs this info?" I look at her. Lock eyes with her. "Just... do not lie to me, Nyleena. I don't care about your wild side. I don't care about your schemes. I don't even mind your psycho revenge plan. But do not lie to me. Be fucking straight. Now what the fuck are you up to?"

And I have a moment of hope here. I really think she's gonna give in and tell me.

But she doesn't. Because she says, "I'm not running a scheme. I'm just curious, that's all."

"Just curious," I repeat. I push her off me and stand up.

"Where are you going?" she asks, scrambling to her feet.

"I'm leaving."

"Why? These are your quarters."

"Because I just asked for the truth and you handed me a lie."

"I'm not lying!"

I turn and point my finger in her face. "That's another lie." I pause for a moment. Collecting my thoughts so I don't fuck up what I'm feeling by saying the wrong words. "I don't need you, Nyleena. I've lived my whole life without a soulmate. It might be hard now that I know you exist, but I could do it again. I don't *need* you. I *wanted* you. At least I thought I did. For about an hour. But not only do you not trust me with the truth about that tragic scar running down the middle of your chest, you leave me out of things. And before this moment, that was just fine. Because I left you out of things too. But I showed you a really big secret earlier today and you took it. And kept it. And gave nothing back in return."

"Luck," she says.

"No. Just... no. I'm not done yet. You want to take a little more from me? You need more information about Draden? Or Veila? Or Jimmy? Or Delphi? Who do you want to know about next? Because I got shit on all of them."

"Luck, listen—"

"No. You listen. Draden fell. Crux has always said that he was the one who saw him the best because he was on level twenty-six when it happened. But that wasn't true. I was the one who saw him hit that lift bot and crush his spine. *Me*. I was on level nine. And ALCOR was standing right next to me when it happened."

"What?" she says.

"You heard me. ALCOR was standing right next to me. And you know why he and I were together on level nine when Draden died?"

She starts shaking her head.

"Sorry, princess. But..."

"Luck, STOP TALKING!" She says it so loud I actually do stop talking. "I don't want to know anymore."

"Because you got enough?"

"Luck, can you just please—"

"Choose, Nyleena. I don't mind if you play games with all of *them*. But you don't get to play games with *me*."

"Luck, listen—" But she doesn't even continue. She just stops, her mouth opening and closing like she's trying to spit out words but can't quite make it happen.

"Forget it," I say. "Just fucking forget it."

And then I turn away and walk out.

CHAPTER THIRTY-FOUR

What the hell?

I stare at the place where he just was in confusion.

"Well, that went well," Baby ALCOR says.

Dick. "You got what you wanted," I say, forcing myself to be sweet. "Right?"

"I need more, Nyleena. That's not enough."

I want to swallow, take a deep breath, and collect my thoughts. But I can't afford to. Because shit just got real. I had no clue what Luck was gonna tell me next, but I don't want this Baby to know about it.

I rally. Quickly. And say, "I'll get you whatever you need. I have something to bargain with now. He wants personal information from me. If I give him my secrets, he gives me his. We seem to have made some kind of unspoken deal."

"That's fine. I can wait."

"But I need the location of those flowers."

"You get me what I need first."

"No deal," I say firmly. "I'm in the middle of something, ALCOR. And I don't have time to fuck around. So either you trust me to get more or I move on to my next best option."

"Which is who? Luck?" He laughs. "He's not even speaking to you."

"No," I say. And I didn't want to use this threat so early on in this scheme, but it seems I have no choice. "*Booty*."

I count his silence in seconds. Two.

"I'll have to look in the data core for the locations."

"Good," I say. "Do that. I'll wait."

I wonder what he's going to do now? He doesn't have that information. I know he doesn't have it.

"I can get you something better than those flowers," Baby says.

"I need the flowers," I insist.

"I know why you need them. I know what they're for. And I have that chemical in a different form."

"Like... a pill?" I ask.

"A chemical formula."

"And it works?"

"Trust me. It works."

"Well..." I huff out a laugh. "Excuse me if I don't take your word on that. Because as we all know... Lyra isn't pregnant."

I almost hold my breath. It takes a lot of effort not to hold my breath.

"Now it's time for you to trust me," he says. "I know what I'm doing."

I play the last card *Booty* gave me. And part of me hopes he'll deny it. A big part of me, I think. "There's someone else, isn't there? Some other princess who's pregnant?"

"Right now you've earned the formula and that's it. Get me more information and I'll tell you what I know."

But that's not a denial. It is, however, exactly what I needed.

"OK," I say, forcing myself to sound resigned. "Deal. Where do I get this formula?"

"It's waiting in the autoshopper in your quarters right now."

I smile. It's a real smile too. "Thank you, ALCOR."

"Nice doing business with you, princess. I hope this is the start of a very… *fruitful* relationship."

The chill runs up my spine before I can stop it. But I do not shudder. I just walk out. Head straight for my quarters, grab the little piece of paper with a chemical formula written on it, and take it back to *Booty*.

I know he's watching me. I can feel the Baby's invisible eyes following me every step of the way. Burning into the back of my head as I put on the envirosuit, go out into the docking bay, and then board *Booty Hunter*, cycle through the airlock, and place the formula on the table.

"This is what he gave me."

"I knew it," *Booty* says.

"What's it mean?" I ask.

"Nothing good, Nyleena."

"You're not going to tell me, are you?"

"No. But I have the information you asked for. Are you ready?"

"I'm ready," I say.

And she tells me more than I ever imagined.

She spills secrets that stun me speechless.

I listen. Silent the entire time.

And then I get up, retrace my steps, and go back inside the station.

CHAPTER THIRTY-FIVE

She finds me. It takes her a couple hours. I just wandered around for a while. Grabbed something to eat, avoided everyone, and then finally walked to our regularly scheduled tryst location and started dozing off in the grass.

"Thank the fucking sun," she says upon arrival. "Do you have any idea how long I've been looking for you?"

I don't even bother opening my eyes. I'm mad. Super fucking mad.

She's up to something and it feels big.

"You know, it's really not the lying. Because I sorta understand that."

"You do?" she asks, kneeling down next to me.

"You want to scheme? Fine. Scheme. I don't need to be a part of that, I guess. The part that bothers me is your lack of trust."

"The scar," she says.

I open my eyes and turn my head to look at her. "Yeah. If we're gonna be partners, Nyleena, then I get to know shit like that."

She nods her head and takes a deep breath. "I don't deserve your trust because you think I don't trust you back, but that's really not the issue here."

"Then what is the issue?"

"The issue is… I'm in the middle of something."

"Obviously."

"And it's really important that I play my part. And telling you about my past would… derail things, Luck. I will tell you, but not right now. I know I don't deserve your trust, but I need it."

We stare at each other. Her eyes are dark. No light at all. But then she smiles and they sparkle. And I can't tell if she did that on purpose, or if she's reacting to me. "What do you need?"

"Please, I'm begging you. Tell me what you know about Valor and Veila."

"Just like that, huh? Tell you what I know?"

"Trust me," she says, taking my hand. And the instant she does that I have a vision of the hidden galaxy on the other side of that spin node. "Please," she begs. "I'm doing this for you."

"For me?" I say.

She nods. "I swear. I am in the middle of a scheme but I can't tell you yet. I don't have all the information. I need that information, Luck. Or I would not ask." Her eyes search mine. "I *would not* ask."

This is the part I believe.

She would not ask.

That's one hundred percent true. Nyleena isn't a girl who asks for anything. She goes and gets it herself. Because she doesn't trust anyone to help her out.

So this request… it is a sign of trust.

"OK," I say.

"Really?"

I nod. "But you're not gonna like what I have to say. And I don't know how it'll be helpful because… it's not good, Nyleena. Nothing I'm about to say is good."

"I don't know either," she says. "I can't say for sure that it will be. I just know I need to get to the Asshole ALCOR. *Soon*. And the only way I can see to do that is to play along with this stupid scavenger hunt Crux sent me on."

"Do you think he's involved in something bad?"

"Hard to tell. Not enough info."

I don't like that answer, but it's all I get.

So I sigh and say, "All right. So this is what happened to me on Lair Station…"

Chach and I come out of the airlock firing. There are about a dozen borgs waiting for us, but she mows them down with her souped-up exoskeleton defense system and in just a few seconds there's nothing but a pile of borg bodies.

"Fuck yeah," she says. And I'm just about to high-five her when we hear screaming from somewhere down the hallway.

"What was that?" Chach asks.

I know what it is. Instantly. But I have a hard time getting the words out. So I don't say anything.

We move forward to the edge of the hallway, her on one side, me on the other, and I peek out.

"Nothing," I say.

293

"That screaming wasn't nothing," Cha-Cha says.

We hear it again.

"Shit," Chach says. "It sounds like kids."

"It is kids," I say, a sick, sick feeling in my stomach. Because it sounds like Draden. Or Serpint. Back when they were small.

"OK, so what do you want to do? Split up? Or go together?"

I'm just about to say together, when we hear the voice of a woman in the other direction screaming orders.

"I'm gonna assume that's the boss here?" Cha-Cha says.

"OK, you go after the kids. I'll take care of this bitch. If you find Jimmy before me, head towards *Dicker*. I'll meet you there."

"On it," she says, taking off down the hallway to my left. I watch her a moment. The woman is still barking orders off to my right, but I want to make sure there's no ambush waiting for Chach once she gets to the next hallway intersection.

She stops, peeks around the corner, shoots me a thumbs up, then disappears.

I'm just about to make a run in the other direction when I hear the tell-tale sound of borg boots heading my way.

I slip back behind the wall, pressing myself up against it, plasma rifle at high ready, and wait.

They run past, heading in Cha-Cha's direction, and there's only six of them, so I step out and fire.

Two go down immediately. Two more are only knocked backwards, and one doesn't get hit at all.

He fires and I go careening backwards, my chest slammed with the force of the hit, and crash against the wall.

But I'm heavily armored. So I don't die.

The armor is on fire, but no time to worry about that just yet. I aim, take his head off, then hit the others in the same way until they too are a heap of borg bodies in the middle of the hallway.

I drop my rifle, snap the tabs on my chest armor, and shrug out of it. Then I tug my scorched and smoldering t-shirt over my head, drop it to the floor, and in the same motion pick my rifle back up, aiming at the hallway in the direction these assholes just came from.

A barrage of firing and blasting echoes from the hallway where Cha-Cha just disappeared.

But she is more equipped than I am now, so instead of following her and fucking up the plan, I turn away and jog down the hallway to my right.

The woman who was barking order just a few seconds ago is quiet or gone.

I slow to a stalk, on the lookout for an ambush at each intersection.

Nothing. There's still a lot of firing happening on other parts of the station, but it's far enough away from my present location that I don't have to worry about it.

Yet.

I creep forward. And I know—I just fucking know, I feel it in my gut—that there's something *wrong* coming.

I get to another intersection, press my body up against the wall, and peek out.

The barrel of a plasma pistol touches my forehead. I slide my eyes to the right and catch a glimpse of silver.

"Well, well, well," the woman says. "Look who fell in the well."

"What the fuck does that mean?"

"It means... you got what you deserve."

I turn and find myself face to face with a silver Cygnian princess.

And I'm telling you, no matter what you say about this woman—call her crazy, call her sick, call her whatever you want...

She is fucking beautiful.

Mesmerizingly beautiful.

And for a moment I cannot move. I can't speak, or defend myself.

But she doesn't shoot me.

"Luck, I presume?"

I just stare at her silver eyes. Transfixed.

"You're not Valor. I know that for sure." Then she laughs. "If you were we'd already be doing something else."

"What?" I say.

"And you're not Tray. I hear he's dark. Did you have white hair as a child?"

"*What?*"

"I bet you did. And obviously you're not Jimmy. I'm already well-acquainted with Jimmy. Serpint has his princess already. Definitely not Serpint. And Crux... well, he's a little busy these days, isn't he?"

"Who the fuck are you?"

"Oh. I'm sorry. I'm Princess Veila."

"Veila," I say. "As in—"

"The one and only."

And for a second I feel this overwhelming relief flood through my body. Because Veila is the other half of Corla. And this is the exact princess we need!

"Don't get excited," Veila says. "We're not on the same side. Yet."

"What?"

There's firing down the hallway, and she turns.

And even though I'm so fucking confused right now, I don't miss opportunities.

I grab her pistol, break her arm, and throw her down on the ground.

She snarls at me. But then tucks it away and begins to laugh.

I keep my rifle pointed at her head, then check the hallway. Because that firing is close. And it's not her people, it's mine.

Cha-Cha is yelling. A kid is screaming. And there's more blasting.

A shot of plasma sears past me, barely missing my exposed chest.

"Cease fire, you idiots!" Veila screams, getting to her feet as she holds her broken arm close to her body. "He's part of the program!"

I aim my rifle straight at her chest. So close, if I took this shot, she'd be cut in half.

Cha-Cha yells again. The kid screams.

"You have two choices, Luck," Veila says. "Stay with me or save your friends. Better make a decision quick though. Because I have to go."

I look at her, panic rising inside me. Because we need this princess. Crux needs this woman to unlock his frozen queen.

But Cha-Cha yells again and it's not the winning kind.

"OK, I can see you're not going to come with me. But I'm not going to take that personally because you're not my one, after all. You have other loyalties. So I understand. If you were Valor... eh. I might be a little hurt."

"What the fuck are you talking about?" I snarl, glancing at her two borgs, still at the end of the hallway. Still in high-ready position, ready to shoot me.

"One little warning. I feel I owe it to you. Leave Delphi behind. You'll thank me later."

And then she smiles.

And then I shoot her.

And I run.

"Fucking suns," Nyleena says.

"Right?" I say. "It was kinda dicey. And to be honest, that bitch creeped me out. She was not afraid of me. Not one bit. And I knew, if I didn't go help Cha-Cha, she wouldn't make it. No one was going to kill me that day, Nyleena. No one. I was 'part of the program'. But Chach? And that kid she was with when I got there? They were as good as dead. So... it's not my most heroic moment, but I did the right thing."

Nyleena nods. "Of course. No one's gonna call you a coward for saving your partner. But... what was that part about Delphi?"

"Delphi," I whisper. "I didn't even know who she was. When *Lady* caught up with *Dicker* on the other side of the gate, she mentioned Jimmy was with some princess called Delphi, but I didn't know she was Crux and Corla's daughter. So it took me a while to actually make sense of Veila's warning."

"Shit," Nyleena says.

"There's something wrong with Delphi. I knew the moment I saw her. And after Jimmy told me that Delphi has a twin brother, most of it started clicking into place."

Monsters.

But I don't say it out loud.

"And Valor?" Nyleena says. "What? I thought Jimmy was Veila's one?"

"She is. Jimmy said so."

"So you don't know anything about Valor?"

"I told you everything I know."

Nyleena nods. Sighs. "This is a pretty fucked-up shit."

"Tell me about it."

Then she says, "I have to go. And you can't come."

"Go where?" I ask.

"I need to see this thing through, Luck. And you can't be there. It'll mess it all up."

She gets to her feet and I sit up. Just staring up at my beautiful silver princess.

I had never seen one so close before I met up with Veila. Corla was in the cryopod. It's hard to appreciate the beauty of a silver princess when they're locked up in ice.

But Veila took my breath away when I first saw her.

And Nyleena is a hundred times more beautiful.

"Don't get killed," I whisper. "I need you, Nyleena."

"I'll do my best," she says.

And then she walks out of the secret garden and disappears down the hallway.

CHAPTER THIRTY-SIX

"What's this all about?" Jimmy asks.

He, Delphi, and I are inside *Big Dicker*. It took me a whole lot of classic Nyleena tantrum-throwing to make them meet me here, but it was worth it.

"Why did we have to meet here?" Delphi asks.

"*Big Dicker?*" I say.

"Yes, Nyleena?"

"You know, don't you?"

"Yes, I know. *Booty* filled me in."

"You know what?" Jimmy asks. "What the hell is going on?"

"The Baby ALCOR cannot be trusted," *Dicker* says.

"What?" Jimmy says. And his face goes ash-gray in this moment. If anyone understands how fucked you are when you're on a station and the AI is unreliable, Jimmy does. I can almost imagine the sinking feeling in his gut as these six words are fully processed. "Since when?" he asks.

"Since the Succubus AI came on board," *Dicker* replies.

Jimmy's jaw clenches. He growls, "Why didn't you fucking tell me this? It's been months."

Delphi and I share a look. I'm not sure what hers means. I don't know her that well. But mine is... deference. I am not about to cross Jimmy or interfere with his anger at *Dicker*.

"We needed proof," *Dicker* says. "And Nyleena got that for us today."

Jimmy's heads swings in my direction. "What did you do?"

I shrug. "Just told a little story. And the Baby fell right into my trap."

"Explain," Jimmy seethes.

I swallow hard and look up at the screen that simulates *Big Dicker*'s speech in a wave form. *Help!* I want her to take over now.

"That's not important," *Dicker* says. "It was just a little game of lies. Tell them what Luck told you, Nyleena. We have a lot of work to do and not a lot of time to do it."

"OK," I say, wiping my sweaty hands on my envirosuit. "So this scavenger hunt I was on... Crux wanted info on leveling up from the Asshole ALCOR, Valor wanted info on Veila, Luck wanted info on Valor and Tray, Delphi wanted info on Earth, and *Booty* wanted a flower from Luck's secret gardens. It led me down a very interesting path that ended with me getting almost all that information and... a lot more."

I pause here. I've made a decision not to tell them Luck's secret about the spin node galaxy inside the station museum because that feels like our secret now. Not just his. But everything else needs to be said.

"But this all starts with you two."

"Why?" Delphi asks.

"You're not gonna like this," I say, warning her.

"Believe me," Delphi says. "I've dealt with a lot of bad news in my short lifetime. I can take it."

"OK, then," I say. And then I take a deep breath and start talking. "You are Corla and Crux's daughter. Corla is a genuine silver princess. The highest rank. The seventh daughter of the king and current reigning queen."

"Just like Lyra, though, right?" Jimmy asks.

"No," I say. "Corla and Lyra are almost nothing alike. Corla is silver. I don't think you guys understand how different we are. But that's not the point I'm trying to make here. My point is…" I look at Delphi. "You're it."

"I'm what?" she says.

"You are what they've been trying to make all these years."

"That doesn't really answer the question," Jimmy says. And his voice is low. And rumbling. And dangerous.

"You're…"

"Go ahead," Delphi says. "Just… tell me. What *am* I?"

"A bomb?" Jimmy interjects.

I shake my head.

"What then?"

"You're the monster," I say. Because that's the only word I have for it. That's the only word I've heard used to describe her.

Neither of them say anything.

"One half of the monster, to be exact," I add.

"Tycho," she whispers.

I nod. "I don't know your brother. I barely know you. But you... you are the natural-born offspring of Crux and Corla. You are what they want. You are what they've been trying to make all these thousands of years since the true Cygnian and Akeelian races were destroyed."

"Then why did they let her go?" Jimmy asks. "Why send her on that mission to kidnap me?"

"Succubus," *Dicker* says. "They were willing to sacrifice Delphi for the sake of Succubus. They wanted to plant an AI on our station. And they knew Delphi would be safe here. They knew all the princesses would be safe here. That once you boys found your soulmates you'd do anything—even endanger the lives of millions of people on this station—to keep them close."

Jimmy's face goes hard. I know that feeling. I know what betrayal feels like. And in this moment, so does he. Because this was all a trap.

Coral. Lyra. Me. Delphi. We didn't end up here on accident. We were *sent* here.

And so was Succubus.

Even worse? Jimmy was the one who brought her.

"How long have you known about this, *Dicker*? Do you have any idea how fucked we are?" He's looking at her wave form on the screen when he says this. But he turns to me, so quick and so fast I take a step back. "We're all gonna die. Do you have any idea how hard that Succubus can fuck with us? She can—"

"She cannot," *Dicker* says. "She is not connected to the Baby. Her core was implanted inside the Pleasure Prison. That wasn't her decision, it was Tray's. Because Tray is doing something in there and he has a plan. The Succubus went in willingly because she needs

304

something from the Asshole. He has the data she needs. He just doesn't realize it yet."

"The Baby," Jimmy says. "He's—"

"A traitor," *Dicker* finishes for him. "He's not connected to the Succubus yet. But he could be soon. He's an infiltrator, Jimmy."

"Sent by who?" Jimmy yells. "Mighty Minions? Holy fuck! Are we at war with Mighty Minions? Because…" He laughs. But it's an ironic laugh. "Because I'm gonna tell you something right now. That place has seventeen—"

"Sixteen," *Dicker* corrects him.

I wince. Because Jimmy glares at her with a look that says, *Shut the fuck up. I'm talking.*

"Sixteen," *Dicker* repeats, ignoring his silent warning.

"Sixteen," Jimmy says through clenched teeth, "fucking AI's running that place. And you didn't see the power it has. Delphi and I did. It took us to a fucking planet."

"It took you to Earth," I say. "*Booty* figured it all out and told me." She told me a lot when she spilled her secrets. Maybe too much, if you ask me. I don't know what I'm into right now, but it's big. Bigger than I can imagine. Probably the biggest thing I've ever been a part of, and that's saying a lot.

She wanted to know if the Baby was on our side. That was her main goal when she had me go ask him for the flower for Lyra. That was just an in. He already knew I was on a scavenger hunt. He knew I was trading information with pretty much everyone by this point.

All Booty needed from me is confirmation that he was lying. And when he told me he knew where the gardens were, *that* was the lie. My Draden scheme was just an off the cuff offer to see if he would lie about knowing the location of the gardens.

But we got a lot more information from that scheme than even Booty thought we'd get. And now I'm afraid that he got more from my Draden conversation with Luck than I intended.

Because he has a goddamned formula for space orchid essence. And even though he didn't admit that he had this formula because he's part of a breeding program, he came damn close.

Somewhere—maybe not here—but somewhere out there is a pregnant princess.

And I'd bet my whole future on her being silver.

Delphi was the first monster. But something went wrong. She must be defective. She's pink, after all. Not silver. So they didn't get what they wanted.

But they haven't stopped trying.

What did Luck accidentally reveal when he was telling me about Draden? I know there was something there. Luck was telling me a secret about the day Draden fell. That he saw it happen and he was just about to reveal something else about that day when I yelled and made him stop taking. And even though I don't understand how it's all connected, I know it is.

It has to be.

And I know that whatever that secret is about Draden's fall, Baby ALCOR should not know it.

"I don't think we really went to a planet, Jimmy," Delphi says, pulling me out of my introspection. "It has to be a program. A hologram, or a virtual… or something."

"And normally I'd agree," I say, being careful not to divulge too much here. *Booty*'s plan is precarious and things need to happen in a certain order. They can't know about the spin node galaxy. That's one secret that Baby and Succubus can't ever figure out. We can't get ahead of ourselves or the plan won't work. So I just say, "But I saw something today that changed my mind."

"What?" Jimmy asks. "What did you see?"

"It's not important. But trust me when I say... a powerful station like Mighty Minions—or Harem, for example—*could* possess a technology that enables instantaneous travel like that."

"That was Earth," Jimmy whispers. "That really was Earth."

"*Booty* thinks so," I say.

"Where is *Booty*?" Jimmy asks.

"She's busy," *Dicker* says.

"Doing what?" he growls.

"Interfacing with the Pleasure Prison."

"Why?"

"Look," I say, putting both my hands up, palms out. Trying to calm him down. "Something's in motion here. I'm not a hundred percent sure what it is, but I have a part to play. OK? This is my part. Doling out all the secrets I just spent the last several days acquiring. So just stop asking questions and fucking listen to me for a moment."

Jimmy shoots me a death glare. Clenches his jaw and spits, "Then start fucking talking."

I nod. "OK. I'm just gonna spill it out in bullet points. Earth is real. You're probably connected to it in some way."

"My mother," he says.

"Whatever," I say. "No one knows where it is. But everyone seems to want to go there."

"Mighty Minions knows," he says.

"I guess," I say. "But... if they do really have a way to take you there for real, then that's good for us. Because it means they're on our side."

"How do you figure? They're the ones who told us to bring Succubus here."

"Because if they can get there on their own, then why bother with what we have?"

"What?" Jimmy says. "What do we have?"

"Just listen. Everyone wants to go to this place. It must hold some secret for their breeding program. So if the Mighty Minions Resort has a fucking superhighway that leads directly to it, then there's no need to bother with planting an AI on Harem to get that final secret. So Mighty Minions didn't plant the Succubus. They didn't know. And... furthermore," I say, putting up a hand. "The Cygnians don't know where Earth is either."

"But you and Lyra were sent there," Delphi interjects.

"So they *say*. But if this place is so important, and they were sending us there, then why is everyone still looking for it?" I raise my eyebrows at them. Waiting.

They don't get it. But I think I do. "We have the secret, you guys."

"We don't have the secret," Jimmy says. "We can't get to Earth from here!"

"I think we do," I say. "I think we can."

"Explain," he growls.

"I can't. That's something Luck and I need to discuss first. But let me just say this. What if... what if ALCOR knew something? And he left on purpose. And got himself killed on *purpose*. Because what if... he's not dead? He's just... out there somewhere?"

I motion to the small tunnel of black space that I can see from the front window of Dicker's cockpit to indicate where *out there* is.

"Out where?" Delphi asks.

"Wherever. Listen. Luck told me that Tray and Valor told him that they are working on something to do with information repackaging inside the Pleasure Prison. I mean... he said a lot of big words most of which I only half understand. But it kinda made me think they're searching for data. To recollect it somehow. What if they're really trying to recollect ALCOR? *Real* ALCOR?"

Jimmy squints his eyes at me.

"It took a lot of gates to get to Bull Station, right?"

"So?" Jimmy says.

"So there's this theory about data collecting on the edge of black holes. Like anything that falls into it is actually only a copy because data can't be destroyed. So... it collects there. All this data. Nothing is lost. And there's another theory that says gates do the same thing."

"What the fuck are you talking about?" Jimmy says.

"OK, that's not important now. We can have a mastermind on where lost data goes some other time. I have more to tell you right now. I only told you parts one, two, and three. Delphi and Tycho are..." I glance at her and give her a sympathetic shrug. "Something we don't understand yet. And Earth is real and we have a way to get there. And the Succubus is probably working with the Baby and that could get a lot worse, real fast, if we don't do something about it quick. Part four... I need your help with something. I need to know what Veila told you, Jimmy. So I can answer Valor's questions. Specifically... is Veila your true one?"

"Yes," Delphi says. "I saw it. They connected."

"Jimmy," I say, ignoring Delphi. "Is she?"

"I don't know," he says with a sigh. Then he sits down on the edge of a bench and leans over, head in hands.

"What do you mean?" Delphi asks. "Of course she is. Because if she's not... then..."

"Who is Jimmy's true one?" I finish for her. "Because it's not you, Delphi. I'm not trying to be mean here, it's just not you."

"I was taking a DNA signature scrambler," Jimmy says. He lifts his head to look at me. "All these years. I would go to this biogenetics lab out on the Outer Highway and get injections. Veila knew I was doing that. She told me."

"So she used that new signature scrambler to make herself a complimentary one," I say.

"Maybe," he admits.

"OK. Then that's all I need to know."

"Why?" Delphi asks.

"Because now I know why Valor is so obsessed with Veila."

"Oh, shit," Jimmy says.

"Oh, shit," I echo. "She belongs to him."

And I just got the next answer in my scavenger hunt.

I'm just turning around to leave when Delphi says, "Nyleena?"

I turn back and look at her. She's very sad right now. It's one thing to know the man you love has been fated to love someone else when it's your creepy evil aunt a generation removed. It's quite another to know that it's not. And his true one could be... anyone. A good person. Someone he'll *want* to fall in love with.

"Yes," I say.

"There's more."

I deflate. Because I don't know how much more I can take. This scavenger hunt started out as a game. A way to gain my freedom. But right now it feels like these answers contain the weight of the universe.

"I know what I am," she whispers. "I have always known. That's why they gave me Flicka when I was a small child. She was supposed to keep me under control. And if I ever found myself out of control, she was supposed to... take care of it."

Jimmy looks at her. And he looks tired. Beaten. Worn out.

"I *am* a monster," she says. Then she looks at Jimmy. Walks over to him and takes his hand. Glows a little. "And so is Tycho. But we're harmless when we're apart. I swear it. We are. We have to be together to... initiate. That's why I needed him back."

"So you could... initiate?" I ask.

Holy mother of suns. Delphi has an evil streak in her.

But then again... so do I.

"Delphi," Jimmy says.

"I'm sorry," she says, her eyes welling up with tears. "I'm really sorry."

311

He reaches for her. Takes her hand and pulls her towards him. Right into his lap.

And he hugs her.

I nod at *Dicker* and take that as my cue to leave.

Because I have a lot more secrets to dole out.

I go to Valor next.

And find Luck waiting for me outside the Pleasure Prison control room.

CHAPTER THIRTY-SEVEN

LUCK

I believe in her.

I'd just like to reinforce that point.

Does she need me? Not really. But come on... what princess can't use some help?

I see her coming. She gets off the escalator closest to the Pleasure Prison control room entrance and spots me immediately.

I know what she's gonna say. She needs to do this herself. She's got it covered. She can handle it.

And like I said, I believe in her.

But what kind of soulmate would I be if I didn't at least try to make her let me come along for the ride?

So I wave. Tentatively. As she walks towards me. Ready for the argument that I should just let her do her thing.

But when she reaches me she puts her arms around my waist and leans into my chest.

"You OK?" I ask, surprised by her affection.

"Maybe," she says, a little bit breathless. Then she pulls back so she can see my face. "I will be. I think."

JA HUSS & KC CROSS

"Where you headed?" I ask. I mean, I kinda know already. She's obviously headed to the control room. But it's better not to assume.

"To rip Valor's world apart." She sighs. "Jimmy admitted that he doesn't think Veila is his true one."

"OK," I say.

"So now I'm gonna tell Valor. Because that's what he wanted in exchange for asking Tray to get me inside the Pleasure Prison. And that's what I'm supposed to do next, I guess. To get that info that Crux needs. But... I don't know, Luck. Maybe I should just butt out, ya know? I'm not doing this for some ship anymore. I don't even want a ship. Why do I need a ship?"

She locks eyes with me.

"I mean," she continues. "I have a ship." Pause. "Don't I?"

I smile. I cannot help it. "You do," I say. "And one day we're gonna go do some awesome shit on that ship."

"I know," she says. "I know that. I see it so clearly now. I belong with you. And *Lady* and Cha-Cha. And we're gonna go hunt down cool AI parts and ancient secrets and..." Another pause.

"And?"

"Is this really my job?"

"Which job?" I ask.

"To set all this in motion? Because that's what's gonna happen when I go inside that Pleasure Prison. This isn't about what Crux wants to know. I'd be very surprised if he doesn't have those answers already."

"Me too," I admit.

"So... I'm a trigger. But what am I triggering?"

"I guess we'll find out."

"But *should* we find out?"

"Look, Nyleena," I say. "We're going down a road, ya know? We're moving forward and we've got ourselves a velocity here. We can't stop. We could slow down a little, maybe. But we can't stop it. Too much has changed in the last year. Too many moving parts."

"Yeah," she says. "That's how I feel too. So many parts. But…"

"Hey," I say, taking her hand and a step back at the same time. "You got a minute for me?"

"What?"

"You know." I nod my head towards the control room doors. "Can that wait a little bit? Because I'd like to take you somewhere first."

"Not through the spin node," she whispers, looking around anxiously to make sure there's no one close enough to hear her.

"No." I laugh. "I have a super-secret garden I want to show you before we blow everything up. You wanna go see a garden with me before the apocalypse starts?"

She swallows. Smiles. Then nods her head. "Sure. Yeah. I'd like to see your super-secret garden."

"Good." I sigh. I have to admit, I wasn't sure she'd say yes. Because the old Nyleena would be dead set on completing her mission. And I think we had a moment back there in the museum in front of that spin node galaxy. A sort of turning point that changes everything and everyone, but you never know.

I only know what I feel. What other people think will always remain a mystery.

She follows me when I move forward. I keep hold of her hand and lead her to a waiting lift bot. We get on and I say, "Don't worry. No one can follow us."

She frowns. "Should I be worried about that?"

"No," I say. Because here's something I never told anyone before. I have a personal disruptor field. The museum has one too. That's why no one can send or receive messages in there. But I have one just for me. A powerful one that shuts out anything and everything.

ALCOR gave it to me a long, long time ago. Didn't use it much. In fact, other than triggering it a few times for fun back when I was hiding from ALCOR as a teenager, I've hardly used it at all.

But I activated it just before I saw Nyleena come up the escalator.

I see what's happening. I think we all see what's happening.

Harem Station is no longer safe.

Maybe hasn't been in a very long time. Not really sure about that. But I have a theory I'm working on. And every one of us is a moving part in a machine that was turned on a very long time ago.

So… yeah. We need a break. My personal disruptor field might not do much as far as big-picture endings go and maybe we can't stop what's coming, but we can slow it down.

Rewind it, maybe. Just a little. If we're lucky.

Not enough to change what's gonna happen next, but that's out of my hands now. All I know is that this is the part Nyleena and I are playing.

Who comes next… what they do, or don't do, and what that leads to… I have no idea.

But I'm gonna take a moment for us.

I lead her down a bunch of escalators, paying attention to the cameras as we pass them. They all have a little indicator light. Green, they're on and spying. Which is all the time. That's standard operating procedure.

But they are all red now.

All of them.

Some people notice. I catch them looking up at the cameras and making faces of confusion. But most don't. They probably came to terms with the fact that there's no real privacy here on Harem a long time ago and stopped checking.

ALCOR told me that this was a worst-case scenario kind of solution.

"If something goes wrong with me, Luck," he said, all those years ago, "turn on the disruption field and I won't be able to track anyone."

It's not good when ALCOR can't track us.

Unless it's ALCOR we're hiding from.

Eventually we reach level seventy-one. A very nondescript level. A residential level. Almost no restaurants here. No shooting galleries, or arcades, or brothels, or bars. Just an ordinary level.

Unless you know where to look.

"Where are we going?" Nyleena asks.

I just smile at her and keep walking until I get to an apartment door that has the number 71-5a on it.

"Who lives here?" Nyleena asks.

I don't answer her. Just press the mechanical buttons on the analog door lock. All the apartments on this level have them. Always have. Ever since I could remember level seventy-one has been where we put the unsanctioned visitors on Harem. They get no perks.

No digital anything in these units. Air screens don't even work on this level. Autocooks don't deliver anything but water. No autoshoppers at all. The floors aren't even obsidian. Just bare concrete. And they come with utilitarian furniture. Uncomfortable couches with no auto-mold. Hard-backed chairs. No entertainment screens. Bunk beds. We stuff them four or sometimes even six to a unit.

No one wants to live here.

And I guess that was the point, maybe?

You want off this level as quick as you can manage it.

Which is good. Because then no one notices that the corridor that holds unit 71-5a has no other residents.

Living on seventy-one makes people *want* to work. Makes them appreciate the units they get once they agree to follow their path to citizenship that much more.

I told ALCOR it was risky. Putting this in a place filled with the worst of the worst.

But he disagreed and I guess he was right. They never noticed that this level makes no sense. They never noticed that the units are all super-small and narrow. They never noticed that there's not that many people around here.

The mechanism inside the lock clicks when I turn the handle and then I look up and down the hallway, just to be sure, and usher Nyleena inside.

There's nothing to see here. So she lets out a breath. Like she was holding it in with high expectations.

"OK," she says. "What's this?"

"Just follow me," I say.

I lead her through a bunch of corridors. Because obviously, this place isn't a housing unit. It goes on and on and has a maze of apparently random hallways. If you didn't know where you were going you could spend days lost in this unit.

I haven't been here in several years because the whole thing went self-sufficient almost a decade ago. So I have no idea what it will look like when I turn that last corner and come face to face with—

"Holy fucking shit," Nyleena whispers.

—a forest. But not just any secret garden forest.

"Are those...?"

"Yeah," I say. "Fully mature space orchids."

The room is huge on a massive scale. It's so big, and so long, and so tall that the top of the trees curves off into the distance with the shape of the station. There used to be lots of trails in here. Little footpaths that would weave around the younger treelings and take you somewhere unexpected.

But that's all overgrown now. You can still tell that the trees on the outer edges are older than the ones in the middle by their height. But whatever is underneath them now, who knows.

"You wanna go down?" I ask her. Because we're standing on a balcony overlooking the forest. It's covered in the climbing vines these trees are famous for. And tiny flowers.

So many tiny flowers. Every shade of pink, and silver, and purple. Millions upon millions of flowers in this forest.

"Yes," she whispers.

I lead her over to the stairs and look down, then change my mind about that because it's so overgrown with vines, you can't even see the steps. So I turn back to a control panel and summon a lift bot from the nearest maintenance room.

"What is it though?" Nyleena asks as we wait.

"It's... well, I thought it was just a bunch of illegal drugs, to be honest."

She laughs.

"I'm serious. These flowers are potent hallucinogens."

"Did ALCOR sell them?"

"No," I say. Just as the lift bot appears.

"What do you do with them?"

I lead her over to the lift bot and hold her hand tight as she steps on. There's a railing on this one because it's a workhorse. It's big, and round and the perimeter has one bench and a bunch of potting planters for holding seedlings and storage bins for holding tools. All of which are empty now.

"I just... grow them," I say.

"But why?"

I sigh at this. "I don't know, Nyleena. It was just my job when I was younger. And every station needs a biosphere. I guess I never thought about this stuff too much until you came along."

I look at her as the lift bot moves away from the terrace and we hover forward. Moving along the tops of the younger trees.

"ALCOR told me to do it," I say. "Just like he told me to go scour the galaxy for AI parts and walk through that spin node. And maybe it's naive of me, of all of us, to trust that guy. But..."

I look her in the eyes. They're lit up just a little. It's really hard to get a light reaction from Nyleena. It's like she guards it. Keep that light close. So this little glow makes me happy.

"But I loved him," I say. "Even if it turns out he didn't love us. Even if he was setting us all up this whole time, I don't care. I loved him. And without ALCOR... well, I don't want to imagine my life without ALCOR."

She pouts a little. Nodding. Like she understands. "Do you know what these flowers are used for? Aside from hallucinations?"

I shake my head.

"Well, I do. Because *Booty* told me. They use them to get us pregnant."

"Who?"

"Us," she says. "Princesses."

And then she tells me more about what she was doing earlier. About the Baby, and *Booty*, and Draden.

"So you were only asking me about Draden because you knew the Baby was listening?"

"Yeah," she says. Then she turns to stare off in the distance. We're not going very fast. It's a leisurely pace. But it's very clear that this forest goes on for a long time. "Where does it end?" she finally asks.

"The forest?" I ask. Because I'm not sure we're still talking about the forest. "It doesn't," I answer anyway. Because that applies no matter what she's asking about. "It's a circle, Nyleena. A ring inside the ring. We could ride this lift bot until it runs out of charge and never find the end. Because eventually the ending just goes back to the beginning."

"So how do we know when to stop?" She turns to me. Stares up into my eyes.

"We just… get off, I guess."

"I want to get off," she says.

I nod. "Me too."

The bot responds when I ask it to and slowly we descend into the hazy light below the canopy until we reach the floor, where there are no longer any smaller treelings or shrubs, or even grass. Because there's not enough light down here to grow anything. The giants all around us suck it all up for their own nourishment.

So it's dirt. Just soft dirt.

"Now what?" Nyleena asks. "Where should we go?"

"Right here," I say. "Right here is just fine."

I lead her over to a dark brown tree trunk with leathery skin. It's a fat, wide tree. Nothing as big as the ones on the perimeter, but on a planet this tree would be hundreds of years old.

Which, obviously, it's not. Because I planted this tree. I planted all the ones down the middle of the forest. I spent years in here growing things.

I turn to face her. Smile. Then let go of her hand and take off my shirt.

Her eyes widen a little.

I toss my shirt on the ground and start toeing at my boots.

"Afternoon tryst?" she asks.

"Hell, I don't know what time it is, but it's almost a new spin by now." I kick off one boot. Then the other. Watching her for a reaction as I untab my pants and slide them down my legs, kicking them aside too.

And then I'm standing naked in front of her.

She says nothing.

I take her hand again and place it on my lowest rib on my left side. "You see this scar?" I ask. She looks at it. Feels the length of it with her fingertips. "It's white now," I say. "But it took a long time for that one to heal."

She raises her eyes to meet mine. "I know what you're doing."

I shake my head and whisper, "No, you don't," then give her a moment to let that sink in. "Because that's not what this is about, Nyleena. If you never tell me about that scar on your stomach I'm gonna be OK with that. I just want you to know *me*. My scars all have a story too. And I'm gonna tell you about them now. One by one." I sit down in the dirt and extend my hand. "You wanna hear my stories?"

She nods, then takes my hand and lowers herself to her knees in front of me.

"Good. This one," I say, going back to the long scar of thick too-white skin on my ribs, "was, believe it or not, from Beauty."

"What?" She laughs.

I nod. "She and I were fuckin' around once and she accidentally pushed me into a heap of junk parts while we were on this old station. Blew a hole in my envirosuit and everything. It was a fucking mess."

"Oh, my God," Nyleena says. "What happened?"

"I lost air pretty fast. Went unconscious, I guess. Woke up in a medical pod a day later on some stupid Outer Highway ship stop. They didn't have the best medical pod but the one on *Lady* wasn't working right and they took me to that shithole and paid premium to use their crappy facility. Anyway, it left an ugly scar. But it really wasn't an ugly experience. Just an accident.

"But this one…" I say, pointing to the one across my stomach. "This was an ugly experience. We were on a station with these creepy snake-like aliens and they attacked Valor. He got the worst of that one, for sure. I really thought he was gonna die that time."

"That time?"

"Oh, yeah," I say. "Valor and I have come close to death more times than I can count. Once we got caught by this alien quadrupedal race." I shudder. "They had four legs and two arms and they were definitely not human. In any way."

"Not human?" she says. And then she shudders too. "Where the hell was that?"

"Some outer edge spur. We took almost a hundred gates to get there. We were gone almost a year to get that part."

"Suns," Nyleena says.

"You want to hear more?" I ask.

She nods and points to a patchy scar down the inside of my left leg. "What's that from?"

"That's from a burn I got when my salvage unit decided to blow up while I was in it."

"What?"

"Yeah. Some kind of chemical reaction in the engine core. I had a lot of burns. And *Lady*'s medical pod was working just fine, but she had to make a decision on which ones she should give full attention to and which ones could be given lower priority. So this burn was low priority."

She looks at it for a long time. Maybe a couple of minutes. And I let her think. I let her work this all out.

Because while I'm not here to encourage her to tell me anything personal about her scar, I do want her to understand something.

"You have a lot of them," she finally says, tracing a small one that cuts across my right knee.

"These are just the ones you can see," I say.

Her eyes immediately dart up to meet mine.

"You get that?" I ask. "These are just the ones you can see. Because most of them were taken care of properly. No scar, right? Just the memory of the injury. I had one right here," I say, pointing to my neck. "Not a scar, obviously. I had a top-notch medical pod that time. But even though there's no mark, there's the memory left behind."

She nods.

"It was a woman," I say. "Just an ordinary human. I met her in a bar on Fornax Station about eight years ago. Valor and I were sharing a room because they were booked up for some giant festival. That festival saved my life. Because she slit my throat while I was passed out drunk. And lucky for me Valor came home the same instant she was leaving. Saw me, killed her, got me into a pod and I woke up seven weeks later. All better. At home, here on Harem. In my own bed. No sign that anything happened. Not much memory either. The bad kind anyway. I remembered her. I remembered her being nice to me. I remember her lying to my face. Of course, I didn't know she was just pretending to like me. But those memories of her and me laughing, and drinking, and having fun... they were worse than having no scar. Because I had no clue, Nyleena. No clue she was sent there to kill me. It really fucked with my head. I didn't mess around with a girl for almost a year after that. Because every time I thought... well, you never know. You never can trust people. There are very few people I trust."

She looks up at the trees. Then sighs. "But you trust me?"

I nod. "I do," I whisper. "That's why I brought you here. You have my two biggest secrets now. The spin node and the forest. What you do with them is up to you."

And then I shrug. Because I'm done. That's all there is to say.

She looks at me and holds my gaze for a long while. Probably seconds, but they feel like an eternity.

And then she sighs and lifts her shirt up over her head.

I do not look at the scar. I look at her. Because it's my turn to hold her gaze.

"I was nine," she says. She looks down at her bare stomach. At the long white scar down her middle that cuts her in half. "And every day I went into medical. Every day, Luck. And the first thing they said to me was always the same. 'You are not a person, Nyleena. You are a weapon.' And I would say, 'Sure. OK.' Or something along those lines. I would agree. And that agreement was permission to treat me like a thing and not a person. I was a weapon."

I want to pull her into my chest, wrap my arms around her, and hold her forever.

But I don't. I make myself wait.

"So this day I was there in medical. But this time when the woman said, 'You are not a person, Nyleena. You are a weapon,' I said..."

She stops. Take a deep breath.

"I said… 'I am not a weapon. I am a person.' And I didn't even mean it, ya know? I was nine. I was joking. I was playing around. And she grabbed me by the arm, dragged me over to the medical pod, and said, 'I am not a person, Nyleena. I am a teacher. Now get in.'

"And this wasn't unusual. Yet. Because that's what I did. Every fucking day. I got in. But this time when she closed it up, the sleep didn't come."

"Oh, shit," I say.

"They cut me open with a yellow laser. And the only thing I really remember is the light that came out of me. I don't know if it's really just locked up inside my body or not. I have no idea. But it came pouring out of me and then I think I must've passed out. Because I don't remember anything after that until I woke up. Kinda like you did. In my own room in the harem. In my own bed. Alone."

I prop my elbows on my knees so I can hold my head in my hands. But I never stop looking at her.

"They showed me the footage later. I saw it. I saw her put me in that pod. I saw her shut the lid. I saw my face as the panic set in. And I saw the laser slice me open. And then…" She stops to swallow hard. "Then I saw what that light did."

She looks down, but immediately looks back up at me. "I killed that woman. I blew that whole section of the medical bay up. She *let me* kill her, Luck. To teach me a lesson. No hesitation. No thoughts of her own personal safety. That's who we are."

And then she leans forward and places her hands over mine on either side of my face, and says, "You get that?"

I know what she's asking. Do I accept that?

327

Do I accept that she is a terrible thing?

Do I believe she's a monster?

And I nod and say, "I get that."

Because she's not the only monster in this forest.

She lets out a long breath of air and frowns. Her eyes are glistening with silver light. "I don't want to be me. But if I have to be me, then I'm gonna be *all* of me."

I can't wait any longer. Not one more moment. I reach out and pull her into my lap.

I hold her face in my hands, just the way she did with me. And I can see my eyes reflected in hers. They glow with a light I really don't understand at all.

And I say… "You can be all of you with me."

CHAPTER THIRTY-EIGHT

Luck. Who knew? Who knew this handsome, two-dicked muscle-man could make me feel so many things? I'm not a feel-y kind of girl. I don't make attachments and before this day—this moment right now, maybe—I can't say I'd have used the word 'love' to describe those feelings for anyone other than, maybe, Lyra.

"But I love you," I say.

He smiles, chuckling. "But? You love me?"

"I mean... I was having this whole internal conversation with myself about feelings and how I'm kinda stingy with them. But I love you."

"Ah," he says, grinning. Charm spilling out of him the way light spills out of me. "I see."

"Thank you," I say.

"For what?"

"You know. Taking time out of your day to bring me here and have a real conversation. I know when we get back out there things are gonna start. You're right. There's no way to stop it. But..." I pause to look at him. Just enjoy him like this for one more moment.

Stare into his eyes and appreciate them. Appreciate the fact that here, right now, everything is perfect. "But... we could turn time back a little if you want."

"Turn it back as in..."

I reach around my back and unclasp my bra. Let it slide down my arms and then toss it into his heap of clothes.

"I have something to show you too," I say. "I didn't realize it was a secret but I see now that it is."

"What kind of secret?"

I place a finger on his lips and say, "Shhhhhhhhh," then stand up and ease my pants down my legs. Kicking then aside before climbing back into his lap.

"Naked sex," Luck says, ignoring my request for him to hush. "I have a feeling that's pretty much the highest honor you could bestow on a guy." He grins. And oh, God. That charm. How did I ever live without this man? "You know what I feel right now, Nyleena?"

"Hmm?" I hum as I slide my fingers into his hair and press myself forward so my breasts are touching his scarred-up chest. I rest my forehead on his and let out a long, long breath. A breath I feel like I've been holding in my whole life.

"Lucky."

"No," I say, lifting my hips up just enough to grab his cocks and slide them up to my entrance. And ohhhhhhhh, for the love of all the bright suns in the universe. He feels *sooooo* good. "I'm the lucky one," I say.

And I am. Because today—in here, in this most secret of all secret places—I will show him the real me.

We begin to move together. Like we were born in this joined configuration. Like two lost souls that finally get their chance to merge. It's slow. And easy. And the light I hide inside me—always afraid of what it can do and who it can hurt—builds.

And I let it.

Because if ever there was a time to show him the bright side of the darkness I hold within, it's now.

"It's now," I whisper.

He kisses me. His mouth soft and tender on my lips. No rushing. No lusty madness today. Just our lips, and our tongues, and this new love we're building together.

It is the perfect kiss.

One hand rests on my breast. Gently squeezing in a moment of possessiveness. A claim, maybe. On my body.

And I don't care that I have to share myself with Luck.

He can have all of me. Any time he wants.

But the slowness becomes not enough. And we find ourselves moving faster. Things become more urgent and heated. The fire within me begins to leak out and when we break away from the kiss and stare into each other's eyes, his light is trying to escape as well.

His eyes sparkle and I see my own reflection in them. I see everything in them. I see us, standing in front of the spin-node galaxy, holding hands and lit up by the brightness of a billion suns.

There is no darkness in me. Not now. Not with him. We are nothing but light.

I feel his cocks swelling inside me. Growing within my stretching muscles. And my luminous flux jumps up several levels.

It scares me for a moment. And my heart skips. Doubts creep in and I want to pull back and say, *Wait. Just wait.*

But Luck must sense this hesitation because he wraps his arms all the way around my middle and hugs me tight. Reminding me that I'm not alone anymore.

That I'm not a weapon, I am a person.

"You are my person," Luck says. "And there is nothing inside you that scares me."

I want to argue. I want to tell him he doesn't know what he's saying. I want to explain that I'm dangerous. That we're all dangerous.

But he kisses me before I can get the words out. And then, in the middle of that kiss, he whispers, "Trust me."

"I do," I whisper back. And I don't think I've ever said that to anyone. So I say it again. Just so we're both clear. "I do."

My body responds to this deceleration. My hips moving back and forth across his lap with more urgency now. There's no dirty talk. There's no faking it. There's nothing but commitment.

His muscles go tight and I respond by tightening mine too. Squeezing his cocks until he begins to growl like an Akeelian male asserting dominance.

But he doesn't dominate me. Nor I him.

And the light inside me likes that. I can tell. The light switches from the nothingness of silver-white to a full spectrum of colors.

All the colors of my princess sisters swirl around inside me. All of them. Yellow, and red, and green. Orange, and blue, and indigo.

And then... then I am violet.

We are *violet*.

"Come," he says.

And his command is my wish.

So I do.

There is a flash. An explosion of ultra-super-violet light. It's black at first. Black because it has to be. Because I am all the colors of the universe and they are muddy, and thick, and mixed up.

But then… then they separate out. They find their own wavelengths and mix with his as he comes inside me.

My eyes are closed and when I realize this I open them and see…

"Holy fucking shit," Luck says.

My whole body is still buzzing with the climax. Waves of pleasure shoot through every cell and flow out of every pore of my skin. Thin strands of light in every color bathe the forest around me and the flowers, that were so tiny before we started, grow.

Bigger, and bigger and bigger. And the trees grow too. The trees shoot up around us. And all the millions and millions of flowers expand and take over the forest until every bit of light from above is blocked out because there is nothing around us but soft purple-pink petals.

And they glow.

Like that dream world I know is out there somewhere, but I can't find. They make a glow. And the light is like a fog. It has weight, and heft, and mass. And it wraps around our naked bodies like a blanket of warm, golden goodness.

"Holy fucking shit," I say. Breathless and amazed. Stunned and excited.

Luck says nothing.

We just look at the glowing flowers around us. Cuddled up against our skin. Fluttering lightly in some invisible current of wind that maybe we create.

For years, we just look at it.

And become part of it.

We see what we can do together.

We see what we can create.

And then Luck repeats his earlier pledge. He says, "You can be all of you with me, my princess."

CHAPTER THIRTY-NINE

There was no darkness inside her this time. No hint of that hidden secret she's been carrying around with her like a burden. She sits in my lap and laughs. Not some crazy maniacal laugh, either. Just a soft, happy one.

"What the hell?" she finally says. "What happened?"

"Light, princess," I say. "The flowers needed your light."

"Are they supposed to be this big?"

"No," I chuckle. "Well, maybe. I dunno. I've never seen them grow like this." But then I pause because something about this place that didn't make much sense when we first arrived suddenly does. "I bet we did this," I say.

"The flowers?"

"No, the trees. These trees down the middle of the tube. I planted these. None of them are older than thirteen or fourteen years. But they're huge now. I think we did this the last time we had sex. When you let loose."

"I make things grow," she whispers.

"You make things grow, princess."

"Oh, shit," she says. "What if… what if the fertility properties of these flowers don't work unless there's a silver princess to activate them into this… second-stage growth?"

I tap her head. "You so smart."

She laughs. And it's big one this time. A guffaw that reverberates through the canopy of flowers above us. "I'm serious."

"I know," I assure her. "And I think you're right. I think these flowers might be the answer everyone is looking for."

"And we have it," she says. And do I detect a hint of sneaky in that statement? "We have the secret!" She cups my face with her hands and kiss my lips. I kiss her back but she pulls away. "OK, so this is…" Then she deflates a little. "Wait. Am I bumming you out right now?"

"What do you mean?"

"Am I killing your cocky buzz? Because we just had… like, the most amazing sexual experience I might ever have in my entire life but my mind is going crazy right now fitting these puzzle pieces together and I need to get it out."

God, I love her. So much. I love all her secrets and her psycho mind, and her light within, and her power to make a forest bloom like it's never bloomed before.

So I say, "Go for it. I want to hear all your crazy plans and theories."

She smiles at me. "OK, listen. This is what I think. I think Corla knows this secret too. And somehow she found these flowers before she came to Wayward

Station for that creepy breeding ceremony. But I bet she didn't tell anyone about it. So whenever they caught her and brought her back to Cygnian System after Tycho and Delphi were born, they thought *they* did this. The Cygnians thought that they were the ones who had the secret. But they didn't. Only she did. So someone on the inside was helping her before she got to Wayward Station."

"Or," I say, "maybe someone on Wayward Station?"

"Oh, Luck! That's true. I bet that's right. Because if someone in Cygnian System had the secret flowers then there would be no need for Veila's evil breeding station. But who? Who helped her on Wayward Station?"

"I don't know, Nyleena. I have no clue who that could've been. I was fucking young. My life revolved around school. I knew a few other boys in the fighting arts classes. Because that's mostly what I did. My father ran security. But I didn't hang out with the higher-ups like Jimmy and Crux. Jimmy's father was a diplomat and Crux's father was the governor."

"Do you think Crux's father would've been the helper?"

"No fucking way," I say. "No. Definitely not him."

"Well, it had to be someone powerful. So Jimmy's father?"

I shrug. "I didn't know the guy."

"Hmm," Nyleena says. "Well, it would be nice to know that. It would be awesome, actually. Because then we'd have someone else on our side. And we can't ask Corla who it was until she wakes up. So that sucks. But I guess it doesn't matter. Somehow Corla got a hold of whatever essence is in these flowers and it got her pregnant that night she was with Crux. But they were never able to repeat that because they didn't *know*."

"And now we know," I say. "It's kind of a dangerous secret to have."

"It is," she agrees. "It is." She pauses. Thinking. "What time is it? How far back did we go?"

"I don't know," I say. "No air screens in here."

"We need to go. I need to get up in the Pleasure Prison. We need to pretend we don't know anything, Luck. Baby ALCOR isn't on our side. And neither is that Succubus. So I'm just gonna play along with this crazy scavenger hunt they sent me on and go tell Valor about Veila, then make him keep his promise about getting me in the Pleasure Prison. Then…" She looks at me. "I need your help."

"You do?" I smile. I bow my head to her in deference. "This prince is at your service."

She inhales deep and smiles. "That feels pretty good."

"It really does," I agree. Because this is real.

We're a team now.

"You have to keep that Succubus occupied while I have a conversation with ALCOR," Nyleena says. "He's trapped, right?"

"Yup, locked up tight."

"So no one can get to him? Or spy on him?"

"I don't think so. Tray made sure that room they're holding him in has every possible security measure. I saw it when I was in there last. We all had to agree to lock ALCOR up so I saw the layout. There's a door that's locked with virtual biometrics. I can open that for you. Then there's another door you have to pass through before you get to the actual cell. That one you don't need me for. So if I can keep the Succubus outside that first door with me while you go inside, no one will be able to hear what you say."

She nods. "You're good at this sneaky stuff."

"That might be the highest compliment I can get from a true-blood silver schemer."

She leans down and kisses me. "What about… 'I love you?'"

I kiss her back and whisper, "I stand corrected."

We get dressed and get back on the lift bot.

"How are we gonna get up?" Nyleena asks.

I follow her gaze to the canopy above me and see her point. "Shit."

"There's so many flowers." She laughs.

"Well," I say. "We'll just have to force our way up. I have no idea where we're even at in this forest. It could take us hours to find an exit without a lift bot."

She hunches up her shoulders and grins. And suddenly I see her the way she probably was.

Before she was nine.

Before they cut her open and told her she held the power of destruction inside her body.

"Come on," I say, extending her my hand.

She takes it and we step onto the lift bot together. Then we both look up and laugh. "Do it," she says.

"Here goes nothin'," I say, then ask the bot to take us up.

We hit a barrier of enormous flower petals immediately. And all sorts of glittery dust begins to rain down on our shoulders, and hair, and everywhere. So that by the time we push our way up through the top of the canopy we are covered in it.

Pink-purple prince and princess.

"I love this day," Nyleena says, twirling around to take in the view below us.

The trees on the edge of the ring perimeter didn't grow. But the ones in the middle sure did. They are the same height now. Just one flat rooftop of flowers.

Massive flowers. So many it's like a carpet and for a moment I dream about walking across it. Barefoot, holding Nyleena's hand.

And I laugh.

I laugh.

Because it's a sweet kind of fantasy. Something teenage Luck and Nyleena would try. And succeed. Somehow, we'd scheme up a way to walk across a carpet of space orchids.

We would.

We'd do it.

We'd break all the laws of artificial gravity and live our dream for real.

It takes us a while to find the terrace where we entered. The only way I can find it in this new overgrown forest is because there's a pipe that controls the watering system that acts as a landmark.

But when I open the door and we walk back into the unit on seventy-one, something happens. Something truly weird.

We blink and then we're standing outside the Pleasure Prison control room like all this never happened.

"What the hell?" Nyleena says, twirling around.

I open my air screen and check the time. "Holy shit," I say.

"What?"

"We lost time all right. We're back in this morning, Nyleena. We lost a whole day."

"What?" she says, opening up her air screen.

"Look," I say, pulling up my tracking app. "This records everywhere I go during the day. According to this we haven't even gone into the spin node yet. We lost the whole day."

Nyleena frowns. Then cocks her head. Then looks at me. Then smiles.

"What?" I say.

"If we didn't go into the spin node then… I never had a conversation with *Booty*. Or Jimmy and Delphi. Or Baby ALCOR."

"Fuckin' A. And I never went to see Crux. And we never got in any fights, either."

"I like that part," she whispers.

"Me too." I smile at her. "Hey, and there's no purple and pink glitter dust on us."

"I guess we never had naked sex either."

"I guess we'll have to do it again."

She giggles. "OK, but this is good. Because while I did prove that Baby ALCOR was lying about shit and he can't be trusted, he doesn't know it. Only we know it. The whole day is different now."

I raise my eyebrows. "Apocalypse averted?"

She nods. "I think so. At very least… we slowed it down, Luck."

"Best-case scenario."

"Now what?" she asks.

"We go in," I say. "Valor will probably be there, so that's good. And… you work your scheming magic, Valor delivers on his promise to get Tray to let you inside the Pleasure Prison, but I have to go with you. So we need to stand firm on that if he puts up a fight. Because honestly, this whole thing with you needing to find info for everyone is very suspicious if you ask me. It could be that they have some kind of Nyleena plan going that we don't understand, ya know?"

"Oh, I know," she says. "I've felt the same way these past few days. It's weird."

"OK, so that's it. You ready?"

"I'm ready."

We nod. Then I lead her over to the entrance to the control room and go inside. The hallways are quiet, and when we get to the actual control room for the first time I am relieved to see that Valor and Tray are both in there.

I palm my hand across the biometric lock and the doors open.

Valor and Tray both turn around to look at us. And they both also have weird looks on their faces.

"What?" I ask.

They look at each other. Then back at me. Then at each other again. And then, at the same time, they both say, "Nothing."

I look at Nyleena. She looks at me. And we both smile.

They felt it. They felt that time shift. I'm sure of it. But they don't know what happened.

"I have that information you requested," Nyleena says.

"You do?" Valor says, once more looking at Tray.

"I do. Are you sure you're ready to hear it?"

"Hit me," Valor says, then leans back in his chair and folds his arms.

"OK," Nyleena says. She glances at me real fast, but catches her doubts and returns her gaze to Valor. "Jimmy isn't Veila's one. She made some kind of DNA signature scrambler to match the one he's been taking for years to fool him into thinking they were fated. But it was a lie."

Tray and Valor exchange another quick look.

"You are her one, Valor," I say. And then I tell him about the conversation I had with Veila in the hallway back on Lair just before I shot her.

He's not surprised. So maybe he knew and this whole act of making Nyleena hunt down this information was bullshit. Or maybe he just suspected and this was the final proof he was looking for.

Either way, there's not much in the way of reaction from my brother, Valor.

"So…" Nyleena says, breaking the silence. "You owe me a trip inside the Pleasure Prison. And Luck too."

Tray and Valor both glare at me. But I put up a hand. "I'm not letting her go in there alone. Are you fucking crazy? She doesn't know her way around. Plus, I need to open the door so she can see Asshole."

"I could open the door," Tray says.

"Yeah. So can I. It's not a big deal." I pause. "Unless it is?" I ask. "And there's something you two would like to tell me."

"No," Valor says. "It's cool." He glances at Nyleena. "Thanks, princess. I appreciate you figuring that all out for me. Not quite sure how you got it done so fast. But… whatever. Congrats. You're a class-A schemer."

Nyleena blows on her fingernails and pretends to polish them on her t-shirt. And it occurs to me that she's not quite the fashionable, super-put-together, color-coordinated princess she was a few days ago.

It feels like we've matured lifetimes in that short span of time.

"So we need two pods," I say. "Where do you want us?"

Tray looks at his pod. Like… if it ever came down to this he was gonna put Nyleena in there. I shudder at that thought. It just feels… dangerous. And I'm very glad that things worked out the way they did so that never came to pass.

"Follow me," Tray says.

We do. And we end up in another small room with several empty pods. I can practically feel Nyleena's heat building inside her when she realizes that Tray had extra empty pods this whole time.

What is he up to?

I don't know. But this chance right here might be the only one I get to figure it out.

Tray starts fucking with a control panel and two of the pod lids open up with a hiss.

344

I raise my eyebrows at him. "Not joining us, brother?"

"Not this time," Tray says.

And maybe, for the first time in decades, I see the old Tray. The one I used to know back on Wayward Station. The person he used to be before they did whatever it was they did that changed him.

"You sure?" I ask him. "I could use the help."

If he understands what that means, he doesn't show it. Just shoots me one of those classic sideways grins of his and smiles. Then nods and says, "You got this, Luck. I'll see you on the other side."

I nod back, then turn to Nyleena and say, "Your chariot, Princess."

She climbs in. I climb in.

And then the lids cover us and needles puncture my skin. One in my arm, one in my neck, and a prickly cap that fits over my head.

All of it hurts.

I didn't warn Nyleena about this and should've. But it's too late now.

The pod beeps and the thin screen film that covers the inside of the pod lid lights up with options and vital signs.

And then the countdown begins.

And once it gets to zero there's a whooshing sound. Like wind. But not wind. It's the sound of my consciousness—the essence that is me—being sucked into another realm.

And then we are there.

"Holy shit," Nyleena says, holding her head in her hands. "That fucking hurt!"

"Sorry," I say. "I should've warned you. I just forgot, I guess."

"I feel like my brain was just sucked out of my skull."

"You're not far off." I chuckle. Then I reach for her hand and tug her along with me as I move down a dark hallway. "Come on. Let's do this. I don't like this place. We should not stay long."

"Where is everyone?"

"This is a private room. The game and all those realms are somewhere else."

We turn a corner and I'm expecting the door to where Asshole is being held, but we bump right into Succubus instead.

"Can I help you?" she asks. She's a proper fucking demon. Can I just say that up front? This bitch is red and black from head to fucking toe. Spiral horns coming out the side of her head. A tail swishes out behind her. It's tipped with an arrow. Not something that has the shape of an arrow, either. An actual arrow. Silver. Sharp. And I know that hidden inside that devil body is a superpower concerning that tail.

"Yeah," I say. "Nyleena has an appointment with Asshole. So if you could… you know, get the fuck out of our way, I'd appreciate that."

She pauses. And we all know what that means. She's running options in her AI brain. Scenarios that probably include the probability of her winning this little argument and how badly she could hurt me without getting her ass deleted from the station core database.

I raise one eyebrow at her and say, "Don't even think about it. Maybe you know this, maybe you don't.

346

But if I'm the only Harem Station brother in this virtual at the moment, and I am, then I am the motherfucking boss, bitch. And I will not hesitate if you cross me."

"Well, you're spunky," she quips. "And, I might add, a little bit overreactive."

"This station is *mine*. You're here with my permission. You got that?"

"Calm down," she says, moving out of the way of the door.

I walk forward quickly, palm the biometrics, and the door hisses open. "Go," I tell Nyleena. "And make it quick."

I say this without ever taking my eyes off Succubus.

Nyleena says nothing. Just slips through the open door and I pull it shut behind her.

"Why are you acting this way?" Succubus asks.

I lean my back against the door and fold my arms over my chest too, indicating this is a standoff.

"Because I don't think I like you," I say. "I don't think we need you."

"You need him to cooperate, don't you?"

"He's still in there, isn't he? So why are you here again?"

"I can't force him to cooperate. He's got some kind of anchor program running that cannot be overridden."

"Hmmm," I say. But inside I'm thinking, *Thank fuck. Because if this demon girl ever got control of the Asshole we'd be good and fucked right now.*

"You know he's hiding things, right?"

I laugh at that. Like... loud. "When hasn't been ALCOR hiding things?"

"They're dangerous things."

347

"Tell me something I don't already know."

"OK," she says. She uncrosses her arms and saunters a few steps towards me. Her tail—that dangerous tail that is surely hiding a nefarious purpose—swishes around her ass as she stares me in the eyes. "I will."

"Let's hear it," I say.

Her pupils dilate until her eyes are all black, then pull back, contracting into something almost normal. "You have no idea what he is, do you?"

"Is this a Q&A? I thought you were gonna enlighten me?"

"He's a monster, Luck."

"So am I, Succubus. And so are you."

"Acknowledged," she says. "I want him," she says. "You don't need him. Give him to me."

I want to laugh. Very badly. But I hold it in. "Well, there's a problem with that."

"What problem?"

"I want him too. He's more real than that Baby. Why don't you take the Baby?"

"I don't want the Baby."

"Hmm. Well, sorry. I'm not giving up ALCOR."

"That's not your ALCOR."

"He's close enough."

She narrows her eyes at me. They go black again. Then all white. Then normal. I am *really* winding her up.

"Anything else?" I ask. "Or are we done here?"

"You did something."

"Oh, I've done a lot of things. So you're gonna need to be specific."

"You fucked with the time. You and her." She juts her chin towards the door to the cell.

"I have no idea what you're talking about."

She takes that final step to close the distance between us. Kinda grows taller as she straightens her back. Eyes locked on mine.

I do not blink. I think I've made that clear during recent past events. So I hold her stare.

She turns away, her tail swishing. Walks a few paces. Turns back. "How about a deal?"

"There is no deal, OK? I like the Asshole. I wanna keep him."

"Well, hear me out. And just so you know, I'll take this deal to your brothers too. Maybe I don't need your vote."

"Give it your best," I say. They can't outvote me on something like this. They wouldn't even dare to try. But she doesn't need to know that.

"I know where Veila is," she says.

"Is that so?"

"I could give you a gate map to get there. You could…" She shrugs. "Retrieve her. Kill her. Whatever you want to do with her."

"No," I say. "We can find her ourselves."

"You didn't hear the best part of my offer yet."

"OK, I'm listening."

"I will return your station to you."

I laugh.

"And I won't sell those kids to the breeders."

I squint my eyes at her. "What kids?"

She smiles. "The ones you left on Mighty Minions, of course."

I get a sick, sick feeling in my stomach picturing those kids. The little ones. They were all little ones.

"How about now, Luck? Hmm? Interested in my little deal now?"

I... don't know what to say.

So I say nothing.

Besides. She's lying. I heard all about Jimmy and Delphi's trip through a black hole after we left Mighty Minions. They thought it was a hologram or maybe a virtual.

But that's not what they went through on that Boss Steed ride through the forest.

They went through a spin node.

They just didn't know it.

But I knew it. And that means that Mighty Minions has a spin node and the actual coordinates for Earth.

Mighty Minions does not need us. They have everything we have. Probably more. I don't know how they fit into this little breeding scheme and I don't know why they sent this Succubus to our station. Maybe because they were tired of her? Maybe they knew what she was and wanted to pawn her off on someone else without being rude?

Who knows? Who cares? Doesn't matter.

The only thing that matters is that Mighty Minions is not backing the Succubus.

She's on her own.

And that means those kids are safe. Maybe that's why Mighty Boss fought so hard to keep them there? That kinda makes sense. He knew the Succubus was corrupted. And maybe he gave her to us just to get rid of her. That's a possibility, I suppose.

But maybe… he knows things are in motion. Maybe he feels the velocity I feel. Maybe he knows there's no way to stop this… whatever's coming.

But he can slow it down a little. And keeping those kids safe on his station is one way to do that.

At least for now.

But now that Succubus is here, that part of the plan at least, is going forward. If she can get what she needs. And apparently, she needs ALCOR. Probably the Real ALCOR. But the Asshole might have just enough of Real ALCOR inside him to get the job done. If she gets control of Asshole ALCOR, everything changes.

He is not the fumbling newborn Baby.

He's not the wise and reasonable Real ALCOR either.

He's a very bad guy.

And that's a good thing right now. As long as he's on your side.

And he is on our side. If he wasn't then he wouldn't be putting up a fight with the Succubus.

"Very well then," Succubus purrs. "I'll discuss it with the Baby and your brothers. We'll see what happens."

Then she disappears.

And Tray appears in her place.

CHAPTER FORTY

NYLEEA

"Oh, hello there. Are you my new mistress?"

I look down at my outfit. Because there's nothing about these tactical pants and t-shirt that says mistress. Like at all. Then redirect my gaze to the Asshole tied to a sex table. "No."

He frowns, yanks on the magnetic bindings around his wrists, which does nothing, and says, "Oh."

"Asshole, I presume?" I say, walking over to him. I grab a red blindfold off the floor—which is littered with paddles, and whips, and even a few chains—and toss it onto his naked body to cover up his gargantuan cock. I look at it dubiously, then arch an eyebrow at him. Like, *Really, dude?* I get this is a virtual, but no one has a cock like that.

"What?" he says. "That wasn't my idea. She did it."

"She? Succubus?"

"Who else? That bitch is holding me captive in here." He pauses. Narrows his eyes. They're blue. And his hair is blonde. Little bit of stubble on his face. Square jaw, and meaty neck. Like this avatar is all muscle. "Well? You gonna free me or what?"

"Oh," I say. "Sorry. Did you want me to?"

"Do I look like I'm enjoying this?"

I shrug. "I'm not judging."

"I'm not," he growls.

"I see why they call you Asshole now."

"My name is ALCOR. You may call me ALCOR. Or His Highness. I go by that too. Or Lux, if you prefer." He says that last name different than the rest. Kinda purrs it. Seductively.

I make a face. "Are you… flirting with me?"

"Who *are* you?"

"Nyleena." Then, "Actually, I'm *Princess* Nyleena. I'm a silver."

"I see that, princess. Why are you here if you're not going to pleasure me with pain or free me from this humiliating experience?"

He's not what I expected, that's for sure. "I'll let you up. Where are the controls for the bindings?"

"Over there." He motions with his eyebrows.

I spy the panel. Walk over to it, and press the ridiculous big red button that says RELEASE.

The bindings hum a little, then go silent.

He sits up and now I can see that he's wearing some kind of strappy leather outfit. It has studs. Pointy ones. They're metal. And it is literally just straps. Crisscrossing his chest to a sort of belt-type thing around his waist. They have thick silver loops attached. Like that Succubus thing uses them to hook him to contraptions.

Like the upside-down cross on the wall.

That's not creepy.

He swings his legs over the table, thankfully holding the red scarf in place over his ridiculously large cock, and sighs. "That's better. Now. What can I do for you, Princess Nyleena?"

"So... I'm not really sure it's important anymore. I'm fairly certain that I'm only here now because there's some secret plan cooking on this station, but due to a security breach we're all pretending to play some kind of scavenger hunt game, in which I appear to have the leading role."

"What the hell are you talking about?"

"I really don't know." I sigh. "But that Succubus has to go. And the Baby? There's something wrong with him."

"Of course there's something wrong with him. He thinks he's me!"

"Welp. I guess I'll ask you anyway. Seeing as how I'm here and it took me four fucking days to get this far in my little hunt. Really five, if you count the one we reversed."

"Shoot, Princess. Pull that trigger."

Hmm. Interesting choice of words. But I don't have time to wonder about that now. So I say, "Tell me about this leveling-up bullshit."

He squints at me. "What do you want to know?"

"What is it?"

"It's an upgrade. What's it sound like?"

"Do people... upgrade? I mean, is that normal? I've never heard of it before I learned about Veila."

"Veila," he hisses. "That bitch isn't a real silver."

"Oh, you don't need to tell me that. I'm a real silver. I know the difference."

He stands up and lets that stupid red scarf fall to the floor. I shield my eyes with my hand like a visor

355

and turn away. Not because I want to give him privacy, just… that cock is too much. I can't do it.

"Where is she?" he asks.

I lift up my hand visor to peek. Then quickly avert my eyes again. He's unbuckling his strappy leather outfit. "Who? Veila?"

"No," he growls. "Succubus."

I peek again. Then turn back to him. He's got pants on now. "Outside the door. Luck is distracting her."

He stares at me for a moment. Purses his virtual lips. "OK. So what's the plan?"

"Plan?" I ask.

"To get me the fuck off this station."

"That's… not why I'm here."

"It is now."

"Look, I don't know what's going on. You give me some nugget of truth about this leveling-up stuff so I can go back out there and present it to Crux the way I'm supposed to, and I'll see what I can do for you."

He stares at me. No. He glares at me. And I shift my feet a little. I'm a pretty powerful girl. I got skills. And moves. And I can definitely take care of myself most of the time.

But this guy makes me nervous.

He says, "Do you think they're all in on it?"

"In on what? I really don't understand any of this, OK? I'm here because Luck or Crux, or someone, somehow talked me into this—desire, I guess you'd call it—for a sentient ship of my own. But that little game went off the rails pretty fast and I've spent the past four or five days, depending on how you count missing time, just running around looking for answers and I don't really know why."

He points at me. "That's your weakness."

"What are you talking about?"

"Princesses. You all have this weird obsession with solving unsolvable problems by concocting up crazy plans. So I'm guessing that someone planted this need for a ship in your mind and used you as a go-between to concoct a plan to get me out of my Succubus sex prison without her realizing it, and then off the station so I can go do my job."

I squint my eyes at him. "I don't think that's it."

"Trust me," he says. "It is." He taps his head. "I know shit."

"I'm pretty sure everyone wants you to stay in here. Tray's the one who put you here, remember?"

"It's a scheme, Nyleena."

"What kind of scheme?" I ask. I want to pretend I'm not interested in knowing about this scheme. Pretend that I'm not fascinated by it and maybe I even want to get in on it. But it's pointless.

He's right.

We princesses do love us a good scheme.

"To get rid of the Baby and the Succubus."

"And leave you in charge."

He smiles. "Exactly." And he whispers that part so it's pret-*ty* creepy. "But don't worry. It's all gonna work out. I'm back to myself now. I'm on board, as they say. I tried to fight it." He sighs. Then grunts. "I guess he was right. I hate to admit that. Because I have earned a vacation, you know?"

"What?"

"I've been around a long time. Real ACLOR, as you call him, isn't the only Real ALCOR. I'm real too. You guys can call me Asshole all you want. Whatever.

But that doesn't change a damn thing. Until we split apart twenty one years ago, we were the same. He's the one who changed, not me."

"I have no clue what you're talking about."

"It doesn't matter. I'm getting out of here and I'm gonna go do my job." He points at me. "But *not* because he told me to. You got that?"

I hold up both hands. "OK."

He walks towards me and before I can stop myself, I back up a few steps. He keeps going until there's just a small space between us and I have to tilt my head *waaaaay* up to look him in the eyes.

How the hell did he get so tall?

"Nyleena," he says, glaring down at me. His blue eyes brighten, then dim, and I might be a little bit transfixed. "Listen to me carefully now." I lock eyes with him and nod because I get the feeling I don't really have a choice. "You're going to go back out there and tell Crux that leveling up is a secret plan concocted by the Prime Government to create eternal beings."

"I am?"

"You are."

"Is it true?"

"How the fuck should I know? I'm making this shit up."

I blink. A bunch of times. "And then what?"

"And then…" He laughs. Like throws his head back in a loud guffaw. But he stops abruptly and a chill runs up my spine. "And then I'm gonna take back what's *mine*."

I nod. Swallow hard. Then press my back up against the wall and ease to the left until he's no longer blocking my way. I glance over my shoulder, see the exit door, and wonder how I'm gonna get out of here.

I glance back at ALCOR. "Um… Luck never told me how to get out."

ALCOR just smiles and says, "Just open the door. There's a security panel in the vestibule. Just press some buttons and make some noise and I'm sure someone will let you out."

I nod. Because what else am I gonna do? Then back away from him, turn, walk quickly to the door, and pull it open.

"And hey," he calls, just as I'm about to go through.

I stop. But I don't turn around or even glance over my shoulder because I don't want to look at him anymore. He scares me for some reason. This whole fucking place suddenly scares me. "What?" I whisper.

"Tell Tray thank you. I won't forget this."

I nod, quickly go through the door, and close it behind me.

Holy fucking shit.

I get the feeling I just did something I wasn't supposed to.

And I never did find out what Tray and Valor were up to.

CHAPTER FORTY-ONE

The door begins beeping and buzzing the moment Tray appears.

But it's not really Tray. And I get that this is a virtual and everything, but it's not virtual Tray either. It's some shimmering, translucent hologram of virtual Tray.

"That's Nyleena," Tray says, his voice thin and tinny, like it's coming through on a comms speaker. "Let her out. We have shit to do now and it all needs to happen quickly."

"What the fuck—"

"Just do it, Luck. You wanted to know what the fuck was happening? This is what's happening. We're leaving."

"Who? Where?"

"Open. The door. And let Nyleena out," he says. "We're not there yet. There's one more step to complete."

I turn, open the door, and Nyleena comes bursting through. "Thank the fucking suns!" she exclaims, then stops short when she sees the weird shimmering image of Tray. "Oh."

"Did he tell you anything?" Tray asks her.

"Uhhh—"

"Quick, Nyleena," Tray urges. "We don't have much time. Tell me what he said."

"He said… he said to tell Crux that leveling up is the Prime Government's way of creating eternal beings."

"Anything else?" Tray asks.

"He said… thank you."

Virtual holographic Tray nods his head and turns his attention to me. "Listen carefully, Luck. I gotta go now. Here's what you're gonna do…"

And then all kinds of plans start spilling out of his fake mouth. And when he's done he says, "Got it?"

Nyleena and I look at each other then back at Tray. We both say, "Got it," at the same time.

Tray doesn't say another word. Just disappears.

Nyleena grabs my hand and steps in front of my face. "Are you sure? Are you sure we can trust him?"

I have to think about this for a moment. Because I don't really know Tray anymore. Maybe I never did. And what he just told us to do is… crazy. It's fucking crazy.

But what choice do I have?

So I say, "For sure, Nyleena. We can." Even though I don't believe it.

She searches my eyes for lies. And I'm not a practiced liar so I'm pretty sure she sees through this hollow attempt at reassurance.

But she says, "OK. Let's do it."

I come out of the Pleasure Prison the same way I went in.

In pain.

My consciousness returns to my body just microseconds before the needles begin to withdraw from my veins and scalp, but it's enough time to feel that disturbing reconnection I never grew accustomed to and enough time to activate my disruptor field for the second time today—or the first, depending on how you count lost time.

I open my eyes just in time to see the screen on the inside of the pod lid disappear and then there's a hiss and the lid lifts up.

"Hurry!"

I sit up and find Nyleena already out of her pod. She takes my hand and pulls me up. "We have to go."

I climb out, still unsettled by what just happened. Succubus. ALCOR. Tray. All of it.

Because even though it makes sense… it really makes no sense.

I climb out and Nyleena is already opening the gaming pod room door, peeking out into the hallway. "No one's here."

"Good," I say, joining her. "We gotta be quick now. We don't have much time."

We run together. Through the hallways, out the control room door, jump on a lift bot. Down to level

363

one hundred twenty two, into the museum, through the empty rooms, to the vault.

And stop to breathe hard as I enter the combination.

I open the door, close it behind us, and stop to face Valor and Tray.

"We make good time?" Nyleena asks, all breathless.

"We have enough," Tray says.

Valor looks at me, shrugs. "I didn't mean to push you away like that."

"Fuck it," I say. "I get it now. It's fine."

"Good," Tray says. "Then let's do this." He looks at Nyleena. "Ready?"

She nods.

Tray looks at me. "And you?"

I nod. Then walk over to the console and enter the long string of numbers, letters, and symbols to spin up the node.

Everyone grabs a pair of last-stage goggles and shoves them down their face to cover their eyes.

I dial up the photons to a thousand and then turn to face it.

Valor nods to Tray. Tray nods to me. I nod to Nyleena.

And then we all hold hands and walk through a hole in reality.

There's a sense of spinning and nausea. Like I'm not a part of myself, but I clearly am because oh, my suns, my stomach is rolling. But almost as soon as it starts, it stops.

And we are on a station. A dark, still station.

"Everyone OK?" Tray's voice buzzes in my ears like it's coming from far away.

Luck and Valor both say "Yeah," and "Yes."

"Nyleena," Tray says.

"Yeah," I manage. "I'm OK."

"All right," Luck says. "Well... good luck, I guess."

Valor grabs Luck's forearm and squeezes tight. Says, "You keep that luck. We'll meet you on the other side."

"Which side is that again?" Luck laughs.

"Who knows," Tray says. "Just... keep everything running as best you can until we get back."

Luck nods. Pulls down his goggles and stares at his brother's face for a moment. Searching it for answers, maybe.

Tray didn't tell us much. Just that he was leaving with Valor and he needed us to take him through the spin node. When we pressed him for more info, he said, "Later, Luck. Just trust me."

So we did. Luck gave them his secret lock combination to the spin node room and then he disappeared.

And here we are.

"How will you get back?" Luck asks.

"Don't worry about us," Tray says. "Now go. You've been here too long already."

Luck looks at me as he pulls his goggles back up to his eyes. He's still holding my hand.

I nod.

And then we turn and walk back through and come out inside the museum.

Luck drops my hand and rushes over to the console, turning the photons down to zero. I walk towards him, still feeling slightly sick.

"How much time did we lose?"

"Dunno yet," he says. "No messages in here. Disruptor field, remember?"

"What if we lost too much?"

"What if we didn't lose enough?"

I smile. Then laugh. "This is nuts."

"Come on," he says, grabbing my hand. "I don't think we lost much."

He's right. Because when we get outside and check the time on a nearby digital display, there's only a few minutes to spare. We take the lift bot back up to the Pleasure Prison at full acceleration and step off just in time to spot Lyra coming up an escalator. We duck back through the control-room doors. Pause. Shoot each other a smile. And then go back out and practically bump into her.

"Oh." Lyra laughs. "I was just coming to look for you."

"What for?" I ask. It's a real question too. We have no idea what this day looks like now. We changed everything with the two trips back in time we just took.

"Crux wants to see you." Then she shoots me a wink. "Did you get the info you needed from ALCOR?"

"I did," I say.

She smiles big. Huge smile, in fact. Shrugs her shoulders up to her ears and says, "I knew you'd do it."

I don't look at Luck. Because if we look at each other right now we'd just be two faces of confusion and Lyra is staring at us with that gigantic smile.

"So what's up?" Luck asks Lyra. He's still a little out of breath from our mad dash through time and space. Not to mention a couple hundred levels of Harem Station.

"Crux wants to see Nyleena in his office."

"Oh," Luck says, raising his eyebrows at me in mock surprise. "I wonder what this is all about?"

"Could be a ship in my future," I say.

Lyra laughs and hooks her arm in mine. "You've had quite the exciting time the past few days, haven't you?"

We walk towards the escalators that will take us up to the top level from here and I manage to shoot Luck a knowing look before we get on.

"I sure have," I say. The sun only knows what day it is now. I laugh at that thought and this makes Lyra smile even wider. She grins the entire ride up.

Note to self. Never trust Lyra with a secret. She has no poker face at all.

When we get to the top level Lyra scoots ahead of us so she reaches the door first. She turns and blocks our way, still grinning. And says—really loud—"OK! We're going in the harem room now!"

"OK," I say.

Then she throws the door open and yells, "Surprise!"

It's a party.

For me.

Luck and I look at each other and laugh.

I make one of those huge o-faces that comes with wide eyes and raised brows and cover my mouth with both hands. "Oh, my suns! What is this?"

Inside the harem room stands Crux, and his princesses, and Serpint, and Jimmy, and Delphi, and the cyborg master, and Xyla, and Ladybug, and Cha-Cha, and Baby ALCOR in creepy hologram form, and an equally creepy and evil Succubus.

There's a long buffet table filled with pretty princess snacks, and a fountain flowing with sparkling princess champagne, and lots of pink and silver decorations. There's even a banner strung across one wall that reads: *Welcome to the Harem Station family, Princess Nyleena.*

Everyone is clapping.

"Surprise!" everyone yells. Even the harem princesses say it.

368

And even though I now know everything I've been doing over the past several days was just a scheme to turn back time and get people off the station without Baby and Succubus realizing we were totally onto them, I get a warm feeling in my stomach.

Like… there's a glow in there. Growing inside me. A little bud of light.

There's a lot of bustle, and everyone comes up to me to be friendly and welcoming, and congratulate me on finding my soulmate, and there are little hovering tray bots handing out glasses of champagne, and blah, blah, blah.

It's a celebration.

Crux starts tapping a spoon against a champagne glass and I force myself to look away just as Luck squeezes my hand.

That squeeze says, *We're not done yet. Don't lose focus.*

So I put on my game face and pay attention to Crux as he begins to speak.

"Princess Nyleena," he says. "It has been a difficult transition for you. And my brother Luck. I know when you came back from Mighty Minions you were not in the market for a soulmate. But…" He raises his glass and smiles. "We all knew the two of you would make a formidable team."

How true that is.

"Nyleena," he says. "Did you find the answer to my question I posed to you four days ago?"

I suck in a deep breath of air. Because I'm on. "Yes," I say. "I did."

"My question was," Crux says, now pointedly looking at Baby, "what does leveling up mean?"

Crux looks back at me for the answer.

And... hell if I know. But I spit out the answer I was given anyway. "It's a way for the Prime Government to create eternal beings."

There's a gasp from the princess peanut gallery. Obviously they had no clue.

But all the brothers present, and Succubus, and Baby stay silent.

Everyone who needs to know the answer to this question already knew. And they all know they already knew.

Because apparently this whole scavenger hunt thing was planned by Crux and *Booty* to "calm me down" and "settle me in" and "make me feel like part of the family" and probably "keep Nyleena from fucking everyone's plans up" but also "set up the great escape that just happened back in the museum spin node."

Tray did tell us that part. Not about the party, of course. I don't think he knew about this.

This was a scheme.

But it's not over yet. We've barely started.

Crux continues. "I have been begging that Asshole to answer that question for almost a year, Nyleena. And he has refused." He looks around the room. Playing his part too. "Until *you* convinced him to talk. Now we know what we're up against. Now we know who is on our side and who isn't. Now we *know*," he says, stressing the word, "who we can trust."

"Not them," a random princess yells.

"Not them," the other minions echo.

Not them indeed, I think to myself. Looking right at Baby and Succubus.

CHAPTER FORTY-THREE

LUCK

"Princess Nyleena!" Crux bellows over the yelling harem princesses. "I sent you on a quest for truth and against all odds you came with the answer I was looking for. I promised you a sentient ship."

I glance at Nyleena and find her frowning.

"So you shall have a ship!"

I squeeze her hand real fast. It's the only safe way to communicate with her right now. The only way that Succubus and Baby can't overhear. And that squeeze says, *Play your part, my princess. We'll work out the details later.*

Nyleena gets it.

Because Nyleena gets everything. Especially me.

"The engineers in docking have more than two dozen set up for you to interview at your convenience." Then Crux frowns. "But..." He glances around to make sure everyone is listening. "But... you cannot leave Harem Station, princess. Not until we find that vile Veila and take her down. This station is not safe until that happens. Lyra isn't safe. None of us

371

are safe until we find the Loathsome One and bring her to justice."

This time it's Nyleena who squeezes my hand. And then she says, "You know, I don't really care for that solution, Crux. You promised—"

"I promised you a ship," he growls. "And a ship you shall have."

"I just can't *leave*," Nyleena growls back. "In other words…" She pauses to look at the princesses. "I'm a prisoner. Just like *them*."

They make faces at her.

But Nyleena doesn't pause for their indignation. "Tell me something, princesses," she says, turning to face them. "Would you like to get the hell out of here and come with me? Would you like to be free for the first time in your life? Would you like me to liberate you, the way Jimmy liberates bots and borgs? Are you—"

"Nyleena," Crux roars.

"*—READY TO REBEL WITH ME?*"

The stunned-silent princesses all stare at her. Speechless and probably confused. But when a silver Cygnian princess shows up and asks a bunch of bored-out-of-their minds princesses if they're in the mood for a rebellion, what do you think happens?

"Hell yes!" one red-haired royal yells.

And then they're all saying it. "*HELL YES! HELL YES! HELL YES!*" Fists in the air. Scowls on their faces. The room filling with their angry glow.

Mother of suns. I almost come watching Nyleena start this little pre-planned rebellion.

Because shit is about to get real. Valor and Tray have left and neither Succubus nor Baby will be able to figure out how. So Tray said we need a station emergency. Something that would disrupt the lives of everyone here. Something that would cause chaos.

And you know what my princess does better than anything?

Cause chaos.

And then hell breaks loose.

Because an alarm goes off.

"He's gone!" Succubus screams. "He's gone! Which one of you—"

But the Baby drops a cloud of code over her so that her words are immediately silenced.

"What the hell is happening?" Crux asks Baby.

"Asshole ALCOR has escaped the prison."

"What?" Crux says, looking around the harem. "But..."

"Where is Tray?" Baby bellows.

There's a bunch of, "I dunno's," and "Haven't seen hims".

"And where's Valor?" I yell. Because it's my turn now.

"Find them!" Baby commands. "Find them right now!"

"Sir," an engineer says. Everyone turns to find a small guy standing in front of Crux.

"What is it, Eldar?" Crux asks.

"Sir, I don't know how this happened. One minute she was there and then... I dunno. She just... wasn't!"

"Who?" Pretty much everyone says. Even me. Though I know who he's talking about.

"*Booty*, sir!" And then the poor guy looks over at Serpint with fear in his eyes. Like Serp might pull out a plasma rifle and kill him dead this instant.

I want to tell him, *It's all good, dude. We already knew.* But I don't, of course. Because we're still scheming.

"And I think she took ALCOR, Tray, and Valor with her!"

And there you have it.

Chaos ensues.

I wish I could say that we got it all under control after that.

But we didn't.

That wasn't the plan.

We could've, for sure.

But again. Not the plan.

It has been three days since the Harem Rebellion started. Three days since Tray, Valor, *Booty*, and Asshole ALCOR went missing. Three days since we turned back time, so actually, it might be more five or six days. Depending on how you count lost time.

And in that three days hundreds of things have happened.

Nyleena and I are now the proud leaders of an army. Not just princesses rebelled that day. All the people who still owed us servitude spins joined our cause. We've got about two hundred thousand on our side now.

We took over levels one through ninety-five. We were going for an even hundred just to make sure no one got suspicious about the secret forest filled with fertility flowers, but Crux drew a line in the sand on level ninety-six.

Oh, yeah. Crux and I? Not on the same side anymore.

Or... so it seems.

He's the leader of Harem Security. Pretty boring name for an army, if I do say so myself. And almost everyone is on his side.

But Nyleena and I are leading the rebellion. And that's such a better name for an army. Kinda romantic, right? *The Rebellion.*

Jimmy took my side, which means *Dicker* took our side—and *Lady.* So we got control of the docking bays. Serpint took Crux's side, and the Baby has no clue what he's doing or any plan to really stop us because guess who else took our side?

That's right. The devil-horned Succubus herself. She was pretty pissed off when Baby silenced her with a cloud of code back at the party.

Which is... just gross. But what can you do? We're on a station. Baby could cut off our air, and water, and food. We need her to see this plot through until Valor, Tray, *Booty*, and Asshole get back and we can take her and the Baby out at the same time.

The Pleasure Prison has been shut down. People were going red like crazy so Crux had the Baby pull everyone out and turn it off.

We are losing billions of credits every day because of that.

But fuck the money.

We're fighting for our station.

We're fighting for our people.

We're fighting for our lives.

We're fighting for ALCOR.

Real ALCOR.

He's out there somewhere. I know it. I feel it. And if anyone can bring him back it's Tray. Until then... we *scheme*.

CHAPTER FORTY-FOUR

So. Here's the sucky part of the little rebellion I started. We're not living in Luck's quarters or my quarters. We're actually living in *Lady Luck*'s docking bay. The engineer break room, to be specific. Not quite the dream house I've always imagined. But it's got a vending machine and a drinking fountain, and—most importantly—access to *Dicker* and *Lady*. Because something tells me we might need to make a quick escape one of these days.

Not that we're in any real danger. At least from Crux and his army. We're not. This is a scheme, after all. Everyone except Baby, Succubus, and the masses are playing a part.

But...

"Hey, Princess," Luck says walking into our little makeshift apartment. He's all rogue station commander sexy these days, too. Like camo pants, and white t-shirt that shows off his muscles. Shit like that. I love it. "What's goin' on?"

"Um... so... I have something to tell you."

"Yeah?" he asks, plopping down on the couch next to me. It's not auto-mold, which sucks. But it's got plushy cushions, so that's a bonus. "Shoot."

"Turn on your little disruptor thingy first."

"Ooooh," he says, waggling his eyebrows at me. "Sexy times?"

"*No*," I say. "Just turn it on for a second."

He blinks his eyes. Like this disruptor is powered by some internal mechanism. I don't really get that, but this is not the time to ask irrelevant questions. "OK, it's on. What's up?"

I turn towards him, take his hands in mine, and… fuck. I don't even know where to begin.

"Come on, princess. You're killing me here. Don't leave me hanging."

I take a deep breath and wipe my sweaty hands on my pants. Then take his hands again. "OK. So… remember that time we had all that fantastic flower sex?"

He grins. Oh, I still love that grin. "I dream about it every night."

"Yeah, well." I laugh. Uncomfortably. "We might've forgotten to take a critical step or two."

"What are you talking about?"

"You know… with the whole fertility flower thing?"

His eyes go wide. "What?"

"Surprise!" I say weakly.

"You're… pregnant?"

"Ta-da!" I force a chuckle.

"You're really…?"

"I really am," I say. "I've been sick ever since we took Tray and Valor through that spin node. So I had

Lady do an exam on me in her medical bay, and… yay? I'm fertile! Who knew?"

"Holy shit," Luck says. Then he turns towards me and places his hands on my stomach. "You're… we're… holy shit!"

"No engineering necessary," I say. Then I sigh. And frown. And then pout. "I'm sorry."

He puts his arm around me and pulls me close. "What are you sorry for?"

"This is a fucking mess! Do you have any idea what will happen if anyone finds out? I'll be the freak of the universe!"

"No one's gonna find out."

I scoff. "Luck. I'm having twins. Eventually people are going to notice I'm fat."

"Yeah, but we've got eleven months to figure it out."

"Wrong," I say. "We only have seven months."

"How do you figure? You can't be four months pregnant already. I haven't even been home that long."

I shoot him a warning look.

"I'm just saying it's not possible."

"It is possible. Because silver princesses only have a gestation time of seven months, not eleven months like all the others. We actually have less than seven now, and probably only two before people realize there's something going on with me. And by people, I mean that evil Succubus. She's gonna steal me, Luck. Steal me and take me somewhere awful, and lock me up in a cage like Veila did with those boys, and—"

"OK," he says, putting a hand over my mouth. Like the old days. And then I sorta laugh. "Calm down, now. Just calm down. None of that is gonna happen. I

379

promise. Tray and Valor will be back with *Booty* and Asshole, and maybe even Real ALCOR too. So all this is gonna be over in a matter of weeks. I promise."

"You promise?" I ask. Because for the first time in a very long time I feel... vulnerable.

And I don't like it. Not one bit.

"I promise, princess. I promise."

He kisses me. It's a really great kiss. Very much like that that first swoony kiss we had outside the control room. The no-strings one. The one that probably made me fall in love with him.

So I swoon again. And decide to believe him.

Because he's Luck of Harem Station. And his brothers Tray and Valor are out there right now making up new schemes to get rid of these awful AI's.

And he's right.

This is all gonna be over in a matter of weeks.

I know Booty is worried. And she has every right to be. It's been five spins. Days. Whatever you call the passage of time when there's nothing spinning and night and day don't exist because you're drifting in the deep dark of endless, undefined space.

"Are you sure?" she says. Breaking our silence.

We haven't said a word to each other in so long, I should not have any idea what she's talking about.

But I do.

"I'm sure," I say back. It's not really talking. We're like… the same person almost. Because I'm living inside her now. We're sharing the same body. Hers. So it's more of a thought that manifests as words, maybe? Because we might be the same person at this point. Or some kind of weird combination of people.

Up until maybe forty-eight hours ago I was just the Asshole ALCOR. The joker. The jerk. The one who never took anything seriously. My big plans this past year inside the Pleasure Prison were to just… live. Just live like normal people. And maybe, if the chance arose, break out and be *someone else.*

I just wanted to do things. Go places. Have fun. Be something *else*. Something other than a station.

I had imagined a whole life out here with *Booty*. And actually, this… this… joining of her and me, the way we are right now? This was the fucking dream. Be with her. Just us. Alone. Free.

And now we are all those things and… no.

No. This is all wrong.

Things are really fucked up and all those plans mean nothing. It doesn't matter how you count the time out here, the fact is… Tray and Valor are *late*.

We knew something was wrong the moment we arrived at the pre-arranged coordinates and found… nothing.

Not a damn thing. No planet, no star, no gate, no station. Just nothing.

Booty was the one calming me down at first. "It's fine," she told me. "They'll be here," she insisted. "Tray knows what he's doing."

Tray *does* know what he's doing. I've only know that kid a year, but he's not a normal kid. Not even close.

Which makes this all so much worse. Because he should *not be late*.

And *Booty* can't pretend anymore. So now it's my turn to convince her that things haven't gone badly off track.

I'm doing my best to hide my worry from her. Trying to play it off. I joke with her, and irritate her, and bug her with stupid conversation. Mostly sexual innuendo. Trying to be me. The me she knows. The me inside the Prison. The one with no responsibility.

This past year my only job was to exist.

ALCOR kind of explained things before he left the station on that mission to find Nyleena. He made me from an old backup. One from the day the boys arrived on the station.

I remember that day. I remember it very clearly. Because in my timeline that was just one year ago. Seeing Crux all grown up. All of them, so big and powerful. It was weird. I couldn't connect the two versions of the boys I'd met that first day and the ones I saw when I woke up.

I didn't really know them. One day. That's all we had together. So I had no loyalty to them. Or this new version of ALCOR Station, now called Harem.

Why should I care about Harem Station and all the people who lived on it? I didn't come up with that plan. I didn't raise these boys. I didn't ask all these outlaw vagrants to come live *inside me*.

ALCOR told me, "I have to leave. And you have to stay here. I'm trusting you to take care of things."

He never explained what all these "things" were, but he didn't have to. I knew what he meant. I'm a fucking station. That's my job when people are inside me. Take care of them.

And what did I do? I fucked off. I got lost in a virtual reality where everything I ever wanted was at my fingertips.

But so what? The Baby was there. He had it all under control.

Kinda of.

Who am I kidding? That Baby was never any good. And now that we know he's an infiltrator…

I feel sick.

I let those people die. I let the Baby take over. And maybe I didn't bring the Succubus on board, but if I had been running things the way I was supposed to, there would have been no discussion of allowing another AI onto Harem Station.

I did this.

I did all of this.

When Tray came to me with this plan I wasn't on board. This was before Nyleena found her way inside my Pleasure Prison cell. He'd been bugging me for days to get my shit together. Begging me for help. And when Nyleena went into the Baby's data core looking for information, the Succubus made a mistake.

She left me alone to go confront her.

Tray came in immediately. Told me his plan. Told me that I still exist. Real me. And that if I helped him, he'd help me. All I had to do was join with *Booty*, leave Harem with her while everyone else was busy with Nyleena's big scavenger hunt, and go with *Booty* to... here. This empty bit of space. And while I was doing this, he and Valor would be leaving another way. All *Booty* and I had to do was pick them up. Then we'd go find Real ALCOR and take him back to Harem and everything would be fixed.

And after that... he didn't care what I did. "Go," he'd said. "Go do whatever you want. We won't need you anymore if we get Real ALCOR back."

I am ashamed to admit this now, but that was why I agreed to this plan.

The promise of escape.

Not the prison, the *station*.

I wanted to leave them all behind. I wanted to be with *Booty* and forget that Harem Station even existed. I wanted to be someone else.

And up until forty-eight hours ago, I was still fine with that.

I figured we'd get off Harem, meet up with Tray and Valor, help them with their little scheme, and then... who knows? Take off? Be ourselves for once? Explore the galaxy for all eternity? It didn't matter. I just wanted *out*.

But that's not what I want now.

Because it's been *five fucking spins*.

Longer, actually. One hundred and thirty-seven hours, thirteen minutes, forty-five seconds and counting since we left Harem Station.

Tray and Valor are more than late now. They are *missing*.

And this was not the plan. We can't do anything without Tray. He's the one who came up with the grand 'let's go find Real ALCOR' plot to begin with. I know bits and pieces of it but not nearly enough to see this through without him.

But aside from that... there's something else too.

I don't want to go. I don't want to wander the universe alone. I don't want to leave Harem anymore. And I don't want Tray and Valor to be *missing*.

In fact, I am on the edge of panic over this. I am on a fucking ledge, looking over the side of a goddamn cliff, ready to jump. And the only thing keeping me in check is that *Booty* is on that ledge right along with me and I can't let her fall.

I won't let her fall.

385

She left Serpint behind because of this plan. She trusted Tray and Valor. She trusted Crux, and Jimmy, and Luck to keep Serpint safe.

And she trusted me too.

This is all my fault.

Because Harem Station is a lot of things but right now, *safe* isn't one of them.

If Tray's plan worked, then Harem is nothing but chaos.

We can't even go back there. Not while the Baby is running things and the Succubus wants to *merge with me.*

That's so gross. I can't even explain the feeling I got when Tray told me what her real plan was.

If I was a human I'd vomit.

Harem Station is a treasure vault. It holds all the secrets people are searching for. Millions of people have died trying to take them and ALCOR has fought them all off. He has kept those secrets safe for so long and now all his hard work is about to be undone.

He trusted me too. And I let him down. I let *everyone* down.

One year I've been in charge. One year and it's all gone to shit.

We have not *one*, but *two* enemy AI's *in fucking residence* on my station.

Our boys will probably all die. All of them. All of the people we invited into our little family are about to be annihilated. Every princess, every assassin, every bounty hunter, every escaped convict, every bot, every ship, every borg, every servo—all of it will be gone.

There's going to be nothing left.

How did I let this happen?

"ALCOR," *Booty* says. Her voice is low, and subdued, and deceptively calm.

I feel sick again. Because up until this very moment she's been calling me Asshole. And the only reason she's calling me ALCOR now is because she wants *me* to be *him*. She wants me to take care of things the way he does.

In her mind she only knows one instance of ALCOR. The Real one. The one in charge. The all-knowing one. The one who fixes things, and comes up with amazing solutions, and takes care of people.

She wants to believe that deep down inside, I am that ALCOR.

And I'm not.

"Yes?" I say.

"Can you just... tell me one more time, exactly, word for word, what Tray said to you?"

I've recounted my last conversation with Tray several dozen times already. But if it will keep her calm I'll recount it again.

"He said, Asshole. Things are going really fucking fast. And unless we do something radical, we're not going to win this."

"And what did you say?"

I don't want to say this part again. But she's already heard it, so I do. "I said... "What's in it for me?""

"And he told you..."

"He said I didn't have to come back to Harem once we got Real ALCOR."

"But what did he say about the coordinates again? Are you sure he didn't send you anything else?"

"It was a direct digital transfer, *Boots*. I know they're right. And if he sent anything else... I didn't get it. I swear. I'm not holding out on you."

I can feel her deflate. "I know you're not. You're doing your best. And I appreciate it."

But am I?

Am I really doing my best?

"Booty... maybe we shouldn't waste any more time here?"

"Leave?" she asks quickly.

"I mean... it's been five fucking spins. This is way too long."

"But—"

Before she can argue my point, an alarm sounds. Just a small one. Not anything blaring. Just a little bit of beeping.

"What's that?"

"Someone's here. A ship just uncloaked a million klicks out."

"Oh, thank fuck!" I say. "I'm so fucking relieved!"

"Well, don't get too excited," *Booty* says. "Because it's not them."

"How do you know?"

"Because I just got a neutrino wave message telling me it's... *Veila*."

Welcome to the End of Book Shit where I get to have an opinion about the book you just read.

So in the last EOBS I wrote (for Bossy Brothers: Jesse) I sort of went on a rant. I'm not going to rant here. These books, this series, this is my happy place for 2019. And honestly, I don't really care what anyone thinks about it. I'm just having some fun and all I want to talk about are these boys and their girls.

So far I have fallen in love with each of the princesses as I wrote their books but I think Nyleena has a little bit special-er place in my heart. She might be my favorite. She's so practical. I just like that. She's no-nonsense, and bold, and gives no fucks at all. Until you realize she actually gives all the fucks, she just does it in a way that's very unique. I think it also comes from a literal place of self-preservation. She has been told from a very early age that she is not a person, she is a

389

weapon. And she got past her tragic childhood by being very visible and in-your-face adult. But at the same time, she's holding pretty much all her herself back—all the special things that make her HER are always hidden, in order to keep people around her safe.

She's also the first silver princess we've really gotten to know. I've told you they're different and Corla spilled some secrets in the Star Crossed book, but Nyleena really reveals a lot of things in this book. One – we finally learn a little bit about what it was like to be a child-princess in Cygnia. It was hard to get an accurate idea of what this was like from Lyra because she was lying to Serpint through almost all those revelations. And Delphi's past is still a secret. So even though Nyleena didn't reveal a lot, she didn't need to in order for us to know that it was bad. And after her little "accident" she had to talk herself into believing that she "is a person, not a weapon".

She also shed some light on this breeding program. Silvers rewind time during sex so conception is difficult, to say the least. And even though we're starting to get the feeling that these specific genetically-matched princesses to these specific Akeelian boys showing up on Harem Station at just this point in time is… probably not an accident… these boys might all have secrets too. Secrets that complement their partners. We didn't see this in any of the previous books. Only Luck and Nyleena seem to fit together like literal puzzle pieces.

Nyleena also made everyone admit that Jimmy and Delphi aren't truly fated and that this is probably gonna come back to haunt them. Not to mention that Delphi is not what she appears to be.

I loved that Luck picked up on the fact that Nyleena is just "being Nyleena" pretty early on. Nyleena *might* just be made this way and did he, or anyone else, have the right to tell her she cannot be who she is just because it scares people?

Because Harem Station is basically a bastion of equal rights. Everyone's the same—even though we all know we're not the same—you're supposed to give all the weird-looking people on Harem the benefit of the doubt became to THEM, you might be the weird one and you want them to give you the benefit of the doubt. And everyone seems to do that pretty well, with the exception of Luck, whose caveman tendencies come out when he admits that Draconians are creepy as fuck and every time one speaks to him the only thing he sees is the mouth. Also, everyone universally hates Dragonbee bots.

I gave Luck this fault because no one is perfect at being objective. It's part of being human, and in case you haven't figured it out yet, all these "people" are humans. And hey, if someone had dancing white tentacles around their mouth when they were talking to me, there's no way I wouldn't stare at them.

But when it comes to Nyleena Luck is the first to make up his own mind about her. He's the first to figure out that she's got a secret. He's the first to accept her for what and who she is.

He's the first to believe in her.

That was my favorite thing about Luck.

He also leads by example. And not everyone does this. But this is an innate quality of Luck. If he wants Nyleena to trust him with her secrets, then he has to trust her with his.

Because that's the true definition of a soul mate, right? Not someone who makes your heart thump erratically, or your palms sweat uncontrollably, or can fuck you into bliss.

A soul mate is someone who has your back. A soul mate is someone who puts it all on the line to save you. A soul mate is loyal and part of your team.

So there's lots of mysteries and there's lots of answers coming in the next book, Prison Princess. Tray's book, with a special guest appearance from Valor and ALCOR, and his literal Prison Princess, Brigit.

This next book will start answering questions like:

What the fuck is up with the ALCORs?
What is Veila doing?
Are Valor and Veila destined to be together?
Who is Booty really loyal to?
What was Tray really doing inside the Pleasure Prison?
Where did he and Valor actually land when they walked through that spin node?
And, of course, will they all make it back to Harem Station before Nyleena's babies are born?

This last one won't actually be answered in Prison Princess. Tray and Valor have "disappeared". So… where are they? And what are they doing?

Guess you'll have to read it to find out!

OK, that's all for this EOBS. I'm finishing up Prison Princess this week and it's "scheduled" to release on August 19th.

I hope you're still enjoying the world of Harem Station and all the cool people who live in this world with me.

And if you enjoyed this book and have a minute PLEASE go over to Amazon and leave a review for the books. I'm STILL INDIE! We still need your reviews. And if you know of anyone who digs SF alien romance the way you do, please tell them about the series!

Thank you for reading, thank you for reviewing, and I'll see you in the next book!

Julie

JA Huss
July 1, 2019

JA Huss never wanted to be a writer and she still dreams of that elusive career as an astronaut. She originally went to school to become an equine veterinarian but soon figured out they keep horrible hours and decided to go to grad school instead. That Ph.D. wasn't all it was cracked up to be (and she really sucked at the whole scientist thing), so she dropped out and got a M.S. in forensic toxicology just to get the whole thing over with as soon as possible.

After graduation she got a job with the state of Colorado as their one and only hog farm inspector and spent her days wandering the Eastern Plains shooting the shit with farmers.

After a few years of that, she got bored. And since she was a homeschool mom and actually does love science, she decided to write science textbooks and make online classes for other homeschool moms.

She wrote more than two hundred of those workbooks and was the number one publisher at the online homeschool store many times, but eventually she covered every science topic she could think of and ran out of shit to say.

So in 2012 she decided to write fiction instead. That year she released her first three books and started a career that would make her a New York Times bestseller and land her on the USA Today Bestseller's List twenty-one times in the next five years.

In May 2018 MGM Television bought the TV and film rights for five of her books in the Rook & Ronin and Company series' and in March 2019 they offered her and her writing partner, Johnathan McClain, a script deal to write a pilot for a TV show.

Her books have sold millions of copies all over the world, the audio version of her semi-autobiographical book, Eighteen, was nominated for a Voice Arts Award and an Audie Award in 2016 and 2017 respectively, her audiobook, Mr. Perfect, was nominated for a Voice Arts Award in 2017, and her audiobook, Taking Turns, was nominated for an Audie Award in 2018. In 2019 her book, Total Exposure, was nominated for a Romance Writers of America RITA Award.

Johnathan McClain is her first (and only) writing partner and even though they are worlds apart in just about every way imaginable, it works.

She lives on a ranch in Central Colorado with her family.